Estelle Ryan

The Netscher Connection

The Netscher Connection

A Genevieve Lenard Novel

By Estelle Ryan

First published 2017

Chapter ONE

"DID YOU KNOW this used to be an Orthodox Serbian church until 1944?" Colin Frey, my romantic partner of five years, notorious thief and unofficial Interpol agent, looked up from his smartphone and studied the cream and mustard façade of the building in front of us. "After the war it became a Roman Catholic Church and is now one of seven churches here in Szentendre."

I enjoyed the factoids Colin got from the travel guide app he'd downloaded on his smartphone. It made our visit to the Hungarian riverside town twenty-two kilometres north of Budapest even more interesting. I adjusted my handbag strap over my shoulder and waited for Colin to take another photo.

It was early autumn and the weather was wonderful. Sunny and warm days, cooler evenings and no crowds. The tourist season was finished, which meant I enjoyed strolling through the quiet village, and very few of the photos Colin took had unwanted people in them. Szentendre was also still one of the less-discovered cultural gems, which made it the perfect place for a person who despised crowded tourist places. A person like me.

"There you are!" Vinnie, the self-appointed protector of our investigative team, stormed across the cobblestone courtyard.

His *corrugator supercilii* muscles were drawn down, forming a displeased frown. "Dude! Why didn't you wake me up? You know I should be here."

"Good morning, sunshine." Colin's smile grew when Vinnie became even more agitated. "Sleeping on the job, were you?"

Vinnie stopped next to us, glowered at Colin, then turned to me. "I know you think it's safe here, Jen-girl, but you really shouldn't take any chances. We've had this conversation before."

"And all three times I pointed out that those men"—I looked at the tall man leaning against the church a few metres behind us, the bald man standing by the stairs and the dark-skinned man under the tree to our right—"are already following us everywhere."

"Émile's bodyguards are good, but they're not me." Vinnie thumped his fist against his chest, the long scar on the left side of his face turning a darker shade.

Eight months ago, I'd decided to go on holiday. I had not anticipated the endless debates, arguments, discussions and even betting that were going to take place. My thought had been for Colin and I go to a remote locale and spend a few days reading and relaxing. That was not to be.

Vinnie had refused to let us go anywhere without his protection. His girlfriend and internationally respected infectious disease specialist Doctor Roxanne Ferreira had agreed, but she was terrible at deception. Her true motivation had been easy to observe—excitement about joining us on a holiday trip. My best friend and top hacker Francine had dramatically pretended to be devastated that

I'd considered going anywhere without her. Her romantic partner and the only law enforcement officer on our team, Colonel Manfred Millard, had argued to let Colin and I go on our own, but he'd been outvoted. He'd been most displeased.

Nikki, the young woman who'd become part of our close-knit group, had begged for us to wait until her baby was at least six months old. She wanted to join us, but not while Eric was still too young. Of all the chaotic arguments, this had caused me the most anxiety. I was still barely coping with Eric's presence in my life. The thought of having him out of his safe, controlled environment had sent me into a three-hour shutdown.

After three full days of everyone arguing and me observing their nonverbal cues, I'd declared that we would all go. On the condition that I chose the location. That was the only way my autistic mind would be able to manage the change in routine, the concern over everyone's wellbeing and the general anxiety I experienced while travelling.

A Sunday morning brunch with Émile Roche had ended weeks of agonising over our holiday destination. I'd met Émile during one of our cases. At that time he'd been in the process of legitimising his businesses that had previously served his organised crime lifestyle.

That Sunday he'd announced that every transaction for the last eighteen months had been one hundred percent legal. When he'd heard about our vacation plans, he'd offered us his newly acquired villa in Hungary. Only when I'd had a video conference with the housekeeper and the chef had I agreed.

We'd been here for six days and I'd not yet regretted the decision. Vinnie and Manny complained about it all the time. I studied Vinnie as he glared at the bodyguards Émile had insisted follow us. "I watched you play computer games with them yesterday. You trust them."

"I don't." Vinnie crossed his arms. "Just because they can work a game controller and know how to strategise an assault and a rescue in a game doesn't mean they know how to do it in real life."

"Drop it, Vin." Colin put his camera in the backpack slung over his shoulder. "You're just pissed that you woke up alone."

"Even Roxy left!" Vinnie put his fists on his hips. "When she finally answered her phone, she told me that she was buying more art."

"I'm not surprised." Colin took my hand and walked towards the stairs leading down to the main square. "There are some really amazing artists in this little place."

"But she's already bought three paintings and two bronze thingies." Vinnie's top lip curled. "Both are these long women in long dresses and long umbrellas."

Colin laughed. I seldom saw him this relaxed. The last few years had been filled with art crime cases as well as more sensitive cases that the president of France sent our way. Our team worked directly under President Godard, investigating complex cases that were not limited to art, but often started with a high-end crime.

Apart from this, Colin was frequently contracted by Interpol to consult on cases that needed not to be immortalised in official reports. At first I had found it disconcerting that such a respected agency would employ thieves. Now I understood that there were situations when Colin had to use his unique skills to break into seemingly impenetrable buildings to retrieve stolen artefacts, classified prototypes of all sorts and even highly sensitive data that had been stolen by countries that planned to use it to start wars. Interpol also used Colin to rescue kidnap victims. The latter made me especially proud.

Colin slapped Vinnie between his shoulders. "I'm glad Roxy listened to me and not you. Those elongated figures are beautiful and evidence of a master bronze caster. True art. And a much better investment than posters of cars."

Vinnie grunted. "Cars are manly."

I listened to the bantering between the two best friends. There were times I found the nonsensical to and fro exhausting, but I'd come to learn how invaluable it was to relationships. I had not mastered that skill. "Where's Nikki?"

"Huh?" Vinnie stopped in the middle of arguing against art and lifted his chin towards the other end of the market square. "The little punk and her tiny punk are somewhere with Francine and the old man. I walked past them when I was looking for you. Franny was buying some glass bowl in one of the million little shops."

"There are not a million..." I sighed at my inability to ignore hyperbole.

"Yoo-hoo!" Roxy's melodic greeting reached us from the end of one of the narrow streets. She waved and rushed towards us. Today she was wearing jeans, a fitted shirt that the ever fashion-conscious Francine had insisted on and running shoes that had caused an animated argument, Francine doing most of the arguing and insulting. Roxy shifted the bulging shopping bags into her other hand and tucked her curly hair behind one ear. "I love this place. Love, love, love. Thank you for bringing us here, Genevieve. There's something beautiful in every single shop."

"I can see that." Vinnie took the shopping bags from her. "We only have so much room in the car, short stuff."

"Who're you calling short stuff?" Roxy stood on her toes and planted a loud kiss on Vinnie's chin. "There will be enough room. If not, we'll just leave Francine behind."

"Why would you do that?" Francine asked from behind me. She was pressing her hand against her chest, her eyes wide in faux-misery. "You love me. Why leave me behind?"

Roxy leaned against Vinnie and snorted. "Because then I can wear comfortable shoes without feeling like I've committed an unpardonable sin."

Francine lifted one eyebrow and slowly lowered her eyes to Roxy's colourful running shoes. "That is a worse crime than an unpardonable sin, Rox. No woman proud of her chromosomes would wear"—a fake shudder shook her body—"those things."

"I see you found them." Manny stopped next to Francine and put his arm around her shoulders. I had never seen any public show of affection from Manny until this trip. Even though he argued daily with Vinnie and Colin, and fretted about staying in the villa of a man who'd once been one of the most powerful criminals in Strasbourg, his overall muscle tension had decreased and a few times I'd seen a soft smile lift the corners of his mouth.

"Doc G!" Nikki walked around Manny and Francine, her

cheeks lifted and the corners of her eyes crinkled in a genuine smile. She was carrying her baby in a large swath of material wrapped around her body and securing Eric. I'd researched the use of baby-wearing slings and then had made sure Nikki had followed the instructions carefully so Eric's little body was properly supported. She stopped next to me. "Look what we found."

I gasped. "Is that safe?"

Eight-month-old Eric was holding a green stuffed toy that looked like a dragon. Nikki kissed Eric's head and smiled. "Of course. It's soft and cuddly. How can it be dangerous?"

"Eighty percent of cuddly toys harbour harmful bacteria. Other micro-organisms on soft toys that have been detected during research are antibiotic-resistant Staphylococcus aureus and other bacteria that can cause food poisoning." I forced myself to stop when I noticed the horror on Roxy's face as she stared from me to the green dragon.

Eric lost interest in the toy and looked around. The moment he saw me, his eyes widened and he leaned towards me, his hands reaching for me.

Eight months. Sometimes it felt like it had been only eight days and sometimes it felt like Eric had been with us for eight years. Nikki had adjusted beautifully to being a mother. She was energetic, caring and responsible. Eric's easy nature had helped that adjustment. He had started sleeping through the night after only five weeks and seldom cried. Mostly he smiled. And cooed. Like now.

I looked at his outstretched hands and took a small step back. Vinnie stepped forward and grabbed both Eric's hands. He gave them a little shake, which drew Eric's attention and also brought a big smile to his face. He loved Vinnie.

Nikki had barely loosened the sling when Vinnie lifted Eric into his arms. "There you are, tiny punk. Is Mommy making you suffer through hours and hours of shopping?"

I watched him walk away, talking to Eric about the fate of men having to help their women shop. I narrowed my eyes as I made a note to discuss the sexism underlying that one-sided conversation. I was glad though that Vinnie wasn't using baby-talk with Eric.

I'd read a Stanford University study that showed addressing babies in normal, educated language developed their own linguistic skills sooner. The use of proper grammar, more varied sentences and full-sentence conversations taught babies context and helped them draw connections between concepts and words.

One of the biggest challenges I'd been struggling with had been obsessing about every aspect of Eric's life. I'd expected some form of my obsessive nature to affect how I related to Eric's presence in my life, but I had not been prepared for how overwhelming it would be at times.

For the first few weeks, I had experienced daily shutdowns. The smell of his diaper, a drop of his saliva on my hand, even the position of his head would cause me the greatest distress and prove too much for my non-neurotypical brain. But his crying had been my undoing.

The eight times Nikki had not been able to console him in less than six minutes had been too much for me. The first seven times had resulted in shutdowns, but the last time, I'd had a complete meltdown.

Fortunately, I'd known it was coming and had escaped to

my bathroom. It had resulted in the destruction of a glass vase and two towels. It had also been one of the longer meltdowns I'd experienced. Colin had tried to calm me in the ways he usually did, but it had not been as effective. Only after I'd plucked at and destroyed the fibres of the second towel had I responded to him.

It had been hard. Even though Nikki knew that neither she nor Eric was to blame, I saw the self-recrimination on her face after each shutdown and meltdown. I wished I didn't cause my loved ones so much despair.

After seven weeks, I'd adjusted mostly to Eric's presence and had found my own new equilibrium. And I'd no longer suffered from daily shutdowns. Not until we'd come on holiday. Change was never easy for me and the new environment combined with my obsessive concerns about the hygiene and safety surrounding Eric had brought the daily shutdowns back. It was exhausting.

Watching my friends laugh and discuss their new purchases, and knowing how much this break meant to all of them, made my own discomfort seem insignificant. Nikki was shaking out the long piece of cloth and folding it neatly while discussing with Colin the many great artists' works on display here. Roxy and Manny were arguing with Francine about where to have lunch and Vinnie was now pointing out old buildings to Eric, telling him that they were hard to secure and discussing the best entry points if stealth was to be kept at an optimum.

"I'm hungry." Nikki pushed her hand against her stomach. After eight months and a lot of dedication, her twenty-two-year-old body had returned to its pre-pregnancy state. She looked over at Francine, Manny and Roxy. "Since I'm going back to Strasbourg tomorrow, I get to choose what we have for lunch."

Francine groaned. "Not lángos again. Please, Nix."

"I love it." She looked at Vinnie. "Vin loves it too. And Eric as well."

"You fed lángos to Eric?" I was horrified. The typical Hungarian food was not only most unhealthy for adults, but should never be fed to an eight-month-old baby. It was deep-fried bread dough, the size of a medium-sized plate, served with cheese, garlic and sour cream.

Nikki looked at me, fake sincerity all over her face. "He told me that he prefers lángos with the extra garlic sauce to the organic vegetable mash I've been feeding him. He really loves it."

It was clear she thought she was funny. I exhaled sharply and turned away from her. "It's not healthy."

"Pah!" She raised her hands and wiggled her fingers as if drawing the others to her. "So? Who's with me? Lángos. Delicious lángos. You guys can eat all the boring healthy stuff when I'm gone."

I was proud of myself for not responding. After giving birth, Nikki had become especially health-conscious. She'd even convinced Vinnie to adjust a few of his recipes to use healthier alternatives for some ingredients. At home, she seldom indulged in junk food, but had been immediately drawn to the lángos stand and had declared herself an addict after the first bite.

"I tell you what, little punk." Vinnie shifted Eric onto his other arm and joined us. "I'll have a lángos with you if you let me choose your avatar for tonight's game."

"Aw, come on!" Nikki crossed her arms. "You're going to put me in some silly costume. That's a high price to pay, Vin. Especially for lunch with the mother of your most favourite nephew."

"You'll have to pay me to not join you for a lángos." Roxy winked at Nikki. "Those things are better than Vinnie's tiramisu."

Vinnie froze. He turned woodenly towards Roxy, his eyes wide. "Never in my life have I ever been stabbed this hard in my back. And here I thought you loved me."

Their melodrama was boring me. This could go on indefinitely if there wasn't a need for food or other means of survival. Nikki was now negotiating with Vinnie about her avatar. They'd discovered Drestia, the multiplayer game Vinnie had referred to, when we'd arrived at Émile's villa. He'd received it for free at a business conference and had never been interested in playing it. The premise of the game had been the reason he'd suggested it to Vinnie and Nikki.

I'd reluctantly given in and watched them for an hour after which I, again reluctantly, had admitted that it was an interesting concept. The players of the game were detectives—amateur and professional—who had to find a secret scroll in the tower room of a castle. They had to fight their way through each room in the castle and find a hidden key which would take them to the next room, the next level.

Every evening after Nikki put Eric to bed, she would join Vinnie, Francine and Colin to play the game. Manny and I sat in the next room, reading. They were too noisy while playing the game and neither Manny nor I had any interest in this game. He'd called it a ridiculous waste of time. I didn't agree. It gave the others hours of pleasure, which in my opinion was not a waste of time.

"It's decided." Nikki punched the air in victory, then turned to me. "Sure you don't wanna join us, Doc G? The dough is deep-fried, which means that not a single bacteria will survive."

"A single bacterium. Bacteria is the plural." I lifted one eyebrow. "I truly hope I'm correct in assuming that you are jestin… You are. It's not funny, Nikki."

She giggled. "It is. A little."

"Come on, punk." Vinnie tugged playfully at her messy ponytail. "I'll suffer through another lángos or three to prove my love to you. I might even give your baby back to you."

It took them another seven minutes of debating before Roxy stepped in. She took Eric from Vinnie's arms and started walking away. As one, the rest followed her, still arguing about which of the several lángos stands and restaurants were their best choice. I inhaled deeply when they were out of earshot.

"Too loud for you?" Colin chuckled. "They were too loud for me."

"They're having a good time. It appears their relaxed state increases their volume."

"Especially Roxy." Colin shook his head. "That woman can chat the ear off a donkey."

"What does that mean?"

"It's a silly saying, love." Colin took my hand, his smile soft. "Why don't we go back to the gallery with the abstracts we both liked?"

I didn't move when he started walking and waited until he

looked at me. "It's not possible to talk any person or animal's ear off."

"And that's why I said it was a silly saying."

"Most sayings are silly." I started walking. "And irrational. And most often impossible."

Colin pulled me closer to him and kissed the side of my head. "I fully agree with you."

I pulled away from him and gave him a displeased look when he laughed. He'd been in a light-hearted mood from the moment we'd walked into the first art gallery in Szentendre. It was his first time here, but he'd known about the historic architecture, numerous galleries and museums for many years. Having so many places representing the rich traditions of visual art within walking distance was clearly making him very happy.

I enjoyed the art. But I had to admit that in some galleries I took more pleasure from watching the owner or artist interact with Colin than I did looking at the pieces. Nonverbal communication had so many nuances. Yet an overwhelming percentage of cues were universal. The lifting of cheeks and crinkling of the corners of eyes produced genuine smiles everywhere in the world.

Our leisurely pace allowed Colin to peer into every shop window, sometimes slowing down to catch an extra glimpse of whatever had caught his eye. My interest was in the people sitting outside the numerous small cafés, sipping coffee. It was mid-week, which was to our benefit. The shops and streets were quiet, yet the service in the cafés was no faster than in the height of the tourist season. Émile had told us that unhurried service was the norm here.

Colin slowed down and squinted into a shop window to our right. I took the time to appreciate the beauty surrounding me. Even though a few buildings were in clear need of maintenance, the flaking paint and very old wooden window frames added to the charm of this village.

A row of trees lined the left-hand side of the street, bicycles chained to every single one of them. The buildings on our side of the street were mostly galleries and boutiques, a few of which had mannequins modelling their wares next to the open doors. On the other side of the cobblestone street, restaurants and cafés had welcoming signs and menus nailed to the walls.

Only one restaurant didn't have outside seating. All the others had a few occupants, giving me ample opportunity to indulge in observing people. Especially the guests at the three occupied tables outside the café closest to us and the one occupant of the café next to them. There were a lot of empty tables between them, affording them a sense of privacy. The couple at the table closest to the café's door were involved in an argument. He was pointing angrily at the open guidebook on the table and she was gesturing at something behind him.

Two tables away from them were three girls I estimated to be Nikki's age. Their beer glasses were almost empty and their laughter genuine. All three had their mobile phones in their hands, taking photos of each other and selfies—all the while behaving silly. They were having fun.

The older couple sitting in the corner rolled their eyes at the young girls, but smiled. In my youth, I'd never known silly moments like the ones the girls were experiencing now. I'd been home-schooled, had gone to university at a young age and had never had a neurotypical sense of humour. I also hadn't had friends. I was happy for the three girls that they had this moment to create memories that they could treasure for the rest of their lives.

Movement from the table at the other café caught my attention. I frowned. The man was sipping coffee, his posture relaxed while reading something on his phone. None of his nonverbal cues were genuine. He was not relaxed and he was not reading. His demeanour reminded me of when Vinnie or Manny were watching someone. The difference was my friends were much better at disguising their interest.

He was in his late twenties, early thirties with an athletic build. His features and toned body would make him attractive to most women. That was why the three girls were now looking over at him and giggling. He didn't pay them any attention. Even though he shifted deeper into his chair, lifted his phone and continued pretending to scroll through something on the screen, it was clear to me that he was watching someone on the other side of the street.

Colin took a few steps to look at another display in the window. I followed him, but didn't take my eyes off the man. His behaviour was disconcerting at best, alarming at worst. His eyes narrowed and he caught himself just in time not to straighten and betray his interest. I followed his gaze.

The street on our side was empty but for a woman standing on the sidewalk, quite a distance from us. She had to be the one who'd caught the man's attention. Francine would like her sense of style. She was wearing a pair of light green trousers, a white blouse and a fitted dark green summer jacket. Her shoes were made for walking, but appeared elegant and expensive. Even the styling of her long, blonde hair looked expensive.

The large sunglasses and her hair being arranged so it covered most of her face made it hard to estimate her age. But it wasn't hard to see the fear in her body language. Like the man, she also attempted to appear relaxed, but failed terribly.

In a movement that was meant to be subtle, but was very obvious, she scanned the street behind her. Her gaze flowed over the café patrons, but she didn't notice the man. Mainly because he was now leaning back in his chair, appearing completely engrossed in whatever was on his phone.

She hid a small shudder and started walking in our direction.

"Maybe we should go in here, love." Colin turned towards me. "They have a…"

I looked at Colin when he inhaled sharply. He was staring at the blonde woman who was now about three metres from us. His eyes were wide, his mouth slightly agape. "Olivia?"

The woman's head jerked towards Colin and she froze. Her reaction mirrored Colin's, just much stronger. She was now close enough for me to observe the micro-expressions on her face. Her eyebrows shot up above the top of her sunglasses and her mouth dropped open. "Jackson?"

All three of us stood frozen for five seconds. I registered a myriad expressions flittering across her face, but didn't have time to process them. My concern was mostly with Colin, whose breathing had increased and whose hand had tightened around mine to the point of discomfort.

A vehicle honking behind us brought intense fear to Olivia's face. She leaned to the side to look past us and gasped, her hand flying to cover her mouth. Colin and I turned around to see what she was looking at. It was a delivery vehicle, waiting to pass a group of tourists heading our way. None of the tourists exhibited any nonverbal cues that would elicit the response Olivia had had.

I turned back. "She's gone."

Colin took a few steps forward, his muscle tension increasing as he looked around the street for the terrified woman. She was nowhere to be seen.

Everyone at the café tables was still chatting, giggling and arguing. But the man was no longer sitting at his table, pretending to be engrossed in his phone. He was gone too. I returned my attention to Colin. I'd never seen him this troubled about meeting someone from his past.

He turned to me, regret, sadness and a deep concern etched on his face. "This cannot be good."

Chapter TWO

COLIN INHALED FOR the fourth time and I wondered if once again he was going to lose his courage to tell the others about Olivia. After a long conversation last night, I had convinced him that the man sitting at the café and Olivia's nonverbal cues of fear warranted disclosure.

"But seriously, dude." Vinnie took another freshly baked croissant, put it on his plate and then took another one. After the first breakfast in Émile's villa, the chef had had to double the number of croissants he baked. His chest had puffed when Vinnie had threatened him with physical harm if there were not enough of these pastries. I'd not been surprised that he hadn't been intimidated by Vinnie. The nine bodyguards who were on the premises were of the same size as, if not bigger than, my friend. He bit into the croissant and closed his eyes for a second. Then he glared at Colin. "Last night was going to be our big win. We were going to get to the last level of the game and you completely flaked out."

"Yeah, it wasn't pretty." Francine lifted her porcelain coffee cup and raised one eyebrow. "You're the one who got us to the door of the last level before. What happened last night? Everything okay?"

Colin looked at Manny. "No."

"Oh, bloody hell." Manny threw the starched linen napkin on the table. "What have you gotten yourself into this time, Frey? We're supposed to take a break from all that rubbish."

"I wasn't looking for it, Millard." Colin took a calming breath, held it and exhaled slowly. "I never expected to see Olivia again. And don't interrupt me with questions. If Jenny hadn't convinced me to tell you, I wouldn't. It's not something I'm proud of."

Manny leaned back in his chair. "I'm listening."

Everyone was listening. Vinnie had even put down the croissant he'd covered in cherry confiture.

Manny, Francine, Vinnie, Roxy, Colin and I were currently sitting outside on the large veranda around a beautifully set breakfast table. Émile was busy with an early-morning conference call and hadn't joined us for breakfast. Nikki was packing the last of her and Eric's things and was late joining us at the table.

The air was fresh, but the sun was already warming up the day. It was going to be another beautiful early autumn day in Hungary. The weather pleased me. The days were still warm enough to wear summer clothes, the early mornings and evenings only requiring a light sweater or jacket.

From the forest at the end of the vast lawn, birds were greeting the day and two deer were nibbling at the fresh leaves of Émile's flowering peonies. No one was paying attention to this. Everyone's eyes were on Colin.

He pushed his hands through his hair. "Nineteen years ago, I was attending classes at Columbia University. I wasn't registered at the university and I wasn't working towards a degree, but I was interested in growing my knowledge base."

He closed his eyes and shook his head. "That's not important. After the first lecture, I met Olivia. Olivia Webster. She was the quintessential American girl next door. Blonde, blue eyes, great sense of humour, pretty, smart, an incredible love for life and genuine. Very genuine."

Six months after Colin and I'd become romantically involved, he'd told me about Olivia. By then he'd known that I found it extremely difficult to conceal the truth. I'd told him that it would be most stressful to lie if someone were ever to ask me about this. He'd laughed and said no one ever would and had proceeded to tell me everything. The same regret I'd seen then was on his face now.

"I was young and far too cocky. I'd known that no one ever succeeded in my line of work—"

"You mean stealing art?" Manny asked.

"—when they became emotionally involved with anyone, yet I didn't walk away." Colin turned away from Manny and faced the others. "Liv and I started talking after class and soon we were meeting for coffee. A year later, we were engaged."

"What the fuck, dude!" Vinnie got up and pointed at Colin. "We've been friends for seventeen years and you never told me."

"Or me." Francine's quiet voice emphasised the hurt visible on her face.

"Well, I for one think that you don't have to tell everyone everything." Roxy grabbed Vinnie's hand and pulled him back into his chair. "What's in the past is in the past."

"Except when you meet your past in Szentendre." Colin didn't continue.

"Okay, so you saw her here." Roxy lifted one shoulder. "What's the big deal?"

"No, no, no." Francine leaned forward and glared at Colin. "You'll answer my question before you answer the questions of someone who's wearing canvas shoes with designer pants." She lifted her hand and held her palm almost in Roxy's face when the latter inhaled to say something. Still glaring at Colin, she lowered her brow. "What happened to the engagement?"

"I broke it off three days before the wedding."

"Dude!"

"Holy hell."

"Shit, Colin." Francine's eyes were wide with shock. "You left her at the altar?"

"He didn't." I took Colin's hand and squeezed it the way he did for me when I needed support. "He ended the relationship three days before."

Francine leaned back in her chair. "That's as good as leaving someone at the altar, girlfriend." She looked at Colin. "Why?"

"I loved her." His soft laugh held no humour. "And I didn't want to hurt her. She knew me as Jackson Roanne, a young art dealer who travelled the world and had no permanent office or residence. Ten days before the wedding, someone I highly respected and who had taught me quite a few tricks of the trade died. In the six years I'd known him, I'd never known he had a family. His wife and three teenaged children found out after the funeral that everything they'd thought they'd known about my associate had been a lie.

"They discovered that the FBI had been investigating him

and everything they'd owned was bought with ill-gotten gains. And that he'd had another wife. The second wife in turn also didn't know anything about this wife and three children. Long story short, I took a good, hard look at my life and realised that I never wanted to be the cause of such devastating betrayal. Not for Liv."

"Did you disappear or did you do this face to face?" Roxy sat unmoving. She was the newest member of this inner circle. Her openness and lack of judgement had helped her settle in and become well-respected within a very short time.

"This is the most difficult part." Colin dropped his head back and closed his eyes for a few seconds. When he faced the group again, shame was now woven together with the regret on his face. "This is one of those actions in my life that I truly wish I could do over. I don't know how I would handle something like that now, but definitely not the way I did. I left her a note."

"Oh, God, Colin." Francine put her hand over her mouth. Her eyes filled with tears. "That poor woman."

Colin pressed his lips tightly together and nodded his head. I hated seeing him this distraught.

"You kept an eye on her, didn't you?" Manny took Francine's hand and interlaced their fingers.

"I did." Colin swallowed once, pulled his shoulders back and looked at Manny. "I needed to make sure she was okay. And she was. Well, after about two months. The first weeks were terrible. She was devastated. The few times I saw her were from a distance, but it was easy to see that she'd lost weight, wasn't sleeping well and generally just looked awful.

I hated myself for being the cause of that."

I knew why Colin despised causing someone else's pain, but it wasn't my story to tell either. I was just once again intrigued at how our life experiences influenced every part of our future. This event in his life was one of the reasons Colin had insisted on there being no secrets between us. It had also made him overly cautious about never being the cause of my distress.

Colin laughed softly. "Then she got angry. I remember one day watching her shout at a taxi driver who'd nearly knocked her over. She ranted for almost ten minutes. That was when I knew she'd be okay."

"But she never saw you again," Manny stated.

"No." Colin shook his head. "I stayed in New York for another four months before I left for Italy."

"To continue your illustrious criminal career."

"Which has no bearing on this specific discussion."

"Don't get your knickers all twisted up, Frey." Manny waved his hand to dismiss the thought. "Most of those crimes you committed are way past their statutes of limitations. Unless you killed someone?"

Had I not been one of the top nonverbal communications experts in the world, I would not have caught Colin's micro-expression of guilt. Sixteen years ago, Colin had broken into a museum's conservation centre to retrieve a stolen painting. It had been at the beginning of his and Vinnie's friendship. Vinnie had joined him to keep an eye out for the few security guards who lazily did their rounds.

One of those guards had changed his route and had come across Vinnie. The older gentleman had been so startled by the huge, muscular man, clearly dressed as a burglar, that he'd had a heart attack.

When CPR didn't revive the old guard, Colin had phoned a detective at Scotland Yard who had been on his trail for a few months already—Manny. Colin had sent Vinnie away and waited for Manny. Once the paramedics had arrived, Manny had taken great pleasure in arresting Colin.

No sooner had they arrived at Scotland Yard than Interpol agents came and told Manny to hand Colin over to them. Manny had been livid and had promised Colin that their paths would cross again one day. Colin had told me this story three times and each time he smiled when he got to the part about their paths crossing. And each time his voice was full of irony as he called Manny his friend.

"Only the guard." Colin's face lost colour. "I'm responsible for his death."

"You didn't kill him, dude." The corners of Vinnie's mouth were turned down. "We've been over this many times. I've made peace with the fact that the old guy's heart would've given out on him anyways. We were just at the wrong place at the wrong time."

Colin shook his head and raised one hand. "We're discussing Olivia, not that."

"Then discuss this Olivia," Manny said. "Why are you telling us about this?"

"I saw her in Szentendre yesterday. After you guys left for lunch. I was looking at the artworks in one of the shop windows and when I turned around, there she was."

"Where were you, Doc?"

"Next to Colin." I had a lot to add to Colin's story, but

decided to wait for him to recount it his way.

"Did she recognise you?" Francine asked.

"Immediately." Colin's hand tightened around mine. "She hasn't changed much. Her hair is a bit longer and she seems shorter for some reason."

"She was wearing flat-heeled shoes."

"Please tell me they weren't running shoes." Francine said the last two words while glaring at Roxy. I recognised Francine's attempt for what it was. She was trying to lighten the atmosphere.

I shook my head. "They were elegant leather shoes."

"See!" Francine threw both hands in the air. "Beautiful women wear beautiful shoes."

Roxy pressed her hand against her chest, her expression insincere affection. "You think I'm beautiful."

Francine tried to control the smile pulling at the corners of her mouth and failed. She winked at Roxy and turned to Colin. "So why are you worried about seeing Olivia? I mean, it could just be coincidence, right?"

Manny made a show of straightening and slowly turned to Francine. "You, the queen of conspiracy theories, used the word 'coincidence'." He slumped back in his chair. "The end of the world is nigh."

"I honestly don't know what to think." Colin raised both shoulders and shook his head. "The probability of seeing her in this tiny village in Hungary does seem unlikely. But the stuff Jenny saw is the real issue."

Everyone turned to me. When I didn't say anything, Francine snorted. "That's your cue to continue the story, girlfriend."

"Oh." I looked at Colin. His lips were tightly pressed together, his eyes revealing his distress. He nodded and I turned back to the group. "I saw a man watching Olivia."

Some of the tension left Colin's face as he chuckled softly. "Tell them everything you saw, love."

Experience had taught me that 'everything' didn't always mean everything. I took a moment to decide which details of yesterday's event were pertinent. "While Colin was looking at art in a shop window, I noticed a man sitting at a café trying to appear inconspicuous. He was watching Olivia."

"Watching like a stalker or like a cop?" Vinnie asked.

"Not a stalker." I shook my head. "There was a professional interest in the way he was observing her as she walked towards us. But he is only one of the reasons I'm concerned. When Olivia recognised Colin, I saw the typical emotions expected when a person comes across someone who'd caused you pain." I stopped when both Francine and Roxy cleared their throats and glared at me. I frowned. "What?"

"They think you're being insensitive, love." Colin squeezed my hand. "Don't worry about it. Tell them what you saw."

"Fear." Recalling Olivia's mouth dropping open, her tense lips and the dread around her eyes brought a tightness to my chest. "The kind of fear someone displays when they believe their life is in imminent danger."

"Before I could ask her anything, a delivery truck behind us made a noise. Jenny and I turned to look at the commotion and when we looked back, Liv had disappeared."

"And the man watching her?" Manny asked.

"He must have followed her." Colin looked at the villa door leading to the veranda. The muscle tension on his face relaxed as he smiled. Nikki was walking towards us with Eric on her hip.

She tilted her head when no one said anything. "What's going on here?"

"Did you pack everything, punk?" Vinnie got up and held out his hands towards Eric. But the baby wasn't interested. He'd seen me and was leaning forward to get out of Nikki's arms.

She walked around the table and stopped next to my chair. "Yes, I packed everything. I swear, it's like packing for seventeen adults. This little monster needs more stuff than I ever did."

Eric was almost horizontal in his attempt to reach me. I took a few calming breaths and pulled my hand from Colin's. At Nikki's enquiring expression, I nodded. "I'll take him."

Nikki laughed when Eric almost fell from her arms to get to me. It had taken me weeks before I felt comfortable holding Eric. I wrapped my hands around his ribcage and tried to settle him on my lap. He didn't want that. He wiggled and turned until I allowed him to face me.

My focus was now completely on the little person in my space. The others were telling Nikki that we'd been discussing our plans for the day once she'd left. She didn't believe them. I didn't care. Eric was staring straight at me with an intensity as if he could understand what he saw on my face. Like most non-neurotypicals, I almost never made eye contact and frequently avoided Eric's curious gazes. Yet now I looked at him looking at me.

He wiggled to get closer and I relented, bringing him eye level with me, making sure he wasn't close enough to put his mouth on me. The one time that happened, Colin had barely caught him in time when I'd gone in a total shutdown from the hot, wet saliva on my cheek. A small smile pulled at my mouth as I analysed the relaxed muscles around his eyes and mouth. He was happy and felt safe. A familiar warm feeling spread in my chest.

Eric opened his chubby hands and rested one on each of my cheeks. He lowered his head and I pulled away. A small frown marred his previously happy expression. I scowled at his mouth. "No kisses. No kisses."

His *corrugator supercilii* muscles pulled his eyebrows even closer and I sighed. Hoping irrationally that he'd understood my repeated order, I moved closer. Immediately the muscles around his eyes and mouth relaxed once again. Not taking his eyes off me, he leaned forward and rested his forehead on mine, our eyes only two centimetres or so apart.

I froze. Eric was a social baby and loved physical contact with everyone around the table. Yet there was something unique about this moment. I'd never observed him initiating such intimacy with anyone but Nikki. There was no conceivable way that Eric would be able to recall this moment, but I knew that allowing him this moment of affection would shape him as an adult.

It was shaping me.

It felt like we sat like that for hours, but in reality it was less than sixty seconds when Eric relaxed in my hands and wiggled again until I settled him on my lap. That was when I realised it was quiet around the table. I looked up to see everyone staring at us.

Nikki was wiping tears from her eyes, Francine was taking

photos with her smartphone and Vinnie was kissing Roxy's curly hair. The gentle expressions of affection were the only reason I wasn't alarmed.

"That's possibly the sweetest thing I've seen in my whole life." Roxy leaned against Vinnie.

"And I got a few really good photos." Francine swiped the screen of her smartphone. Her expression softened even more and she turned the screen towards Manny. "I think we should print this one and get it framed."

"Ready for the road, Nikki?" Émile Roche came out of the house, carrying a laptop bag. "We'd better get going if we want to stop in Vienna for cake and coffee."

Émile's light blue eyes sought Eric. The laughter lines around his eyes deepened when he saw the baby on my lap. At seventy years old, Émile was still very active. Margot, his wife of forty-four years, was just as active. She'd hurt her back playing tennis two weeks ago and returned to Strasbourg to their specialist. I imagined it was another reason Émile wanted to go back. His devotion to his wife and family was strong.

He walked to me and touched Eric's cheek with the tip of his index finger. "You're going to miss your auntie Genevieve, aren't you?"

Eric smiled at Émile and rested his cheek against my chest. I stared at his fist tightly gripping my thumb.

"I'm ready, Émile." Nikki got up from her seat next to Francine. "Let me smooch everyone, grab my firstborn and we can blow this joint."

Émile chuckled and shook his head. He had taken an immediate liking to Nikki and she to him. They'd spent most of the week talking about their shared love for old gangster movies. When they'd started quoting the movies, I'd stopped paying attention. It had become too difficult to determine when they were jesting, having a genuine conversation or trying to out-quote each other.

Ten minutes later, we were standing next to Émile's bulletproof SUV. This vehicle and two just like it that would lead and follow Émile and Nikki were part of the argument she'd used to placate Vinnie and Manny. Both men had expressed their concerns over Nikki and Eric's safety the moment she'd decided to go home early. The arguing had come to a climax last night.

Roxy had been the one to remind everyone the reason why Émile was returning to Strasbourg. His daughter was giving birth to a boy and he would do everything in his power to arrive there safely. I had confirmed Émile's sincerity when he'd said he considered Nikki as family and Eric as an honorary grandchild. I knew Nikki and Eric would be safe with him.

"You tell Pink he'd better listen to the doctor's orders or I'll put him back in hospital when I get home." Vinnie gave Nikki another hug.

"I'll tell him that." Nikki walked to me. "And then he'll kick your butt the next time we play Drestia."

Pink was the IT technician of the GIPN team we frequently worked with. Similar to the SWAT teams in the US, the men and women on the French GIPN teams put their lives in danger on a daily basis. During our last big case, six months ago, Pink had been injured quite severely. He'd been in a coma for four and a half weeks before he started the very slow road to recovery.

Five weeks ago, he'd walked again for the first time. Francine had been there and had shown me the video she'd taken. I'd been deeply upset by the discomfort bordering on pain I'd observed on Pink's face as he'd leaned heavily on the walking aid, slowly making his way towards the camera. Since then he'd worked extremely hard with his physiotherapist to strengthen his body. At first the doctors had said Pink would never walk again. Then they'd said he would always have difficulty walking, possibly always needing a walker or crutches. I didn't know what the doctors' latest prognosis was. Pink had proven them wrong the first time. I hoped he would do so again.

When he'd started making significant progress, a lot of arguments had erupted about where he would go once released from the inpatient rehabilitation facility he'd moved to after his long stay in the hospital. His team leader and best friend Daniel had insisted on Pink moving in with him, but everyone agreed Daniel's modern apartment was not suited for someone in recovery.

Vinnie had announced that Pink would move in with us. On Vinnie and Nikki's side of our joined apartments was an unoccupied room Vinnie used as his home gym. That same day he'd moved his equipment into his bedroom and got Nikki to help him arrange the room and take pictures to send to Pink.

No matter how much Pink insisted on going back to his own place, Vinnie would hear nothing of it. I'd grown tired of the constant bickering and had told Pink he would be wise to stay with us for a few weeks. There was more than enough space in our joined apartments and if ever I felt overwhelmed by the many people in my home, I would retire to my bedroom and lock my reinforced bedroom door. All three locks.

His micro-expressions when he'd agreed had been enlightening. He'd resisted out of concern for me and was relieved when I'd reassured him that he would be wise to make use of Vinnie and Nikki's offered help.

Three days after we'd arrived here at the villa, Pink's doctors finally permitted him to go home. When he'd phoned to say he was being released, Vinnie had wanted to leave immediately. Nikki had convinced him that Pink already felt guilty for intruding in our space. Having Vinnie leave this long-awaited vacation would only exacerbate that guilt.

She hadn't made any rational argument for her being the one to pick Pink up at the hospital and settle him into his new room. I still didn't know her true reason for ending her vacation early to help Pink, but I was proud of her.

We walked to the front of the villa. The SUVs were parked in the circular driveway, the bodyguards chatting next to them. Nikki took Eric from me and secured him in his car seat. She handed him the green dragon, then straightened and walked to me. She stopped in front of me. "Gonna hug you."

I appreciated the warning and took a moment to brace myself. She threw her arms around me in her usual exuberant manner and held me tightly against her. I took a deep breath and put my arms around her, awkwardly patting her back. The hug lasted for a mere twenty seconds, but my uneasiness at such physical closeness was already turning into panic. I took a step back when she released me. “Keep me updated on your progress.”

“I’ll send you loads of photos from the road.” She looked at Eric shaking the dragon in our direction. “If this is the same as our trip here, he’s going to sleep most of the way.”

It took another ten minutes for everyone to bid their farewells. I found such emotional moments most uncomfortable and unnecessary. We would see Nikki and Eric in another five days when we returned to Strasbourg. Such long embraces and tearful goodbyes seemed excessive. I was glad to watch the three cars leave the long driveway—not glad to watch Nikki go, but glad for the melodrama to end.

Manny and Vinnie were talking about Pink’s physiotherapy, and Francine was begging Roxy to go shoe shopping with her today. I leaned closer to Colin and simply enjoyed standing in the morning sun, listening to my friends.

I turned towards the road when the gentle rumble of a car drew my attention to the driveway. My first thought was that, despite Nikki’s numerous assurances, she had indeed left something behind. But it wasn’t one of the three large black SUVs that entered the property.

By now everyone was watching the light grey sedan making its way towards us. Vinnie reached behind his back and rested his hand on his weapon that was holstered there. Manny stepped in front of Francine and nodded at the two bodyguards who came around the side of the villa. They spread out behind us, their hands also resting on their weapons. Whoever was in the car should by now know he or she was not getting a warm reception.

The sun was reflecting off the windscreen, making it hard

to see the driver. I squinted and saw the sleeve of a man's blazer. The sedan slowed and turned to park in front of us. I inhaled sharply and clutched Colin's hand. Dark edges entered my peripheral vision.

I didn't want to shut down now. Not out here and not when I knew this was important. So I mentally played Mozart's Symphony No. 6 in F major with great determination.

"Doc?" Manny didn't take his eyes off the vehicle. "Do you know our visitor?"

I swallowed past the tightness in my throat as I watched an athletic body exit the vehicle. "It's him."

"Who, love?" Colin asked softly.

"The man from the café. The man who was watching Olivia."

Chapter THREE

I MANAGED A few shallow breaths as the man got out of his vehicle. He was wearing jeans, a dress shirt and a blue blazer. He moved with the easy grace of someone who was very fit. What he'd managed to hide yesterday was the confidence in his movements. He looked at me and nodded as if confirming something to himself. He closed the car door, his body language attempting to bring the message across that he was relaxed. He was not.

He was alert and curious, and the tension around his mouth and in his shoulders increased when he noticed the two bodyguards and the many hands resting on holstered firearms. With a sigh he raised both hands. "I come in peace."

Manny nodded towards the man's hip that was clearly visible now that his raised hands had moved his blazer. "That's not what that pistol on your side tells me. A P9RC if I'm correct. Hmm. That weapon has quite the reputation for its aim being off."

"Yeah, well, you see, this is part of my work outfit, so I kind of have to wear it every day." He lifted one shoulder, then pointed to his blazer pocket. "I'm going to reach into my pocket and get out my ID. Please don't shoot me."

"Who are you?" Colin took a step forward, his arms away from his body, his fists clenched. "What do you want?"

The man used only his index finger and thumb to take a leather folder out of his pocket. He opened it and held it out towards me. "I'm Detective Andor Garas. I'm from the Special Affairs Department at the Budapest Police Department."

I didn't move. I wasn't interested in his credentials. I was much more intrigued by his excellent command of English, the manner in which he observed everyone looking at him and the way he then seemed to make decisions about each one. He didn't look overly concerned with the two bodyguards, but his eyes kept straying back to Vinnie and Colin.

Manny stepped forward, took the leather folder and glanced at it before he handed it to Francine. "So, Andor Garas, you heard the question. What do you want?"

Andor's shoulders dropped a bit. "Seriously, guys. I come in peace. I know who you are and I'm here to ask for help. I'm not interested in a pissing contest." His eyes narrowed at Francine while she tapped and swiped her tablet. "What are you doing?"

"Making sure you are who you say you are."

"Um… I'm pretty sure what you're doing is not legal." There was no judgement on his face, just curiosity.

Francine didn't look up from her tablet, but smiled. "It will only matter if you… huh… okay." She lifted her tablet. "He checks out."

Manny turned to me. "Doc?"

"Yes?"

Manny raised both eyebrows and, when I still didn't say anything, glared at me. "What do you see?"

"In Detective Garas' nonverbal communication?" I tilted my head as I turned to Andor. "You're being truthful. But you should practice your deceptive skills. You're not successful in hiding that you are nervous of all of us and in awe of Manny."

"What the hell?" Manny grabbed the leather folder from Francine and tossed it at Andor. "Awe?"

A blush crawled up Andor's neck and reddened his cheeks as he easily caught the folder and put it back in his blazer pocket. "I needed to know who I was dealing with, so I ran your names. You have quite an impressive résumé, Colonel Millard."

"You know who we are?" Francine's voice was a pitch higher than usual.

"You hack anything and everything to help your team." Andor looked from Francine to Vinnie, his eyes pausing on the long scar on Vinnie's face for a second. "He's your team security, Doctor Ferreira lends her medical expertise when needed, Doctor Lenard analyses the data and people and"—he looked at Colin—"I'm not sure what you do, but you seem important."

"What do you mean?" Colin's tone was quiet, dangerous, his body language threatening.

I eagerly waited for Andor's explanation. There had been a nuance to his statement I wanted to understand.

"I have a fantabulous idea." Roxy avoided Vinnie's hand grabbing her arm and walked towards Andor. "You're not here to kill us, right?"

His eyes widened. "Right."

She turned to me. "And you're saying he's harmless."

"I said no such thing."

"See? We're all going to get along just fine." She extended her right hand to Andor. When he took a moment too long to shake her hand, she widened her eyes and looked pointedly at her hand.

He chuckled and shook her hand. "It's a pleasure to meet you, Doctor Ferreira."

"Yeah, yeah. Everyone says that." She waved towards the villa. "Now let's go inside and talk." She looked at Colin, Manny and Vinnie. "Nicely."

No one moved. The tension in the group was most discomfiting. I took my time analysing the detective's nonverbal cues. "Detective Garas means us no harm."

"Please call me Andor."

Colin stepped in front of Andor, preventing him from entering the villa. "You—"

"Truly." Andor held out both hands, showing the insides of his arms. Non-confrontational. "I deal with douchebag alpha males every single day. I'm not one of them. I don't think it proves my smarts by playing my cards close to my vest and trying to wrangle things so I can get all the glory. I'm here because of a case that now involves you and I'm convinced you and your team can help me."

The sincerity on his face and in his voice convinced not only me. Collectively, the men's bodies marginally relaxed. But still no one moved.

Colin studied Andor for a few seconds, then nodded his head. "Let's get inside and talk."

Three minutes later everyone but Vinnie was seated around the square dining room table. It was a beautiful walnut wood table that seated twelve people with ease. As soon as we'd entered the villa, Manny had directed Andor to one side of the table and had made sure no one else sat on the same side as the detective. Vinnie was standing behind Roxy's chair, one hand resting on her shoulder, the other ready to grab his weapon.

Andor settled in his chair and waited. He exhibited a confidence usually seen in very accomplished individuals and people who had no need or reason to prove their value. It made me curious about him as a person.

Manny slumped in his chair and sighed heavily. "Why do you need our help?"

Andor blinked once then faced Colin. "Olivia Webster is missing."

"What do you mean missing?" Manny knocked on the table when Andor didn't look at him. "Speak."

Colin's face had lost colour. That was the only external indication that Andor's statement had affected him. Even before he'd met Manny, Colin had mastered the art of disguising himself—not only his identity, but also his nonverbal cues. When I'd first met Colin, my expertise had played a significant role in analysing his micro-expressions. I'd come to know him well enough to recognise the deep distress he was masking now. I also saw his usual casual interest to be much keener.

Andor leaned forward in a manner friends did when sharing anecdotes. "So, my boss' big boss is friends with Ms Webster's boss. My boss is pissed off that this got dumped in our lap, but I think he's more pissed off that the big boss blackmailed him with revealing how badly he lost at the last interdepartmental poker game." He shrugged. "But that's just my take on things."

"You haven't told us anything useful yet." Manny sounded bored, but the slight contraction of the *orbicularis oculi* muscles around his eyes betrayed his piqued interest.

"Very true." For the first time, Andor showed the excitement he'd been attempting to hide since he exited his car. "I'll start with the bosses and then tell you my side of it."

Manny nodded and Vinnie sat down next to Roxy. Andor was building rapport with my team at a faster rate than most people. Even though scepticism was still clear on most faces, it was slowly being replaced by interest.

"So, Ms Webster… what the bleep, I'm just going to call her Olivia. Anyway, Olivia's boss phoned my boss' big boss when Olivia didn't check in with him last night. She's here… oh, wait. Do you know why she's here? Do you know what she does for a living?"

No-one answered him.

"Okay then. I'll just tell you as if you don't know. Olivia is a lawyer at a prestigious legal firm in Manhattan. Most of her cases are white-collar crime cases. Sometimes she's hired by families to dispute last wills and testaments. She's currently in Hungary because of a case like that." He lifted an index finger. "I'll tell you about the case in a sec. Anyway, Olivia's boss is also her mentor and thinks of himself as her godfather. When her case brought her here, he made her promise to check in every morning and every evening. She's been in Hungary for three days and so far has spoken to her boss twice a day, every day."

"Until last night," Colin said softly.

"Until last night." Andor nodded. "Her boss became increasingly worried when Olivia didn't phone him at their usual time or at all during the evening. He didn't even wait until this morning before he phoned my boss' big boss."

"Why don't you just say Commissioner Drozdik?" Francine pointed at her tablet. "If that's the big boss you're talking about."

"It is.' Andor's smile was mischievous. "It's more fun calling him my boss' big boss."

Francine's smile was wide and genuine. "Can't argue with that."

Manny knocked on the table again. "Speak."

"So, one man's favour became another man's order and my boss woke me up to shout at me to find this woman."

I added everything he'd told us to what I saw in his expression. "Your boss doesn't know that you already knew Olivia was in Hungary and that you were surveilling her."

"You saw me yesterday." He didn't look surprised. "I wasn't surveilling her. I was waiting for her to meet with me."

"She was going to meet with you?" Colin asked.

"Yes." He waved his hand as if to stop something. "Wait, let me tell this right. Firstly, my boss didn't know that I was going to meet Olivia yesterday. I didn't know what to make of it when she contacted me and asked for a meeting. She sounded scared on the phone and then wanted all kinds of silly counter-surveillance steps to make sure that I wasn't followed to that café. Honestly, she sounded paranoid and I wasn't going to tell my captain and make anything official until I knew what she was up to."

"Tell me exactly what she told you when she phoned." My expertise was in nonverbal communication, but sometimes I was able to derive important information from someone's words.

He closed his eyes for a moment, then focused on the ceiling. Recalling. "She phoned me yesterday morning at around ten, saying that she asked around and heard that I was the right person for controversial and sensitive cases." He smiled at Francine when she picked up her tablet. "You can check. I've worked on eleven high-profile cases that involved crooked politicians, a religious leader and even a doctor who played God. On a few of those cases I co-operated with the National Bureau of Investigation. I wasn't surprised that my name came up when she asked around. I was, however, going to ask her who she had asked."

"But you didn't get the chance."

"Nope. I saw her talking to you and"—he looked at Colin—"you. Then the delivery truck honked and just like that she ran."

"Did you see where she went?"

"She ran into the small alley that goes to the church. I followed her, but I'm sure you know Szentendre has so many winding little streets that I wasn't surprised that she disappeared."

"Finish telling me what she said when she phoned." I needed to hear everything.

"Oh, sorry. Yes. She gave me her name and told me that I can confirm that she's a lawyer from New York. She said she was working for a family who was disputing a last will and testament. She'd uncovered something and didn't know how to proceed with the information in Hungarian jurisdiction. She didn't want to disclose anything else on the phone. Even though she didn't say it, I got the feeling that she was worried about someone listening in on the conversation."

"There's more." I could clearly see it on his face.

"Yes. She told me that if for some reason she didn't show up yesterday afternoon, I was to meet her this morning at six next to the church."

"Let me guess." Manny pushed his hands into his trouser pockets. "She wasn't there."

"There was no one there." Genuine concern contracted the corners of Andor's mouth and eyes. "That early in Szentendre, almost everyone is still sleeping. It was easy to hear footsteps and see anyone approaching the church. I was there at five-thirty and waited until seven. Until six-thirty only three people were in the vicinity. Then a few cleaners and two delivery trucks showed up. But no Olivia." He looked at Colin. "I saw that she recognised you. She spoke to you. Did she say anything? And how do you know her?"

Colin stared at Andor for a few seconds. I could see he believed the detective's story. But he was undecided on how much to reveal to this stranger. "She only said my name. The delivery truck honked before she said anything else. We turned to look at the truck and when I looked back, she was gone."

"Yeah, she moved bleeping quick." Andor opened his arms and rested his hands palms up on the table. "Look, I know you guys don't know me and therefore have no reason to trust me with anything. But I have a feeling that this is important. Not only do I think that Olivia is in real danger and we should do what we can to find her, but I think the case she's looking into might be important. And is the reason she's missing."

For a moment no one spoke. Francine's interest was undisguised, as was Roxy's. Vinnie and Manny both clearly communicated their reluctance, but I could see their curiosity. It was Colin's dismay and the myriad nonverbal cues from Andor that affected me the most. I needed time to process what Andor had told us and compare it to what I'd seen on his face as well as what I'd learned from meeting Olivia.

"Doc?"

No. I silently shook my head. I wasn't ready to give an opinion. I needed time. And I needed Colin alone so I could ask him what he wanted to do. The idea of putting him in a position that caused him any kind of emotional turmoil brought darkness to my peripheral vision.

I ignored Manny when he asked me again for my opinion. I also ignored the concerned looks I got from everyone. I got up and left the dining room without looking back.

Chapter FOUR

I WASN'T SURPRISED when Colin entered our large ensuite bathroom nine minutes after me. When Émile had declared this room ours, I'd been pleased. The room was spacious, with large windows and a sliding door that led to a balcony overlooking the extensive grounds. The furniture and finishings in the room were of the highest quality and comfort.

But it had been this bathroom that had immediately served to relax me in this unknown environment. The cream-coloured tiles and minimalistic finishings soothed my mind. The bathtub was large enough to easily accommodate two people.

Like so many times in the last few days, I was sitting in the empty bathtub, hugging my knees to my chest. The other times Colin had found me in the tub, I had been rocking and keening while in a complete shutdown. Now I was only sitting here to think.

The moment he saw me in the tub, he kicked off his shoes and climbed in with me. Every time I'd come out of my shutdown or meltdown in the last week, Colin had been in the tub with me. He sat down facing me and studied me for a moment. "Are you okay?"

"The question is too generic. If you want to know whether I'm going to shut down, the answer is no. If you want to know whether I'm upset, that question would also be too generic, but the answer would be yes."

"Is it because of Olivia?" Immediately, he closed his eyes and shook his head. "Don't answer it. It's another bad question. Um… I suppose I should rather ask what you are doing in the tub."

"I need to think."

He nodded and leaned back against the tub. When he closed his eyes and dropped his head back, I knew he was going to give me the time I needed to process the events and information from the last twenty-four hours. I also knew he needed this moment for himself.

I thought about Olivia's strong response to seeing Colin, the open fear on her face and the other expressions that I'd registered. My thoughts turned to Andor and I wondered what it was that he was not yet telling us. And why he seemed immune to the hostility he'd received from almost everyone on the team.

"I loved her." Colin's quiet statement drew me back into the present. He was looking at me, his emotions raw and unhidden on his face.

"I know." When he'd told me about Olivia, I'd known he was sharing the basic minimum, but I'd seen that his emotional connection to her had been deep and strong.

"I think I hurt her really badly when I just disappeared."

I nodded. "I saw the memory of that pain on her face yesterday."

"Shit." Colin pushed his fingers through his hair. It felt like there was a vice tightening around my chest when I saw the internal turmoil pulling at his mouth and eyes. "I want to grab Vinnie, rush out and find her. But I also want to run the other way."

"Why?" My question applied to both his instincts.

"I hate the idea that she might be in danger. But she also represents a part of my past that… well, I was young and stupid. I'm not proud of what I did to her."

I valued the complete honesty in my relationship with Colin. I never had to worry about hidden meanings behind his words. I knew it wasn't always easy for him to be as open with me as he was. But he knew that I didn't expect him to share every detail of his life with me. I'd told him that events, experiences and thoughts about the past that were pertinent to our lives, affecting our relationship, were all I was interested in. It helped me understand him better and formulate an effective strategy to deal with challenges that arose because of his past.

I'd been frustrated when he'd told me that he agreed and disagreed with my approach. He agreed because unnecessary information was exactly that: unnecessary. But he disagreed because knowing little bits of useless information about my life helped him get a much better overall picture of who I was.

After some thought, I'd conceded to his point. I always insisted on as much data as possible in order to gain an accurate holistic view of a case. Why would it be any different in relationships? I never asked him to share parts of his past he wasn't willing to and he didn't push me. Yet thinking about it now, I realised how much we'd trusted each other with our pasts. How much I'd confided in him and he in me.

He rubbed the back of his neck and nodded downstairs

towards the others. "There are things I don't want them to know."

I studied his face. "No one downstairs has the right to judge you for any mistakes you made in the past. I've wasted countless hours, even days, micro-analysing and re-analysing mistakes I've made in my life.

"Every time I do something that is not completely correct or controlled, something that draws the scorn of peers, I find it hard to disconnect. I've come to the conclusion that I should allow myself to make mistakes, but it is not that easy. The only way I can ever release the obsessive analysing, the regret and the suffocating feeling of being inept, is by putting all my effort into learning from my mistakes.

"I look at your life, at the way you treat the people you love, and I have no doubt that you've learned from your mistakes. Regret and guilt I can understand, but the shame you're exhibiting? I feel confident in venturing that that is a waste of valuable emotional energy."

He stared at me. I had been told numerous times that I was hard to read. I'd never allowed my deepest emotions to communicate themselves through my nonverbal cues. But now I made an effort. I allowed Colin to see my trust, my acceptance and my love.

He swallowed and blinked a few times before he reached for my hands. He pulled me closer and pressed my hands hard against his chest. "You are the best thing that ever happened to me. You're the best part of my life."

"What the bleeding hell are you doing in here?" Manny walked into the bathroom and glared down at us. "Why are you in the bath? Dressed?"

"Why are you in our bathroom?" Colin twisted to half-shield me from Manny. This instinctual action confirmed my earlier proclamations.

Manny shook his head, his shoulders dropping as he grumbled. He walked to the toilet and sat on the closed lid. "That Garage character is telling us all kinds of interesting things and he's making calls to people I just know are going to piss me off."

"Garas. His surname is Garas." I huffed at the distraction and focused on Manny's nonverbal cues. "You're interested in this case."

Manny didn't answer. He looked around the bathroom, then looked at us, his *corrugator supercilii* muscles pulling his eyebrows in and down in a deep frown. "I really want to know what you two are doing in that bath."

"Jenny just needs some time to think," Colin said before I could answer.

"Hmm." Manny leaned forward, rested his elbows on his knees and stared at me. "Is this getting too much for you, Doc? Should we just pack up and go?"

His softly spoken question revealed so much more than just his concern. "You know about my shutdowns."

"I'm a bit of a detective, you see." A small smile lifted the one corner of his mouth. "I saw you disappearing when Eric drooled on you the first day. Then the next day you disappeared as soon as we got home. I wasn't surprised the crowded marketplace got to you that day. I nearly punched a few people's lights out there. Frey would disappear with you and then you two would only join us hours later. It didn't take much of my detective skills to put two and two together."

"Do the others know?" I wanted my friends to enjoy their holiday. I didn't want them to be worried that I was in a constant state of overstimulation and anxiety.

"What do you think, Doc?"

I put my hands over my eyes and dropped my head forward.

"They know you're handling this as best you can, love." Colin took my hand from my eyes and leaned down until I looked at him. "No one's worried about you. Well, not in the way that would spoil their fun."

"Why didn't you tell me they knew?"

"And add more stress?" Colin shook his head. "We're all having a wonderful holiday. Just a few quirks."

"And now a big quirk." Manny sat up. "Are you up for questions, Doc?"

Whereas sitting in the bathtub made me feel protected while I was overwhelmed, I was now feeling vulnerable. I got out of the tub and sat on the edge. Colin joined me. "What questions?"

"Is there anything in that detective's body language that's giving you red flags?" He lowered his brow. "Do I need to explain red flags before you piss me off?"

Colin chuckled.

"I understand the expression." I had an exceptional vocabulary and an above-average grasp of linguistics. But because my brain processed everything on a literal level, it was often hard to catch the euphemism while I was processing the rest of someone's speech as having a straightforward intent. "Nothing in Andor's nonverbal cues gave me any indication that he's being deceitful or that he has ill intent."

"But?" Manny must have heard the reservation in my voice.

"He's withholding information." I caught myself before I crossed my arms. I put my hands on my lap. "I don't like speculating, but I venture that he's keeping that information from us as a way to bargain for our assistance."

"Yeah. That's my take on that little bugger too." Manny raised both eyebrows. "If he gives us everything he knows and we decide to take on the case, will you be able to handle it?"

I was barely coping with the change of environment and my constant concern over my friends. I considered Manny's question even though I knew there was no possible way for me to predict how my non-neurotypical mind would deal with challenges. There were weeks, even months that went by when I didn't experience a shutdown. Then something as seemingly insignificant as my favourite brand of camomile tea not being in stock would cause a shutdown that would last hours.

The unpredictability of my mind was frustrating. It was impossible, however, to imagine how trying my shutdowns had to be for my neurotypical friends. I brought my thoughts back from this digression and once again deliberated our involvement in finding Olivia and helping Andor with his case. And whatever he was yet to reveal. I inhaled deeply. "I can only predict that my mind will handle this case in a manner similar to our other cases. I can't say what effect the different environment would have. If you are determined to help Andor, I will support you in that decision."

"Determined to help." Manny snorted. "I wouldn't use those words exactly, Doc." He looked at Colin. "And you?

Are we going to have to give you hugs and cuddles so you don't fall apart while we deal with your ex?"

Colin's mouth opened slightly in astonishment. "You are without a doubt the biggest arsehole I know."

"Thanks. Now answer my bloody question."

"No, Millard. I won't need hugs and cuddles. Olivia was part of my life a very long time ago. She was important to me then and if there is anything I can do to help her now, I will do it." He took my hand. "We'll do it."

"You're good with helping the ex, Doc?"

"I don't understand your question."

"Bloody hell."

"Genevieve is not like us, honey." Francine walked into the bathroom. It was getting crowded. She stopped next to Manny and rested her hand on his shoulder while looking at me. "She's not jealous of someone who played an important role in Colin's life before she became the most important person in his life. Right, girlfriend?"

I frowned. "Why would I be jealous?"

"See?" Francine shrugged as if my response had been exactly what she'd expected. She poked Manny's shoulder. "I've been shamelessly eavesdropping on you guys and am dying to know why you chose the bathroom for this discussion, but I came here to get you. Andor has been on the phone with someone for the last two minutes and is demanding to speak to Genevieve."

"Doc?"

I turned to Colin. "This is your decision."

He got up and took my hand. Twice he inhaled to speak, but in the end just nodded his head.

I didn't reveal a lot about myself to others simply because I seldom considered it relevant. Colin, on the other hand, was obsessively private. I believed it was a combination of his character and spending more than half his life living as one of his many aliases. If I were going to find this case challenging, Colin was going to find it most arduous.

We went downstairs to find Roxy laughing at something Andor had said. Vinnie also looked decidedly less aggressive towards the younger man. The true proof that Andor had built a positive rapport with Vinnie was the plate of Vinnie's homemade cookies in the centre of the table. A tray of coffee mugs sat next to it, steam still floating up from the hot liquid.

"Ah, you're here." Andor put his coffee mug down and smiled at me. "I have much to tell you."

"So I hear." I took one of the mugs and sat in the same chair as before. Colin settled next to me, nodding when Vinnie gave him a concerned look.

Andor waited for everyone to sit down and prepare their coffee and Manny his milky tea. "I can understand that you guys don't want to trust me yet. So I'll start with a confession. I researched your team the day you arrived here. You see, I've been keeping an eye on Émile Roche."

He looked around the elegant dining room and towards the large and opulent entrance of the villa. "His name was flagged because of his previous run-ins with Interpol. My boss was again pissed off with me about something or another and as my punishment, I had to do a full check on Émile. The brass wanted me to keep an eye on all Émile's comings and goings as well as any people he was in contact with or who visited him. I quickly learned that all his businesses were now on the up and up and this villa was bought legally with clean money. I was curious about his change of lifestyle and asked around. It took a while to determine which team employed Émile's help in one of their cases."

He was using speech more colourful than I was accustomed to, but in context it was easy to understand. I wasn't that interested in his euphemisms and other verbal expressions. It was his facial expressions that caught my attention. I wasn't one to speculate or anticipate what a person was about to reveal, but the current expression on his face brought an uncomfortable feeling to my chest.

"When you guys arrived here at Émile's villa, I was immediately informed." Andor took another sip of his coffee. "And that was when I started thinking about asking for your help."

"Help with what?" Manny asked. I wondered if Manny had also noticed that Andor had wanted our help before he'd even known about Olivia's disappearance.

A troubled look replaced all light friendliness on Andor's face. "I think we have a serial killer in this area."

There it was. The confirmation of my suspicion that there was something much larger than Olivia's disappearance motivating Andor. I waited for the panic, the darkness to take over, but none of it came. I felt strangely calm and interested.

No one else responded. Manny slumped into his chair and glared at Andor. Vinnie crossed his arms, his lips in a thin line. Of all of us, Roxy looked the most perturbed by Andor's statement.

Colin put his coffee mug down on the table. "Tell us everything you know."

"Does that mean you'll help me?"

"Why do you need our help?" Manny asked.

His expression was so revealing I spoke before I thought about it. "He hasn't told his superiors or they don't believe… aha, it's the former."

"Why haven't you told your superior?" Colin asked.

Andor raised one shoulder. "Because I have no bleeping solid proof that these murders were even murders. They all appeared one hundred percent to be deaths by natural causes."

"Dude, bleep isn't a good swear word." Vinnie's top lip curled. "It has no oomph."

"That's why I'm using it." Andor chuckled. "Someone complained about my strong language and I was told to change it."

"So you started using bleep?" Roxy laughed. "How does that translate into Hungarian?"

Andor's smile was mischievous. "Really badly."

It irked me when people got so easily distracted. I needed to stay on topic. "So what makes you think these deaths are murders?"

Andor sobered. "All three victims were extremely influential individuals. Rich, powerful and connected. That is a very loose similarity between them." He looked at Francine. "All three deaths were livestreamed."

"Someone was broadcasting a live feed of these people's deaths?" Francine's eyebrows rose high on her forehead. "You're sure about this?"

"I found the camera still streaming in the last victim's house. I then checked the data flow from the IP addresses of the first victims. The IT experts assured me that both victims were streaming live video at the time the medical examiner said they'd died. Both victims died in rooms with cameras in laptops, TVs and phones, so it could've come from any of those devices. When I tried to delve deeper, I was strongly and clearly told that even the medical examiner classified these deaths as natural and I should mind my own business."

"What did you do to create such a fragile relationship with your colleagues and superiors?" It was easy for me to see the way he was avoiding full disclosure.

"You might as well tell us all your secrets, dude." Vinnie's biceps bulged as he flexed his crossed arms. "If you want our help, you gotta know that we're going to find out every little detail about your life."

Andor looked at Manny and pulled his shoulders back. "I advanced through the ranks very quickly. There is some resentment among my peers because of that. I got where I am today because I'm good at what I do. I look at cases and can quickly determine if there is something fishy about them. I've taken on cases that everyone else thought were nuisance cases. Those were the cases that got me promoted, that got me noticed. My colleagues who dismissed those cases as rubbish are the ones with the most resentment."

"Your superior?" Manny asked.

"He's a good man." Andor's micro-expressions revealed his respect. "But he's convinced he was being punished when I was placed in his department. I don't want to cause him any problems with his bosses by taking cases to him that might turn out to be nothing."

"You mean this case," I said. "Your suspicion of a serial killer."

"Yes." He rubbed his palms on his thighs, a self-soothing gesture. "I suppose I should also tell you that my father is the National Commissioner of Police."

A small smile lifted one corner of Manny's mouth. I didn't understand why he would find Andor's apparent embarrassment humorous. He leaned back in his chair. "Does anyone know?"

"Only my captain." Andor shrugged. "I begged him not to tell anyone in the department. I got to where I am because I'm good at what I do."

"You don't have the same surname." Francine lifted her tablet. "Here it says his name is Victor Drozdik."

"I'm using my mother's maiden name. I didn't want to live under my dad's shadow."

"And you don't want people to think Daddy promoted you," Vinnie said.

"That and I don't want anyone to think that I'm going to run to my dad at the slightest sign of a disagreement or confrontation."

His candidness and discomfiture at his lineage strengthened the respect Manny, Colin and Vinnie exhibited. Manny nodded. "Okay, what else do you have?"

"Nothing. Just the loose connection of them being VIPs, the livestreaming and my gut screaming at me." He straightened his shoulders. "When Olivia contacted me yesterday and said she wanted to talk to me about István

Koltai, my gut screamed at me again. And now she's missing? It's simply too much of a coincidence for my liking."

"Let me guess." Roxy pushed a strand of wayward curls behind her ear. "István Koltai is one of your victims?"

Andor nodded. "The third victim. He died two days ago. He was—"

"The CFO of Július, the largest and oldest investment institution in Hungary." Francine swiped her tablet screen. "It says here that Július handles the investments of more than forty percent of the country's richest people. It is also known for its programmes educating students about pension funds and other investments for their and their children's futures. Huh. Sounds like a solid company. And from this István Koltai's bio on the company website, it sounds like he spearheaded a few of these programmes."

Andor pointed at Francine's tablet. "What you won't find on his bio is that István Koltai had a severe peanut allergy. I was surprised when I found a recording of the livestreaming. It's as if the killer is bleeping taunting us."

"Where did you find the recording?" Francine asked. "How?"

"Google." Andor snorted. "It was pure luck. I thought I'd deleted István Koltai's name from the search box when I entered 'peanut allergy,' but I hadn't. His name and allergy brought up a YouTube video under a numbered account."

"That's awful." Francine shuddered. "I want that detail. Maybe I can trace the killer through the video."

"Sure." Andor turned from Francine to face me. "The video showed him eating a snack and almost immediately suffering an allergic reaction. That snack should've been clear of any peanuts. The company that produces the snack denied any wrongdoing. Their factory is inspected once a month on their own insistence. They want everyone to know their products are safe. This was the first death that involved one of their products."

"Did you find anything to indicate the snack was tampered with?" Colin asked.

"No. It is of course possible that the needle mark where the allergen was injected was destroyed when István Koltai tore the wrapper." Frustration was clear on his face. "We have nothing. All we have is that video showing him going into anaphylactic shock, grabbing his EpiPen and injecting himself. But it didn't help."

Roxy's eyebrows rose. "It should've helped him immediately. Why didn't the epinephrine work?"

"The medical examiner told me that he tested the EpiPen and there wasn't any epinephrine in it. It was a vitamin B12 solution."

"What?" Roxy's voice rose a fraction. "Who would do such a thing? It's murder."

"Yup, that's what the ME also said." Andor's lips contracted into thin lines. "And still he refused to classify István Koltai's death as a homicide. He said the snack killed Koltai. Not the EpiPen."

"And this was all livestreamed." Francine shook her head. "It's just…"

"Yeah, I know," Andor said. "And the recording? It's as if the killer wanted us to see nobody was there. That it wasn't a murder."

It was quiet around the table for a few seconds. The sound of trumpets announcing the arrival of a king broke the silence and caused me to jerk in surprise. I reached into my handbag and took my phone out. Much to my annoyance, Colin had once again changed the ringtones of my phone last week. He had set this ringtone for the wife of the president of France.

I answered the call. "Isabelle. Why are you phoning me?"

"Are you enjoying your holiday, Genevieve?"

"Yes. No. I don't think it's a holiday anymore."

"Aha. So Andor has already talked to you?"

"He's here." I frowned. "How do you know Andor?"

Andor leaned forward, his eyes locked on my face. I turned away from his curiosity and faced Colin. He took my free hand.

"I met Andor's mother, Vera, at a conference on childhood neuropathy twelve years ago. We became friends." Isabelle paused. "I trust her with my life, Genevieve. Her husband is one of the few law enforcement people in Hungary who will never be found guilty of taking any kind of bribe or doing anything illegal. They're good people. And Andor is just like them. You can trust him."

"I don't know him." And therefore had little reason to trust him.

"Then trust yourself. I know that you've been reading him the whole time he's been talking to you. Vera doesn't know why he needs your help. He refused to tell her because he knows she would tell his dad, who would then get involved, and he doesn't want that. She also told me that he would never ask assistance from someone he didn't trust could help and he would never ask for help if he didn't need it."

I didn't reply. I needed to consider this. Isabelle was correct. I'd studied every micro-expression Andor had exhibited and had not once found him to be deceptive.

"Can you put me on speakerphone?" Isabelle's question interrupted my thoughts. I nodded, lowered the phone and tapped the speakerphone icon.

"Hi, Isabelle!" Roxy leaned towards the phone and winked at me. "Genevieve put you on speakerphone. Nikki's gone home, but the rest of us are here with Andor."

"Hello, everyone." Isabelle cleared her throat. "Manny, the president told me to give you the go-ahead if you consider this something worth looking into. Provided, of course, that the local officials approve of our involvement."

"Did my mom tell my dad I phoned?" Andor appeared younger in his concern about his parents.

"No, she didn't. But you know she will. You'd better phone her again and ask her to give you a few days before she spills the beans."

Andor's shoulders slumped. "It's most likely too late."

"Well, that's what you get for asking your mom's friend to convince these people to help you." Laughter lifted Isabelle's tone.

Andor raised both hands when Vinnie and Manny inhaled deeply. "Guys, I'm desperate. I was willing to risk my dad sticking his nose in my business just to get your help."

"Doc?" Manny looked at me for a decision, but I saw the curiosity on his face. He was ready to agree.

"If Andor's intuition has led him to other cases that were

being overlooked, I'm willing to take the risk." And I was intrigued. Already I was thinking of the different types of searches we could run to find connections between the victims.

Chapter FIVE

I DIDN'T EVEN try to modulate my facial expression. My *levator labii superioris* muscle raised my top lip as if I was smelling something bad. I was. The police station in Budapest was modern and appeared clean, but the smell of homeless bodies permeated the air. All European capital cities had a fair number of homeless people. Budapest was no exception, hosting over ten thousand homeless people, of whom a substantial percentage were Roma.

As we entered the police station, two police officers in front of us ushered three men and two women to a waiting area. They appeared to be homeless. I'd noticed the officers' latex gloves and had wondered if anyone would consider it discriminatory. I considered it wise. Living on the streets was most unhygienic and it was clear those five people hadn't washed in a very long time.

I swallowed as I watched one of the women wipe tears from her cheeks, smearing the dirt. It was hard for my logical mind to accept that people could endure such living conditions. Yet I had learned, not only from my social studies, but also from my own life, that not much in life was clear-cut. The decisions—our own and those of others—that had led us to this place in our lives had far too many nuances for strangers to comprehend.

Colin's hand tightened around mine and he tugged gently. I dragged my eyes away from the five people and followed Colin deeper into the station.

As soon as we'd agreed to help Andor, he'd phoned his captain, who'd insisted on meeting us. A few times during that phone conversation, Andor had held the phone away from his ear, shouting coming through the small device. I was not looking forward to meeting Andor's captain.

At the moment, Andor and Manny were at the reception desk, taking the visitor badges they'd been arranging for us. This was the reason Francine and Vinnie weren't with us. They didn't want their names registered in any police station unless there was no other alternative. And they didn't want to be in a police station. Roxy wasn't needed for this meeting and had been happy to keep Vinnie company.

"Henry Vaughan, here is your badge." Manny scowled at Colin as he handed him a plastic-covered ID badge, then held one out to me. "Yours, Doc."

I glanced at the homeless people, then at the yellowed lanyard that was supposed to go around my neck. Clearly that strap had been around many other necks. I shuddered and refused to take it. "I'm not touching that."

"I'll wear both." Colin took mine and hung both around his neck.

"This is so against protocol." Andor blinked, narrowed his eyes at Colin and lowered his voice. "My research identified you as Henry Vaughan and also gave me very, very little information about your career as an art historian. But at the villa, you were called Colin and Frey." He pointed at the badges around Colin's neck. "Are you Colin, Frey or Henry Vaughan?"

"Henry Vaughan, of course." Colin's nonverbal cues confirmed his truthfulness. If not for my expertise and intimate knowledge of this man, I would've been convinced. I always hated it when he used one of his seventeenth-century poet aliases, but I marvelled at his deception skills. "You can call me just what you want."

"Hmm." Andor stared at Colin for a few more seconds then turned around. "Let's go face the beast."

"Let me do the talking." Manny followed Andor, but stayed closer to us. "But Doc, I need you to read this captain and tell me if we're going to waste our time helping Garas."

We walked through a hallway that appeared to have been renovated recently. I had to admit that I was surprised at how modern and generally clean this police station was. Even the front of the station seemed well-maintained and clean. Despite the smell.

When I didn't answer Manny, he turned to me and glared until I frowned. "You know I always take note of people's nonverbal cues, even more so when it's a situation like this."

Andor slowed down and shook his head while looking at an open door at the end of the hallway. A booming baritone voice reached us. The man was shouting his displeasure in Hungarian. My language skills didn't extend to Hungarian, but the last six days had tempted me to master this language. This man was the first person who didn't make the language sound melodic. Instead he made every sentence sound like an assault.

Every now and then a tenor voice answered, too quiet and

mumbled to understand. From the booming voice's response it appeared the other man was apologising, which infuriated the loud man even more. A final, even louder order came through the door a few seconds before a muscular man exited the room. He was wearing jeans and a dress shirt. His shaved head and the tattoos peeking out from under his shirt collar were not the typical image of a police officer. But the gun holster on his hip and the way he immediately assessed us led me to believe he was indeed a police officer.

His red face, thinned lips, flared nostrils and every other nonverbal cue communicated his powerless frustration. His eyes widened slightly when he noticed us. Then his frown intensified when he saw Andor. He marched over and stopped in front of Andor, poking him in the chest. He lowered his chin and asked a question through his teeth.

Andor's reaction intrigued me. He wasn't intimidated or scared. In fact, he appeared bored as if this happened all the time. He allowed the other man to finish speaking before he nodded and answered in English. "I wouldn't be surprised if he is pissed off because of me. I'm sorry he took it out on you. I saw the video of that arrest. You didn't use excessive force, no matter what that stupid journalist says. It was a clean takedown."

By the time Andor finished speaking in his respectful and calm tone, the other man's breathing had slowed and his muscle tension decreased. He pulled his shoulders back, glanced at me, then looked at Andor. "Yeah. Whatever. Good luck. You're going to need it."

Andor watched the other man leave, then turned back to the open door. "Well, let's do this."

I felt conflicted. On the one hand, I didn't want to enter a space that hosted a person who considered shouting at his subordinates a good leadership skill. But on the other hand, I was curious. Andor didn't appear scared and watching him interact with the bald man had me wondering how he would handle a shouting superior.

"Come in, Garas." The loud voice reached me just as Andor stepped over the threshold. "Where are your friends?"

I didn't know whether the captain calling us Andor's 'friends' sounded condescending because of his heavily accented English, because of the volume of his order or because he was actually being disdainful. I needed to get into the room and observe this man's nonverbal cues. This time I was the one tugging on Colin's hand as I followed Manny and Andor.

The office surprised me. At first glance, it appeared to be a conference room. I took another step into the room. We were roughly in the centre of the room. To our right was a seating area with seven chairs and a coffee table that looked like it had suffered years of abuse. And not one of the chairs matched. A map of Hungary with torn and curled corners filled most of the wall.

I looked closer at the wall and realised it was retractable. My initial impression had been correct. This was a conference room that could be enlarged by sliding those walls on the floor and ceiling rails out of the way. I wondered why the commanding officer of a department would have his office in a conference room.

Large windows let in natural light, but faced another building which clearly needed renovation. It wasn't a view that could be enjoyed. To our left was a long light wood table that could easily seat twelve people. A man in his fifties was sitting with his back to a wall that had four large monitors mounted on it.

"I think I must say welcome." His accented English made me question the intention of his words. I decided not to trust his ability to communicate clearly with his words. I focused on his nonverbal cues as he got out of his chair.

He wore a suit that Colin would, no doubt, later criticise for having been made in the previous millennium. His full moustache didn't hide his *orbicularis oris* muscles contracting his lips to display his annoyance. He pushed his thick glasses up the bridge of his nose and scowled at Manny as he walked around the table. "So you are the team of superheroes coming to take over my department."

"They're not coming to take over anything, Cap." Andor moved to step between his superior and Manny, but stopped when the other man pointed an index finger at him.

"I'll shake your cage when I want you to speak, Garas." He stopped in front of Manny. "I'm Captain Zorán Palya. I assume you are Colonel Millard."

"At your service." Manny slumped and scratched his stubbled jaw. "Your detective is right. We're not here to take over anything. If you don't want us here, we'll just march on right back out the doors and continue our holiday."

Manny was lying. I knew this not because he was communicating clear deception cues. After working with him for five years, it had become easy for me to know when his disinterest was true and not. As he was watching Captain Palya for a reaction, Manny's interest was obvious to me. It was in his slightly narrowed eyes, his fists pushed into his trouser pockets and his shoulders drooping even more to create the false impression of his ennui.

Captain Palya grunted loudly as he took a step back and leaned his hips against the table. "No, no. You have to stay. As much as I would like to think that I'm running the show here, I don't."

"I swear I didn't do anything, Cap." Andor took a step back, waving both hands in the air as if to ward off the irritated glance his superior gave him.

Captain Palya turned his full attention to Andor. "I got a phone call this morning from the colonel." He lowered his brow, his top lip curling. "Before breakfast, Garas. I got that call before breakfast. And then exactly two hours later you phoned me, telling me you have a super team that's going to help you find this woman."

Relief lessened the tension in Andor's face as he turned to us. "The colonel is Captain Palya's superior and about two tiers below my dad."

"Does your father know about this?" Captain Palya clenched his fists.

Andor shook his head. "You know I don't involve my dad. I haven't told him, but the way things are happening, I won't be surprised if he finds out soon."

"Most likely from the colonel." Behind Captain Palya's bluster and loud displeasure, his respect for Andor was unmistaken. In this moment, he was addressing his subordinate as a peer. He slammed his fist against his thigh. "It pisses me off when people use their connections to get crap done."

"You're not talking about Andor." I winced as Manny turned to me, his lips tight. I turned my focus back to Captain Palya's expression. "It's quite clear that you're irritated with this morning's events. It might save us all time and energy if you forgo the show of rage and simply tell us what you know."

"Who the hell do you think you are?" The redness in his cheeks darkened as his volume increased with each word shouted at me.

"You know who I am." I nodded when his reaction confirmed my statement. "The moment you were notified about us, you found out as much as you could."

Captain Palya glared at me, his nostrils flared. "Oh, I know about you, all right. Doctor Genevieve Lenard, well-respected and highly disliked world expert on nonverbal communication."

"If I may." Colin leaned in to put himself slightly between me and the irate captain. I needed only one glance at Colin's face to know that he was locking down his emotions and was now fully immersed in his alias. He was the suave, soft-spoken Henry Vaughan. "Emotions are running a bit high, but it is not helping Ms Olivia Webster. While we are indulging in this unpleasant show of power, she might be in dire need of our help."

Captain Palya's top lip curled even more as he turned his attention to Colin. When Colin didn't lower his gaze or take a step back, the older man's brow furrowed. For three seconds, he moved his bottom jaw, breathed loudly and exhibited more cues indicating his internal debate. Then he came to a decision. His facial muscles relaxed and he nodded. "Fine. Doesn't mean I like this."

"To be honest, neither do we." Colin's tone was respectful. "Our holiday is being interrupted by this case, but there are too many elements that make it a matter of urgency."

"Urgency?" Captain Palya tilted his head as if he realised there was more involved than what he was aware of. "Before I get into that, I need for you superheroes to understand I'm not a complete idiot. I know you are extremely good at what you do. What I need to know is whether you're going to loop me in or make this your own show."

I inhaled to ask him to explain the numerous expressions he was using, but Colin's hand tightened around mine. I bit down on my lips and focused instead on analysing every micro-expression on Captain Palya's face.

"I don't want a show." Manny pulled out a chair and sat down hard. "All I want is to help find this woman and also find out what else might be involved in her disappearance."

"So you don't think she's been kidnapped?" Captain Palya took a chair and sat down facing Manny.

"I don't know what to think yet. We have far too little information."

"Hmm." Captain Palya pushed his glasses up the bridge of his nose. "It seems like her boss is convinced that she's been kidnapped. That's why I got the call this morning. Her boss is friends with the commissioner. Instead of waiting the usual twenty-four hours before reporting her missing, he went straight over everyone's heads to the commissioner." He narrowed his eyes at Andor. "I know that look. What did you do?"

"He also went over heads," Manny said. "He got his mother to make a phone call to help convince us to help him."

"Why?" Captain Palya winced. "Is this another one of your idiotic gut feelings?"

Andor smiled. "My gut feelings have solved many cases for us."

"At the cost of my sanity." The captain's voice rose as he shook his index finger at Andor. "You better start telling me everything. Now."

Andor did. He told Captain Palya about Olivia calling him, how he'd waited for her at the café, her escape and then her not showing up at their meeting point this morning. I was most intrigued that he didn't once mention Olivia's job, her mention of István Koltai or his own theory about the loosely connected murders.

"Why did she want to meet you?" Captain Palya had clearly picked up that he was not receiving all the information.

"Olivia is a lawyer who was looking into a last will and testament." Colin ignored Andor's resigned sigh. "She wanted to speak to Andor about a man who Andor is convinced died under suspicious circumstances."

"Who is this dead person?" Captain Palya looked at Andor.

"István Koltai." Andor straightened his shoulders.

"What the hell!" Captain Palya got up and walked to Andor. "You and that stupid gut. How many more times must I tell you to never keep things from me? I can't protect you when I don't know what the fuck you're up to."

"I didn't want to come to you with just a theory."

"We've been over this, Garas! When you think you might have a thought, you come to me. Clear?" He waited until Andor nodded. "Now tell me everything."

This time Andor told his superior everything he'd shared with us at the villa. I saw no calculation or any indication that he was withholding information. While he was talking, Captain Palya walked back to his chair and sat down. When Andor finished his retelling, the older man didn't say anything. He pinched his chin between his thumb and index finger, his elbow resting on the table. He was considering everything Andor had said. He sighed heavily. "Is this going to be like your Roma case?"

Andor blinked a few times and took a step back. "Dear God, I hope not."

"What Roma case?" Colin asked.

Andor swallowed. "In 2008 and 2009, eight people of Roma descent were murdered by a gang of Neo-Nazis. It shocked our nation, but it also led to accusations that the police had failed to protect this historically persecuted minority. I agreed. It was awful that a gang managed to kill eight people and wound many others in carefully planned attacks and were only stopped thirteen months after their first murder. The victims included a four-year-old boy. Four years old."

"And this idiot"—Captain Palya shook his index finger at Andor—"was still in the police academy when he started with his stupid gut."

I couldn't abide it anymore. I pointed at Captain Palya's face. "Your micro-expressions communicate respect, yet your words are outrageously condescending."

"Condescending. Hah!" His short laugh was genuine. "Nope, not condescending. Pissed off. After he made the entire police department look really bad, the higher-ups decided to give him to me. The gift that just keeps on giving."

I paid careful attention to Andor's reaction, but observed no anger, resentment or even irritation. He was used to Captain Palya's verbal abuse and the contradiction in his verbal and nonverbal communication. I was most confused. And intrigued by this dynamic.

"I noticed a pattern and tried to get someone to pay attention to this," Andor said. "Cap was the only one willing to listen to me. I was in my second month at the academy. Nobody took me seriously."

"Not even your father?" Manny asked.

"I didn't go to him." Andor shrugged. "He wasn't commissioner then, but he was fast on his way. When I applied to join the police, I knew that my dad's high position would always count against me. I knew that if I was ever going to gain anyone's respect, it would have to be because I proved myself to be able to function without the help of my father."

"What happened with the case?" Three weeks ago I had read a book about the two hundred thousand Roma people who'd been killed during World War Two. So much of history was focused on the horrifying loss of Jewish lives that the millions of other lives lost were often overlooked. From an article I'd scanned, I recalled that it was estimated that half a million to a million Roma were currently living in

Hungary. I needed to know that the murderers of those eight people had been caught and incarcerated.

"Oh, we caught those sons of bitches." Captain Palya's *levator labii superioris* muscles drew his mouth into a sneer. "But it took Garas' non-stop nagging and sadly eight victims before anyone would admit terrorists were killing people because of their ethnicity."

"Don't downplay your role, Cap." Andor raised an eyebrow. "You nagged just as much as I did."

"And look where it got me!" He slammed his fist on the table. "Stuck with you. And a case that my gut is telling me is going to give me a bigger stomach ulcer that I got with the Roma case."

I decided not to comment yet again on the conflict between Captain Palya's words and expressions. The short time in this conference room-style office had shown me that there was a deep respect between Andor and his captain. For reasons I could only imagine had to do with the politics within the police hierarchy, neither of the two men showed their true feelings towards each other.

"So I have your okay?" Andor asked.

"Like you would've stopped investigating if I told you not to pursue this." Captain Palya touched his moustache. "Yes, you have my okay. But your first priority is to find this woman. If we still want our jobs, you'd better do it quick. And you're running this case from here. And when I say here"—he pointed at the floor—"I mean from my office. Not from your car or your teensy flat or any of that crap you've pulled before. I want you here so I can keep an eye on the investigation."

I didn't like that. I really didn't. Not only was I in a different country and had agreed to work on a case far outside my comfort zone, I was now going to have to work from an unfamiliar space.

"Doc?" Manny turned to me. "Is this place good for you?"

Once I started shaking my head, I couldn't stop. It took Colin's strong touch on my forearm, the first four lines of Mozart's Violin Concerto No.1 in B-flat major and numerous deep breaths before I calmed down.

"What will make it better for you, love?" Colin asked gently.

"Nothing. I don't want to be here. I don't want to work here. I don't want to work with different people." I raised my hand when all the men inhaled to respond. I took a moment to collect my thoughts and force more calm into my mind. "I know this case is important. I will find a way to work here."

"Well, don't hurt yourself trying." Captain Palya jerked back when Manny, Colin and Andor turned furious expressions his way.

"Doctor Lenard's brain doesn't work like ours, Cap. She needs an environment where she feels safe to work."

The captain slapped the weapon holstered on his hip and looked at me. "You're safe here."

I didn't answer him. I had no desire to educate someone about autism in all its variations.

Colin's hand tightened on my forearm. "You're sure, love?"

I looked around the conference room. "It's empty. There's no clutter. I can make it work."

"Oh, goodie. I'm honoured." Captain Palya got up. "Now

scram. Get out of my face. You're not going to find Olivia Webster here."

"We'll start at her hotel room." Andor waved towards the door. "I've spoken to the hotel. They're expecting us."

I frowned at Captain Palya, looked at Andor, then back at the captain. I didn't understand their relationship. It was rife with nuances, sarcasm, misdirection and yet there was a sense of deep friendship between them. I was genuinely interested in the case Andor had presented and I also wanted to help find Olivia. But now I wanted to study the dynamics between Andor and Captain Palya. I needed to understand how such a relationship could work when the friendships I had were simple.

As I followed the men out of the room, a strange emotion settled in me. It took almost the entire trip to the hotel for me to identify it as anticipation and excitement. How odd.

Chapter SIX

OLIVIA'S FIVE-STAR hotel room was spacious and elegant. The hotel manager had confirmed that her legal firm had booked and was paying for the room. From what I'd learned so far about her, I wouldn't be surprised if she could afford this on her own income.

There was a small coffee table and two reading chairs in front of the window. Against the wall facing the window was a desk that had the usual hotel and tourist reading materials, but also a novel and folder belonging to Olivia. Housekeeping had been in her room, so if there had been any evidence of a struggle or someone searching through the room, it had been removed. The king-sized bed was neatly made, the minibar fully stocked and the bathroom spotless.

Andor opened his arms and turned around the room. "We're not going to find anything here."

"Not true." Colin walked to the wardrobe and opened the door. "If Olivia didn't change completely, I'm sure we'll find something here that can help us find her."

Manny walked into the room and I flinched. Even though the room was large for a single occupant, I still felt crowded. Not because of Manny or Colin. It was the presence of someone I didn't know that was threatening to overwhelm my senses. Andor.

Colin was removing everything from the wardrobe, going to each item individually before placing it on the bed. It turned the immaculate room into a chaotic mess. My mind did not appreciate the disorder. I needed something to occupy my mind so as to not give in to the threatening shutdown.

I turned to Andor who was sitting at the desk, looking through the folder. One by one he took documents from it—a plane ticket, a printed-out hotel booking confirmation and a few leaflets for sightseeing tours. I studied him, analysing everything he'd revealed about himself, verbally and nonverbally. "You researched Olivia."

When he didn't answer me, Manny walked over to the desk and grabbed the now-empty folder from Andor's hand. "The good doctor is talking to you."

"Huh?" Andor looked at me. "Sorry, I wasn't listening."

I almost rolled my eyes in a manner similar to Nikki and Roxy. "I don't understand why you are lying."

"Bleep it. I keep forgetting you see everything. Fine. I admit that I researched Olivia."

"Why lie about it?"

"Years of conditioning, I suppose." He shrugged. "In the beginning, I would share my methods, but it freaked everyone out. Either I was working too much, researching too much, reading too much or doing something else too much. I realised that people were more comfortable accepting my method being my gut instinct rather than me spending hours and hours studying a case and making connections."

I understood that. My peers at university couldn't accept that I gained immense pleasure from hours of study. I, too, had stopped talking about the time I spent on work.

"What did you learn about Olivia?" Colin put a pair of light blue shoes on the bed. I looked away immediately. The sheer number of contaminants on the streets that we carried into our homes that were now on that stark white bedcover sent a shiver down my spine. I turned my full attention back to Andor.

He bit down on his bottom lip and looked up, recalling a memory. "She's thirty-eight years old, married and has two children. She travels a lot for work, which makes me think that she's very committed to her career. Her social media privacy settings are quite high, so I didn't learn much there. But the photos I saw there were all of her with her kids and husband. Everybody seems quite happy. And before you say anything, I know that those photos could be there to create an image that is not real."

I nodded. This was one of the reasons I found social media such a fascinating field of study. Many articles had been written, based on a great deal of research, that had proven again and again that the vast majority of people represented themselves on social media in a light that was not a true reflection of their lives.

"She's been working for Freeman, Scott and Associates for the last nine years," Andor continued. "Before that she worked at a smaller, but also prestigious legal firm. She started there as an intern while she was still studying, then worked her way up the ladder. Freeman, Scott and Associates head-hunted her just before she was made partner in her first company. They offered her an immediate partnership as well as many other lucrative incentives to join them. She's not disappointed them."

"How did you get that information?" Colin didn't even try to hide the suspicion on his face.

"Her boss." Andor shrugged. "Since he phoned my boss' boss to force our hand in looking for Olivia, I thought I'd phone him to reassure him that she was our top priority."

Manny snorted and sat down on one of the chairs in front of the window. "You're going to catch flak for this."

"I don't think so. He was extremely happy to tell me anything I needed to help us find Olivia." Andor looked at me. "I'm no expert in body language and such, but his tone and the consistency in his wording and his concern made me think that he cares deeply for her. He's really worried."

"Did he tell you more about this case she was looking into?"

"No." He pressed the tips of his fingers hard against his temples and massaged. "I phoned him this morning at five, which was eleven in the evening there. He was at home and didn't have access to any of her files. He said that he would send it as soon as he gets into his office this morning… well, our afternoon. He only knew that she was looking into a client's last will and testament and that she'd seen something that had made her question an item that was listed to be inherited."

"That's vague." Colin put the last of Olivia's clothes on the bed. She had packed wisely—pants and skirts that would easily match the elegant blouses now losing their immaculate appearance while all thrown onto one heap.

"Tell me about it." Andor reached for his temples again, but dropped his hands and sighed. "At least I got some info on her activities while she's been here."

I took a step closer. "Do you know who she met?"

"Not everyone, no." He raised his eyebrows and leaned forward as if he was about to share extremely important information. "She arrived in Budapest three days ago after a direct flight from New York. As soon as she landed she booked into this hotel, then had a meeting with someone. Her boss couldn't tell me who, because that information is also in his office."

I stared at his face. "You're sceptical about something."

"Yeah. He said that he couldn't remember where, or even if, he wrote down all the names she was spouting at him. I don't know. It just sounded like he so completely trusts Olivia that he wasn't really paying attention to what she was doing, only to whether she was okay."

"Did he give you any names at all?" I was growing impatient.

"István Koltai." He nodded when Colin turned from the cupboard to face him. "I asked him twice and both times he was convinced Olivia had spoken to Koltai."

"That means she saw him before he died." I wondered what they'd discussed.

"Exactly. Man, I really wanted to speak to her yesterday. But now I have so many more questions." He sighed. "Olivia's boss couldn't tell me why she visited István, only that he remembered the name."

"We need to find out what she was working on." Colin was right. It was becoming imperative that we knew why she was here.

"Did you get any other useful information from Olivia's boss?" I hoped he could provide more data.

"Not much more, no. But you can be sure that I'll be on the phone to Mister George Freeman if I don't get an email or something by noon New York time." He leaned back in the chair. "I finished my call to him just after half past five and decided that it was as good a time as any to phone István Koltai's boss."

"And you wonder why people don't like you." Manny shook his head.

"I'm not doing this to win popularity contests." Andor shrugged in a manner that was becoming familiar. "After the CEO of Július finished complaining about the early hour, he told me that everyone was shocked about Koltai's death. He said that he'd told Olivia the same when she phoned him the day after Koltai died. Apparently everyone in the office knew about his nut allergies. People were very careful with their lunches and snacks.

"He said that Koltai was the perfect CFO. He was obsessively careful and always did extensive due diligence before approving funding for any new project. Even though it frustrated a lot of the employees, he was so highly respected and liked that everyone accepted his methods. He was always fair and when he was presented with a well-developed or researched project or financing request, he would very likely approve the application."

"You're not convinced." It was quite easy to read that on his face.

"You're damn right I'm not convinced." Andor tapped his index finger hard on the desk. "I don't know. It's just hard for me to believe that someone is or was that well-loved and respected by everyone all the time. I'm not saying it's not possible. All I'm saying is that in my experience, the higher trees catch more wind."

"What do trees…" I thought about the expression, but didn't want to presume that I knew the meaning. "Explain."

"Seriously?" He blinked a few times. "Okay. People in higher positions or more in the public eye are subjected to higher scrutiny and, more often than not, stronger criticism and even hatred. So, after I finished speaking to István's boss, I phoned his personal assistant. It didn't sound like she was lying when she told me that she really liked István and had enjoyed working closely with him for more than eight years."

"But?" Colin asked.

"She said that he never talked about his family and whenever the topic came up, he was almost aggressive in the way he put an end to that discussion."

"Here you are!" Francine walked into the room, waving her tablet in the air. "None of you responded to my SMSes, so I had to track your sexy butts here."

"What are you doing here?" Manny slumped against the back of the chair. "I thought you didn't want anything to do with the cops?"

I took a step back, but bumped into the bedside table. The room felt too small for me. Even though Francine didn't physically command a lot of space, her flamboyant personality made the room appear much smaller. The mess on the bed didn't help. I took a deep breath and waited for her answer.

She raised one shoulder and winked at Andor. "I dug a bit deeper into your life, Detective Garas. All my sources agree that you're cool. So here I am."

I was familiar with the badly concealed excitement on her face. "What did you uncover?"

"Nothing too scandalous, I'm sad to say." She paused when she noticed that I'd pushed myself into the corner of the room. Her eyes narrowed for a second, then she sat down next to Manny. She swiped her tablet screen. "I managed to find most of Olivia's whereabouts the last three days."

"How did you do that?" There was only interest in Andor's question.

"I know somebody who knows somebody who knows somebody who gave me legal access to all the street cameras in Budapest."

"And let me guess." Manny glared at her. "You then went and found more cameras without the proper authorisation."

"Do you really want me to respond to that?"

He pushed his fists into his trouser pockets. "No, I don't."

"It doesn't matter." Colin took a step closer to Francine. "What did you find?"

"That girl has a great sense of fashion. And she visited four places of note." She glanced at her tablet. "Her first stop was István Koltai's office. Then she went for lunch and a bit of shopping before going to a small art gallery."

This caught Colin's attention. "What art gallery?"

"Elite-Art." Francine winked at Colin. "I thought it would get your attention. So I made sure to find out as much as I could about the place. The owner is Pál Elo and he's quite well known in the Hungarian art industry."

"I know Pál." Colin tilted his head. "He's a legend when it comes to authenticating masterpieces. He's made many enemies and many friends over the years."

"Well, Olivia was there for only three minutes. I got her from the city camera on the other side of the street. Quite good-quality footage I might add. Anyhoo, she spoke to a young woman who I assume manages the gallery when Pál Elo isn't there. This young woman shook her head a few times and when Olivia left, she looked frustrated. I reckon she was exhausted after the long flight from New York and jet lag was getting to her, because she then came to the hotel and stayed here until the next morning. Then she visited two places that I'm still working on getting the details for."

"We need to find out why she was looking for Pál." Colin walked back to the wardrobe. "And what she was investigating."

"I might be jumping the gun here with assumptions and such, but it looks to me like Olivia was trying to figure out whether a painting in her client's last will and testament was stolen, forged or something like that." Andor looked at Colin, his expression speculative. "The question is what artwork or painting she was looking into and what had made her so paranoid."

"The more important questions are why she disappeared and where she is at this moment." Colin took a large dark blue suitcase from the back of the cupboard, put it on the floor and opened it. It was empty.

"Um." Andor waited until Colin looked at him. "I know I'm a complete outsider, but can you please tell me what your connection is to Olivia Webster?"

Colin straightened and looked at Andor for a few seconds. "We almost got married."

"What the bleep?" Andor stood up, then sat down again. "That's… well, that's huge. Why didn't you tell me before?"

"You're a complete outsider." The corner of Colin's mouth quirked to soften the words Andor had used himself. "Just think of it as extra motivation for me to help you."

"Hmm." Andor tilted his head. "You still care about her."

"Hey, watch it, buddy." Francine's expression was fierce as she pointed a manicured finger at Andor. "There's no need to get personal here."

Colin chuckled. "Well, if I almost got married to our missing person, it is kind of personal. But thanks for standing up for me, Francine."

"You betcha." She shook her finger at Andor. "And you better not think about climbing into Colin's character. He's the best human being you'll ever meet."

Manny snorted, then winced when Francine kicked his shin. "Frey is level-headed. And much smarter than you, Garas. You'll lose every time you even think of catching him out."

Colin wasn't fast enough to mask his shock at Manny's compliment. I'd seen it. Andor had also seen it. His eyes narrowed again in the manner I now recognised he did when he was contemplating something.

Being non-neurotypical, I experienced life very differently from my friends. I didn't need to communicate my thoughts or emotions to feel understood and appreciated. I also didn't need reassurances or platitudes to give me confidence in who I was and what I did. But I was non-neurotypical.

Colin was neurotypical. Yet he was so unlike many of the neurotypical people I'd studied and known. His altruism bordered on self-sacrifice. And he never expected acknowledgement, gratitude or even a mention of all the assistance he gave everyone. I'd never heard anyone in our circle of friends outright vocalise their appreciation for him.

I thought about Colin's role in my life. "Your unconditional support has made me a stronger individual."

Colin jerked and turned to me. His expression softened and he walked around the bed to stand in front of me. He took both my hands in his and placed them against his chest. "Thank you, love." He smiled and shook his head when I inhaled to speak. "This is maybe not the time or place for intimate conversations."

I looked around the room and cringed. Manny appeared most uncomfortable and Andor's eyes were narrowed to thin slits as he watched us. I needed to change the topic. "The suitcase?"

"Yes, the suitcase." He kissed me lightly on my nose and walked back to the large designer piece of luggage on the floor.

No one spoke. We watched as he ran his hands along the outside of the expensive piece of luggage. He lifted the lid again and inspected every centimetre with the tips of his fingers. "Nothing here." His whisper was barely audible. He flexed his fingers, then gently touched the lined sides of the case.

I saw the moment he discovered something. His body tensed and his breath hitched. He leaned closer, obscuring my view. I couldn't stand not knowing. "What did you find?"

"I'm not sure." He shifted to the side so I could see, carefully prying away the lining. "But I think it might be a notebook or something."

"Then get it out, Frey." Manny leaned forward, resting his elbows on his knees. "No need to protect her suitcase."

"And there's no need to destroy it." He straightened, holding a small notebook in his hand. On a deep inhale, he opened it and immediately smiled. "It's in code."

"Bloody hell." Manny frowned. "Why do you think it's funny?"

"It's just such a Liv thing to do." Colin turned a few pages, then focused on a single page for a few seconds. He nodded. "She's using the code I taught her."

"Um." Andor got up and stood next to Colin, his *corrugator supercilii* muscles pulling his brow down in a deep frown. "Do you know what it's saying?"

Colin sat back on his haunches and looked at me. "I'll need a few hours to translate the whole book."

I nodded. I wouldn't mind a few hours at my computer. I needed to find out as much as I could about István Koltai, his company Július, Elite-Art Gallery, and everyone else so far mentioned in this case.

"Can't you do any of that now?" Manny tapped his foot and glared at the notebook.

"No. I need…" Colin frowned and stared at the notebook. "Shit. I don't need to translate this." He looked at me. "She was looking into a Caspar Netscher painting."

"She didn't write that in code." I thought about this. "Why not?"

"Maybe she did this as a safeguard. In case something happens to her and someone discovers her notes, they will at least be able to follow up on that one clue."

"How the hell does that help us?" Manny slumped into

the chair. "And who is this Casper the Friendly Ghost?"

"Caspar Netscher was a seventeenth-century Dutch artist." Colin closed the notebook. "Today there are more than two hundred paintings undoubtedly attributed to Netscher. But there are another four hundred that are speculated to have also been painted by him. Some scholars speculate that the number of works is much higher than that."

As usual, Colin's features became more animated as he talked about art. He smiled. "No one really knows when Netscher was born. It was either 1636 or 1639 and it was either in Heidelberg or in Prague. What we do know is that he was a master at portraying the social interactions of the Dutch elite. He was known for his outstanding portraits and in high demand by the who's who of that time.

"His play with shade and light, his use of accurate and often brilliant colouring made his portraits come to life. He had a light touch and his patrons loved the way he portrayed them. He was one of the few artists who managed to become rich and famous while he was still alive."

He stopped when Francine's phone pinged. She took her phone from her cherry-red handbag and looked at the screen. "Vinnie is asking when we're going to be finished. He's ready to start cooking dinner for us."

"It's too early for dinner." I looked out the large windows, but couldn't determine the hour. Even in early autumn, I still lost track of time when the days were still a bit longer.

Colin looked at his watch. "Not really. If we pack up here and leave for the villa, we'll be there at around half past five. It's an early dinner, but we didn't have lunch."

"And I'm starving." Francine put her phone and tablet in her handbag.

"What did you mean pack up here?" Andor looked at Colin.

"I'm not leaving Liv's things here. Not while she's missing."

"Is this a crime scene?" Manny didn't even wait for Andor to shake his head. "Then there's no reason to leave anything untouched. There's no evidence of a struggle or a crime. Her handbag, passport and phone are not here, so she could be on a day trip for all we know. We take her stuff with us. Once we know where Olivia is, we'll give it all back to her."

I frowned and tilted my head. "Why are you lying?"

"Bloody hell, Doc." Manny's lips pulled into a thin line. "I'm not lying. I just don't plan to give her notebook back to her."

Colin and Manny started arguing about the notebook. Soon, Francine got involved and even got Andor to voice his opinion. I didn't care about their argument. I was far too troubled watching Colin and Francine stuff Olivia's belongings into the suitcase. Her blouses were crushed into small bundles, her trousers folded in a manner that would leave horrid creases.

When Colin started folding another pair of trousers, I could no longer watch. I grabbed the piece of clothing from him and put myself in front of the suitcase. While they continued their inane arguing and even moved on to different topics, I carefully packed all Olivia's belongings in her suitcase.

It gave me time to plan everything I wanted to research. I

also thought of a few questions I needed to ask Colin, but decided against it. He would be too distracted deciphering Olivia's notes. My questions about her investigative methods were not as important as the information we could glean from what she'd written in that book. I hoped it wouldn't take Colin too long to decode.

Chapter SEVEN

I INHALED DEEPLY and held my breath. The early morning air in the forest next to the villa had a specific scent that was pleasing to my senses. I'd been walking for the last fifteen minutes, trying to clear my head of the influx of information.

We'd spent most of the night trying to decode Olivia's notebook. That had happened after a quick video call with Nikki and Émile. They'd decided to stay the night in Vienna instead of driving straight through to Strasbourg. Manny and Vinnie had been most displeased. Nikki had giggled and assured them that she was safe. The intensity on Émile's face when he promised to keep her safe had been sincere. It had pleased me that I could focus on the notebook without any more concerns about Nikki and Eric.

Colin had been surprised and impressed with the sophistication of the code in Olivia's notebook. She'd taken what they'd used and had changed it in such a manner that Colin had been stumped. After an hour of not making any progress, he'd called for my help.

At one o'clock this morning, Manny had come in and shouted at us to sleep. Even though it had been a restless sleep, it had been enough for my brain to continue its search for the key to the code. I'd woken up at seventeen minutes to five, knowing how to decode the notes.

Colin had joined me and we'd spent the last two hours translating Olivia's thoughts. Francine had joined us and had taken over from me, typing as Colin dictated. The pages in the front of the book had been minimalistic notes on her worries about the painting in the last will and testament of a Nathan Donovan.

It had been most frustrating to realise that we would need her to elaborate on these notes for them to make sense. There was a certain aimlessness in her notes that Colin had confirmed was not typical of the Olivia he'd known.

Francine and Colin were still working on decoding the notes in the back of her notebook. Those seemed to all be her personal impressions of Budapest, the food, the people, even the weather. It had been a great disappointment that her encrypted notes had yielded very little useful information. It had been equally disheartening when Olivia's boss had informed Andor that Olivia's assistant had revealed that she'd taken her client Nathan Donovan's file with her and had removed everything about this client from their servers.

I'd grown bored and left for a walk. Vinnie had followed me. He was walking about fifteen metres behind me, giving me space to be alone, but had resolutely told me he refused to let me wander around the jungle alone. I'd been unable to let that go and wasted four minutes explaining the difference between a forest and a jungle to him.

The narrow footpath veered to the right. This forest was mostly beech and oak trees. Earlier I had smiled at the fright I got when a deer rushed away when I'd interrupted it nibbling on small white flowers. The rest of the wildlife around me was all in the trees. The first few mornings in the villa, I'd woken up around five-thirty in the morning when the birds became active.

Their chirping was so loud that even now, when they were no longer announcing the break of dawn, the many different sounds demanded my attention. Instead of it overwhelming my senses, I found it grounding me. It was a similar experience to when I focused on mentally writing Mozart's compositions. My mind became so involved in trying to separate each individual bird and recognise their calls that there was no space for obsessing over the case, Olivia's disappearance or Colin's deep concern for her.

I followed the path for a few more minutes. I wanted to give my brain the time to filter through all the information we'd learned in the last twenty-four hours. What had been interesting and perplexing was the mention of two deceased Hungarian nationals in Olivia's notes. It was with growing frustration that I wished we could find her so I could ask her what these two people had to do with István, Nathan Donovan and Andor.

Movement to my left caught my eye and I slowed down. If it were a wild boar mother and I was too close, she might feel the need to protect her offspring by attacking me. This was not an experience I desired. I stopped completely and looked deeper into the shadowed woods. Behind me, Vinnie's light tread also slowed down. I held out my hand behind me, hoping that he'd see my gesture for him to stop. He did.

A rustle drew my attention to a copse of trees about five metres from where I was standing. A rush of adrenaline increased my heart rate, my breathing turning erratic. I was just about to call out to Vinnie when a woman stepped from behind the trees.

Olivia.

She was wearing the same light green trousers and white blouse as two days before in Szentendre. But now the trousers were dirty around the legs and a long muddy smear ran across her left thigh. Her blouse was wrinkled and stained under her arms. Her eyes were wide, her arms tucked in close to her body. "Please don't hurt me."

I took a moment to study her. "Your nonverbal cues are telling me that the meaning behind your words is not related to physical harm only. What do you truly mean?"

"I'm going against every instinct I have to trust you. My biggest fear is that you will betray my trust and leave my children without a mother."

"That makes more sense." I frowned when I noticed the expectation on her face. It took me two seconds to realise what it implied. "You want me to reassure you."

Her surprised laughter was genuine, but short-lived. She crossed her arms in a full-body hug. "Yes. I know who you are. You're Doctor Lenard. I read an article you wrote when I did a business psychology course a few years ago. I also know that more recently you've been working on criminal cases. Please tell me that you'll live up to your reputation. Tell me that you'll help me out of this hole that I dug for myself."

I looked at the ground at her feet and wished people wouldn't use expressions that needed interpreting.

"Jen-girl?" Vinnie's soft question from behind me didn't surprise me. It did, however, send a flash of immense fear across Olivia's face. She took a step back, her entire body ready to run. She reminded me of the deer I'd startled earlier on.

I lifted both hands in a gesture communicating my harmless intent. "Vinnie is my friend. He is Colin"—I realised she wouldn't recognise this name—"he is Jackson's best friend. If anything, he'll protect you."

"Please tell me I can trust you."

"I can tell you that, but I don't know what your expectations of this trust are. I can tell you that I—and my team—will do everything we can to find out the truth behind whatever is causing you such fear." I looked at the forest around us. "It has to be an overwhelming fear to make you find out where we are staying and, if I'm correct, make you sleep here."

She exhaled, covered her face with both hands and started crying. Her shoulders shook as she sobbed. Vinnie walked past me and lightly bumped my shoulder. "I got this."

He walked to her and gently pulled her into a loose embrace. At the first contact, she tensed, but then collapsed against him and cried even harder. I stood frozen. Intellectually, I knew all the right things to say to someone in distress. I could even manipulate my nonverbal cues to communicate empathy. But none of it would be natural or genuine.

When facing a threat, I analysed it and sought the best possible way to either avoid or deal with it. I never cried. If overwhelmed by information or danger, my mind simply shut down. In a way I supposed there was some similarity to the actions Olivia had taken. She'd run away and found a place of safety. My mind did the same. I wasn't certain, however, that the fearful woman would agree when I told her that. I'd been told that my tone always sounded professional and distant.

It was clear that Vinnie was giving her what she needed at the moment. Softly spoken words of reassurance, physical contact and patience. I didn't have that to offer her. But I knew that Colin had spent most of the last twenty-four hours deeply distraught about this woman's safety. So I offered her what I had. "I will do everything I can to find the truth, to find a way for you to return safely to your children."

She took a shaky breath, pushed away from Vinnie and looked at me. "Thank you."

"How long have you been in the woods?" Vinnie asked.

"Two nights." She looked at me. "You were right. But it wasn't easy to find out where you stayed. As soon as I did, I made my way out here."

"Were you followed?" Vinnie looked into the trees, his eyes narrowed.

"No. I bought a bicycle and cycled out here. It took me almost four hours because I took a few smaller roads and doubled back a few times as well." She looked back to the copse of trees she'd been hiding behind. "My bike and backpack are there."

"Well, let's get them and go to the villa. I'm sure everyone is interested in hearing your story." Vinnie walked to the trees, I assumed to collect her bicycle. He was typing on his smartphone and I was quite sure that he was alerting Francine, Colin and Manny that we'd found Olivia and were taking her to the villa.

Olivia stepped towards me, her hand outstretched. "I know you know who I am, but I still want to introduce myself. Olivia Webster."

I leaned away from her and put my hands behind my back. "The type and quantity of micro-organisms in soil is quite large and diverse. These include viruses, archaea, fungi, bacteria and even larger organisms such as protozoa. Exposure to these can cause anything from a classic infection to tetanus, botulism, gastroenteritis and respiratory syndromes. Your hands are covered in dirt."

Her top lip curled and her shoulders pulled up to almost reach her ears. She aggressively wiped her hands against her trousers. "That's really gross. God, I'm really gross. I don't think I've ever been this disgustingly dirty in my entire life."

"We have lots of showers." Vinnie pushed a thick-wheeled bicycle from behind the trees and joined us. He shrugged and looked at the red backpack slung over his shoulder. "Is this all you have?"

She nodded. "I bought a space blanket, a toothbrush, toothpaste and lots of water before I cycled here. All my stuff is in my hotel room."

"Not anymore." I turned towards the villa. "We packed everything and brought it here."

"Oh, thank God!" Her eyes widened in excitement. "How far is it? Is it okay if we walk fast? I want a shower. No, I *need* a shower. A really long shower."

We did walk fast. At first I didn't say much. Vinnie was successfully putting Olivia at ease. He had suggested that we wait for Olivia's explanations until we were at the villa. I agreed. I loathed having to repeat myself or retell a story.

The muscle tension in her body had decreased significantly, her spine had straightened and her arms were swinging slightly as she walked. The reprieve from the fear she felt for her life would most likely last only until we reached the villa and she had to tell us what had caused her fear. I followed behind the two of them, paying close attention to Olivia's body language.

Halfway to the villa, a lull in the conversation brought my attention back to the birds. Our presence didn't seem to inhibit their singing. Their beautiful sound no longer distracted my mind from all the questions I had.

There was no gradual decrease in the forest. It ended abruptly on the edge of the villa's large lawn. The moment the imposing mansion came into view, Olivia's arms moved closer to her torso and her shoulders rose towards her ears. She slowed down and waited until I was next to her. "I should've asked this earlier… God, I should've asked a lot of questions earlier. But first just tell me if Jackson is okay with seeing me."

I wanted to correct her, but didn't know if Colin wanted me to reveal his name wasn't Jackson Roanne. So I considered my answer for a few seconds, then nodded. "He'll be most relieved that you are well."

"Hmm." She exhaled loudly, then stopped and turned to me, her back to the villa. "Are you married to him?"

"No."

"Do you know about… us?"

"Yes."

She waited for more, but when I didn't elaborate, she closed her eyes for a second while taking a deep breath. When she looked at me, she appeared more relaxed. "It took me a long time to get over him. He was my entire world. When he walked out on me like that, it killed me. It was only when my first child was born that I felt completely whole again. And honestly, I think my husband is a saint. To have put up with my emotional crap in the beginning could not have been easy."

I raised my hand to stop her rambling. "What is your real concern?"

She huffed a laugh, looked at Vinnie who was waiting for us a few metres away, then looked back at me. "Honestly, I don't know. I suppose this is just a bit awkward. I don't even know if you two are an item and here I am all worried that you won't like me." Her voice dropped to a whisper. "That you won't want to help me."

"I don't know you, so I have no reason to like or dislike you. And your past relationships have no bearing on my commitment to find the truth about this case that you're involved in. Why would they?"

She stared at me for a few seconds, blinking slowly. "You're different."

"Hey." Vinnie walked back towards us, but stopped when I shook my head and looked behind him. He turned and nodded when he saw Colin walking towards us. Olivia had her back to the house, her focus completely on me.

"You're right. I am different." I studied her face. "You showed no nonverbal cues to indicate malice. You appear relieved."

"I am." She crossed her arms, again giving herself a full-body hug. "I still don't know why Jack really left me. After years of trying to figure it out, I only went with what I knew about him. He was the most caring man I'd ever met. The only reason I could think he'd left me was that he was trying to protect me from something."

"I was." Colin stopped next to me and stared at Olivia, a gentle expression on his face. "Hello, Liv."

"Jack." She pressed her hand hard against her mouth, but wasn't able to control her reaction. Tears streamed down her cheeks and her shoulders shook.

"Shit." Colin pushed his hands through his hair, then closed the distance between them and hugged her hard against him. "I'm so sorry. Sorry that I left. Sorry for how I left."

She shook her head against his chest. "That's not why I'm crying."

"Okay." He drew out the word and leaned away from her to look at her face.

She wiped her cheeks, looked at me, then looked back at Colin. "I'm crying because for the first time in almost two weeks I feel safe."

"Yoo-hoo!" Francine was standing on the veranda waving at us. "Bring the party here, people."

Roxy was standing next to Francine, blowing kisses to Vinnie. From this distance, I could not see their facial expressions, but their body language loudly communicated curiosity.

Colin hugged Olivia once more, then let her go. He stood next to me and took my hand. "Olivia, I would like to introduce myself." He held out his right hand, showing no concern for the dirt on her hands. "Colin Frey."

Her eyebrows rose high on her forehead. "Jackson Roanne isn't your name?"

He shook his head, remorse etched on his face. "And I've never been an art dealer."

"Wow." She looked at his hand for a long time before shaking it once, then putting both her hands behind her back. "Was everything a lie?"

"No." The word came out strong, with conviction. "Only my name and occupation. Everything else was true. Deeply true."

Vinnie was following the conversation with intense interest. And a genuine concern for Colin. His brow was furrowed as he waited for Olivia's reply.

She wiped her eyes and laughed softly. "This has honestly been the weirdest two weeks of my life. But this here?" She pointed at Colin, then at me and her. "This has to top it all. By a lot."

"I'm sorry." The contrition on Colin's face was genuine.

"Oh, stop saying that." Olivia sniffed. "God, it's been twenty years. I'm totally over you."

They stared at each other, then burst out laughing. I didn't know what had caused their amusement, but the strange tension that had tightened around my chest released at their laughter.

Colin's hand tightened around mine and he pulled me closer to his side. "It's really good to see you, Liv. I'm just sorry that it's under these circumstances."

"Weird, right?" She looked at our hands, then at Colin. "She told me you're not married. What are you?"

"Happy." His smile was genuine. "Olivia, meet the woman

who is daily making me a better man. And also the woman who will outsmart all of us. Genevieve Lenard."

Olivia smiled at me. "It's truly a pleasure to meet you, Genevieve."

I nodded. So far her presence in my life had not brought me pleasure so I simply couldn't return the polite greeting. Being polite was most definitely not a priority for me at the moment. We needed to get Olivia settled and get all the information she'd gathered. "You need to shower."

"Oh, God, don't remind me." She turned towards the villa and noticed Francine and Roxy waiting for us. "Urgh. This is not the way I like to make first impressions."

She straightened her shoulders, took a deep breath and nodded before she started walking towards the villa. Vinnie pushed her bicycle and we walked next to her in silence until we reached the veranda. Francine inhaled to say something, but stopped when Olivia raised one hand, her thumb tucked in and the other four fingers separated in pairs to form a 'V'.

"I'm Olivia. I come in peace. Take me to your leader."

Chapter EIGHT

"WHAT'S WRONG?" I stared at Francine for three seconds before I turned to Roxy on my other side. I was sitting at the dining room table, searching for information on Ferenc Szell. He was one of two deceased Hungarians mentioned in Olivia's notebook. I planned to find out as much as possible about them before asking her why they'd been important enough for her to mention. I would ask her as soon as she finished her shower.

I'd been reading about Ferenc Szell's success as a highly respected architect for the elite in Hungary when Francine and Roxy sat down either side of me. Roxy glanced at the kitchen where Vinnie was helping the cook prepare breakfast, the nonverbal cues on her face loudly communicating internal conflict and guilt.

She glanced at the kitchen again when Manny raised his voice. Colin was also in the kitchen and the three men were discussing strategy for keeping Olivia safe. Roxy leaned closer to me, her eyes wide. "We like her."

"Who?"

"Olivia." Francine slapped her hand on the table, her eyebrows pulled low. "She's funny, pretty and smart. She's genuinely interested in who we are and what we do. Like really interested. She thinks it's supercool that you're a body language expert. And did I mention she's funny?"

"Your point?" It was clear to me that these were not the reasons Francine was upset.

"And we like her!" She threw her hands into the air, her bracelets jingling. "I don't want to like her."

"Why not?" I didn't understand what was happening.

"She's the ex. That's why." She sounded exasperated.

"Ex? Wha…" I stopped and thought about this. And thought some more. Then I shook my head. "I can't find a rational reason for you to dislike the woman who'd been engaged to Colin."

Francine straightened in her chair and stared at me. "You're really okay."

Even though she'd stated her opinion, her expression told me she needed an answer. "Yes."

"Wow." Roxy poked my arm twice, then leaned against the table and stared at me with wide eyes. "I think you're a superhero."

"There is no such thing."

Roxy laughed. "Well, I think you are. I wish I could be like you."

I shook my head. Then had a hard time stopping. It took mentally writing two bars of Mozart's Violin Concerto to stop the involuntary movement. "I don't understand why you would want that."

"Yeah, I think I spoke faster than I thought." Her expression sobered. "I suppose I envy the way that you manage to look at things so rationally. I'm an emotional, hot mess. I talk too much, giggle like a teenager and offend certain people with my footwear." She winked at Francine.

"You're so organised. And Colin is always so calm. I swear I've never seen him rattled."

"What does that mean?"

"Huh?"

"It means she's never seen Colin flustered." Francine blinked a few times. "You know, that's true. He's always so serene."

I didn't know what to say. They were talking about someone I not only respected immensely, but also loved. Someone who was extremely private.

"Just the other day Colin really came through for me." Roxy stared towards the kitchen. "I had a patient who needed very specific treatment, but couldn't afford it."

"Surely that happens a lot," I said.

"Yeah. But not to adorable seven-year-old girls. Man, it broke my heart when her parents sat in my office crying because they didn't have any way of getting the thousands of euros needed to help their child." The helplessness she'd felt then was reflected on her face now. "I told Vinnie about it that night. Colin was also there and asked me a few questions. The next day, the parents came rushing into my office with the news that a famous local artist was looking for a charitable cause to improve his online profile and had picked their daughter.

"The artist was sponsoring all the child's medicine as long as he could paint her and take a few photos to post on his social media sites. I don't even know how Colin discovered the parents' names, and I actually don't want to know. I'm just glad that child is now getting the treatment she needs."

"And let me guess." Francine pressed her lips together in

an annoyed pout. "Colin didn't know what you were talking about when you asked him."

Roxy laughed. "Yeah. He just gave me one of those gorgeous smiles of his and said he's happy it all worked out."

"Typical." Francine became more annoyed. "He does this all the time. Helps everyone out and never asks for anything. He doesn't even want anyone to know that he did something amazing."

"Like the stuff he does for Martin." Roxy's anger confused me. She acted as if Colin was committing crimes.

Again I remained quiet. Colin was helping Eric's father, Martin, with many things. Phillip Rousseau, my previous boss and a man who'd become a father figure in my life, often met with Colin and Martin to help the younger man. Martin had just graduated from the first part of his law studies and was relying heavily on Phillip for guidance on how to proceed with his career.

Since we'd discovered Nikki was pregnant with Eric and that together she and Martin had decided not to get married, Colin had made sure to set up meetings with Phillip and help Martin in any way he could. Colin had been the one to find a comfortable apartment close to us so it was easier for Martin to spend time with Eric.

I'd seen the pleasure it had given Colin to help Martin. But it was Nikki's reaction that was really his reward. She had been extremely proud that Martin was proving to be such a responsible young man and father. I didn't know if she knew that Colin had played an important role in that behaviour.

"He's always been like this." Francine was looking up and left, recalling memories. "I've known Colin for a long time and I can't think of any instance where he didn't go out of his way to help someone."

"Like he did for Vinnie." Roxy's strong emotions lowered her pitch. "He allowed Manny to arrest him so Vin didn't have to go to prison."

They both stared at the kitchen. Then Francine straightened and knocked on the table. "We were talking about Olivia and that we don't want to like her so much."

"You'll never succeed." Olivia walked into the room and sat down across from me. She looked at Roxy, then at Francine. "I'm amazing. I'm extremely likeable. You won't be able to stop yourself from totally falling in love with me."

"See!" Francine pointed at Olivia, but glared at me. "That's what I'm talking about. She's wonderful. But you're my best friend and I feel like I'm betraying you."

I froze and for ten seconds studied Francine's face. "You're serious about this."

"Of course I am."

I looked at Olivia, trying to make sense of this strange situation. She looked much more relaxed after her shower. She'd insisted on cleaning up before telling us everything she'd discovered and had followed Vinnie to one of the many guest rooms. Her blonde hair was only partly dried, her make-up fresh, and she was wearing jeans and a dark-green silk blouse. Her smile was soft and genuine. "They feel weird that they like me when usually a friend's ex-fiancée is a total bitch."

"None of this makes sense and we are wasting time with this kind of nonsense." And it frustrated me that I didn't comprehend this. I planned to go and read up on this.

"What nonsense?" Manny walked into the room, followed by Colin.

"Nothing." Francine winked at Manny. "Just girl talk."

"Ah." Manny nodded. "Nonsense."

Roxy got up and moved to the chair she usually used when we all sat at the table. Colin sat down next to me and looked at Olivia. "Feeling better?"

"Much."

"Did you speak to your family?"

She shook her head. "I don't want to risk phoning home. I think my phones and my husband's are bugged. So I called my sister's husband to tell him to let my husband and my boss know I'm fine and that I'll contact them soon."

"I'll set you up," Francine said. "You'll be able to chat with your family on a secure line in no time."

"Thank you. That would be great." Olivia put her hand on a notebook that I hadn't noticed before. "I'm ready to talk."

"Not yet." Vinnie walked into the room, carrying a tray of steaming coffee mugs. "Let's get breakfast on the table and then we talk."

Seven minutes later, everyone was dishing up from the numerous hot and cold dishes Vinnie and the cook had prepared. Every morning, I had a bowl with fruit and natural yogurt. Today I might, however, also have one of the cook's fresh croissants. They were truly delicious.

"Do you need a special invitation or are you going to tell us why the bloody hell the first lady of France ordered us to look for you?" Manny scowled at Francine when she slapped his arm, then turned his irritated look back to Olivia. "Well?"

Olivia closed her mouth and put her uneaten croissant

back on her plate. "Wait, the first lady of France? What are you talking about?"

"I'll tell you later." Francine leaned past Manny to see Olivia and nodded towards Manny. "He'll get all huffy and puffy if you don't start sharing."

Olivia lifted one eyebrow, then looked at me as if for approval or permission.

I frowned. "What?"

"Nothing." She shook her head, took a sip of her coffee, then nodded. "I don't know how much you know, so I'll tell you everything. Five weeks ago, Nathan Donovan died from what the coroner determined was a massive heart attack. He was twice the weight a man of his height should be, didn't walk anywhere he could drive and had a history of high blood pressure, so the heart attack didn't come as a surprise.

"His last will and testament also didn't come as a surprise to me or his family. I'd helped him set it up about six years ago and had recently updated it to include new acquisitions in his art collection." She looked at Colin. "He managed to build up quite an impressive collection of artworks over the last two decades."

"Your boss wasn't able to send us Mister Donovan's client file." I noticed her flinch and made a mental note about her discomfort at deleting the file from her company's server. "Tell me more about him."

"Um, well, honestly? There's not much to tell." She raised one shoulder. "Nathan inherited his father's real-estate business. His father had a bit of a reputation during the seventies and early eighties for colluding with the Mafia in New York, but was never arrested or even investigated.

"I've had no reason to look that far into his history, so I don't know much more than this about his father and family history. What I do know is that Nathan took over the business in 1987. It was only three years after he'd graduated from some business school or something. If you need the exact university, I can get that for you."

"Not right now." I didn't know if that information would be pertinent at a later stage.

She smiled. "Okay. Maybe later then. Well, anyway, Nathan turned the business around. By the middle of the nineties, Don Estates was given the Manhattan Business of the Year award for its transparent and honest business practices in New York. Nathan had worked hard to create and then maintain a reputation of integrity. In the real-estate industry that was not easy and even today it is not at all common for a company to be that open with their dealings and finances."

She took a bite from her croissant and chewed it only three times before washing it down with coffee. I wondered if she knew how unhealthy that was. Yet I didn't say anything. I was too interested in every detail she shared.

She tilted her coffee mug and frowned at the inside. "May I please have more coffee?"

"I'll get it." Roxy jumped up and grabbed Olivia's mug. "Back in a sec."

"Thanks." She leaned back in her chair and looked up to the left—recalling information. "When Nathan's wife phoned with the news of his death, I immediately got the ball rolling. I strive to give my clients' loved ones closure as soon as possible after their deaths. Already they're dealing with a traumatic event. Having to fight with their insurance companies isn't something anyone wants and I definitely don't want to add to the stress in their lives."

Roxy returned and put Olivia's refilled coffee mug next to her plate. Olivia nodded her thanks. "But I do have an obligation to ensure that no laws are broken in the execution of a last will and testament. Hmm." She blinked a few times and looked at Colin. "I don't know how much you know about me, but I work white-collar crime cases and investigate iffy last wills and testaments."

Colin nodded. "I knew that you worked at Freeman, Scott and Associates, but the last I checked, you were working only white-collar cases."

"That was eight years ago, just after I started at FSA." She narrowed her eyes. "About a year after I started, one of my clients died and I discovered laundered funds hidden in an account that he'd bequeathed to his lover. It was extremely well-hidden and had taken quite a lot of digging to find. I found it and we got the FBI involved. I fought hard to clear the family from any involvement in the laundered money. The lover had given herself away the first time I spoke to her, so I helped the FBI to get proof that she'd helped this man clean his dirty money. This caught my boss' attention and within a year, I was spending more than half my time on investigating suspicious claims."

"Do you still rely on your left pinkie to tell you when people are lying?" Colin asked.

Olivia burst out laughing. "Oh, my God. I'd forgotten about that." She looked at me. "I used to tell Jacks… Colin that my left pinkie finger ached when he was lying to me."

"You were lying." I could see it on her face.

"Oh, totally. But I've always had a good sense for when people were bullshitting me." Her smile disappeared as she returned her gaze to Colin. "Somehow, my radar never went off with you. Well, not about the important stuff. I knew when you were fibbing about my looking good when I looked crap. But I honestly never once doubted that Jackson was your name."

"I'm sorry." He swallowed. I wondered how many more times Colin was going to apologise to her before he forgave himself.

"In the past." She took a sip of coffee and straightened her shoulders. "Back to Nathan. So, when we worked on his will, he gave me notarised copies of all the sales documents and provenance papers for every single one of his artworks. Imagine my surprise when, after his death, I went through the documents and started Googling these pieces."

Her narration was interrupted by two bodyguards making their way to the front door moments before the doorbell rang. Manny and Vinnie got up, their hands resting on their holstered weapons. It had made sense that Manny had gained permission to carry his weapon across borders, but I still didn't know how he'd got that permission for Vinnie.

Olivia's *frontalis* muscle raised her brows and upper eyelids in an expression of fear that was becoming familiar. Her hand was shaking so much, she put her coffee mug on the table and tucked her fists under her crossed arms.

"It's just Garage!" Manny's call from the front of the villa was an uncommon show of consideration for a stranger. If not for Olivia, I could think of no other reason for him to announce Andor's arrival to the rest of us. Colin, Francine, Roxy and myself exhibited nonverbal cues of interest and curiosity even though there was an alertness visible in all of us that had not been there before. It showed our trust in the protection offered by Manny and Vinnie.

I tried to keep observing Olivia's body language, yet I couldn't stop myself the moment Manny walked into the dining room. "Andor's surname is Garas."

"Don't worry about it, Genevieve." Andor followed Manny into the room. "The way my surname is pronounced in Hungarian sounds mighty close to 'garage'. Here we say a 'sh' sound for an 's', like in my surname."

Manny didn't look pleased with this. Francine laughed and played with Manny's collar when he sat down next to her. "And here you thought you were annoying him. In the meantime you're the only one pronouncing his surname correctly."

"Put a sock in it, supermodel."

"Ooh." She winked at me. "First time in months he's called me that. He must be really annoyed."

I shook my head at the way she was drawing out the 'really' and looked at Andor.

Colin pointed to the chair that Nikki had used while she'd been here. "Have a seat. There's more than enough food for you."

"Oh, thank the stars!" Andor sat down and looked at all the dishes on the table. "I got here as fast as I could. I was already up and dressed when Colonel Millard phoned, so I just jumped in the car. I haven't even had a cup of coffee yet."

"I'll fix that for you." Roxy got up and left for the kitchen.

The next ten minutes was spent briefing Andor on everything that had taken place since we'd parted ways yesterday afternoon. I took that time to savour my croissant and start a second cup of coffee. I also watched Olivia. It took her most of the briefing to relax enough to eat again. She didn't say anything while Colin and Manny did most of the talking. Instead she studied Andor.

I wondered what she saw. Earlier she'd mentioned that she was a keen observer and was able to determine if a person was deceitful. I wondered about her conclusions when she nodded to herself and put another croissant on her plate.

"I'm pleased to meet you, Olivia," Andor said when Manny finished most of the retelling. "I'm just sorry that we couldn't meet three days ago so you could've felt safer."

Olivia nodded. "Thank you. And in turn I'm sorry that I ran out on you like that. I just didn't want to take the chance that…" She hesitated, blinked a few times, then moved her lips into a polite smile. "Well, that it wasn't safe."

"Why are you lying?" I didn't understand why she would start being untruthful now.

She closed her eyes, groaned loudly, then laughed and looked at Colin. "Is it at all possible to hide something from her?"

"Never." Colin's smile was genuine. "So you better tell us everything."

Roxy leaned closer and touched Olivia's hand. "We trust Andor. You can trust him too."

Olivia looked at me, her micro-expressions communicating a desire for reassurance. Again. I took a calming breath. "He has not exhibited any deception cues. As a matter of fact, he's been uncommonly forthcoming with us."

"Thanks, Genevieve." Andor smiled at me, then turned to Olivia. "I don't know how much you've been told about what we've found so far."

"Nothing." The surprise on Olivia's face was soon replaced with a grunt of acknowledgement. "Of course you guys would've investigated my disappearance. Oh, God. Did you find all my skeletons?"

I gasped. "What skeletons? You've murdered people?"

Everyone laughed, except Manny. He slumped deeper into his chair and narrowed his eyes. "Answer the doc. What skeletons?"

Olivia didn't appear concerned. She counted off on one hand. "My abnormally large collection of amber jewellery, my obsession with finding a lipstick that will stay on my lips for longer than two cups of coffee, my shameful love for buying kitchen gadgets that I never use and last, but most definitely worst, my love affair with pedicures."

Manny looked disgusted. I was confused. How were those skeletons? While Francine got into an inane discussion with Olivia about pedicures, I took a moment to analyse the expression. Soon it made sense and I was exasperated. They were wasting time.

"Ooh, yes! Paraffin pedicures are the best." Francine noticed my expression and smiled widely. "Um, I think we should shelve this conversation for later, girl." She tapped her index finger on her lips. "Before you continue, please first tell me who you visited when you went to Erkel Street and Király Street in Budapest."

Olivia frowned. "How do you know I was there?"

"We know everything about your movements since the moment you landed." Francine gestured as if it was obvious. "We were trying to find out what happened to you."

"Huh. Okay. Well, I met a lawyer friend of one of my colleagues in New York. He helped me get access to national archives. I was looking for information on a painting in Nathan Donovan's estate. I didn't find anything there. The same when I went to Király Street. That library has microfilm of newspapers printed all the way back to before the First World War. I didn't have enough time to go through everything. I would need at least a week. I was planning on returning there, but alas. Here I am. Here we are."

"What about your visit to Pál Elo?" Colin asked. "We know that he wasn't at his gallery, but why did you want to meet with him?"

Olivia thought about her answer. "I think it might be best if I tell everything as it unfolded."

"I would appreciate that." I loathed stories being told out of chronological order.

"Well, where was I?"

"You talked about Googling the paintings in Nathan Donovan's estate."

"Oh, yes." She smiled at me. "That was my first clue. Ooh, wait. I suppose it's important for you to know when I did this. Well, it was about ten days ago. All the artworks in the Donovan estate had their provenance documentation. Everything was legal. Or so I thought. For some reason, I decided to double-check. I found nothing suspicious on any of the works except *A Woman Feeding a Parrot* by Caspar Netscher."

"Are you kidding me?" Colin's eyebrows rose high on his forehead. "That painting has a horrid history."

"Exactly." The muscles around Olivia's mouth tightened. "On the second page of results, I found an article that suggested that this specific work of art had been taken by the Nazis during the Second World War. The journalist then disputed that theory with documentation that the painting had been through a few legitimate sales."

"That was an inaccurate article. That painting was thought to be lost after the Nazis took it from the owners in 1940." Colour crept up Colin's neck, his muscles tense. "Did you search for more information? Better information?"

"Yes." She nodded. "And that was when things went to pot."

"What does that mean?" I asked.

"It went crazy." Colin frowned and leaned closer to Olivia. "What happened?"

"I decided to do some more internet sleuthing and started checking into any and all names mentioned in the article. I was busy with this for about three, maybe four minutes until my computer just blinked out." She looked at Francine. "I turned my computer back on and my really good antivirus software was screaming at me that I had a virus. I shut everything down and immediately contacted the IT guys."

"This was your work computer?" Francine's eyes were wide with interest.

"Yes." She pulled the notebook closer to her. "The IT guys went through my computer three times and said they couldn't find any virus of any sort."

"You didn't believe them." I could see it clearly on her face.

"I had a feeling. A bad one." She sighed. "The rest of that day I didn't do anything interesting on my work computer. When I got home and I turned on my laptop at home, there was an extra icon on my desktop screen. I know this because I only have five icons and they are all in a specific order. That made me wonder and I checked my smartphone. The same thing. I had a new icon."

"What icon?" Francine's tone emphasised the impatience on her face.

"The computer's and the phone's cameras. I have it set that I need to give permission every time the computer's cameras are used. The same with my smartphone. I don't want the cameras turning on for whatever reason. I checked the settings on my devices and everything was as I left it. That's when I suspected that I'd been hacked. There and then I decided that I would have to work offline." She lifted the notebook. "I kept two notebooks. This one and the one I suppose you found in my hotel room."

Colin's *zygomaticus major* muscle lifted one corner of his mouth into a half-smile. "You did a really good job changing the code. I didn't manage to find the key. Jenny did. I then started decoding it."

"You won't find a lot of useful stuff there." Her smug smile had me paying close attention. "I did that notebook as a decoy. In case someone found it, it would keep them busy for a long time and the info they would find there would be enough to make them think that was all I had."

"Your real notes are in that notebook." I looked at the leather-bound journal she was now holding against her chest.

"Yes. And I didn't let this thing out of my sight for a

second. As soon as I thought I was being cyberstalked, I moved my laptop into the kitchen so that person could only ever see me cook and eat. I also booked a lot of my meetings out of the office."

"Is that why you deleted Nathan Donovan's file from the company's servers?" Andor asked.

"How do you know that?" She lifted her index finger and groaned. "Of course George told you."

"Not that he told us a lot." Manny scowled. "Does he know about your cyber-stalker?"

"No." Her shoulders rose until they almost touched her ears. "I had no proof. Only a huge dose of paranoia."

"So you booked a flight to Hungary," Colin said.

"Not immediately. I thought I was overreacting and wanted to give myself some time. But then I got in my office one morning and my computer was turned on. I never leave my computers on. Ever. I checked the security cameras of the night before and no one had been in my office."

"Someone had turned your laptop on remotely," Francine said.

"Which means that whatever software that person had uploaded into my devices left me completely naked whenever I was close to any of them."

"Where's your smartphone now?" I swallowed at the tension in my throat.

"Stripped of all data and dumped in the Danube."

Francine nodded her approval. "Good for you. Whatever is left on that phone will be destroyed by the water. We hope. When did you toss it?"

"When I saw Ja… Colin and Genevieve in Szentendre."

"What made you think there was danger? Why did you run?" Andor asked.

"A feeling. I really didn't see anyone or anything real." She looked at Colin. "It was the shock of seeing you added to the growing fear of what I was uncovering that made me run."

"What have you been uncovering?" I asked.

"The first thing I uncovered was that *A Woman Feeding a Parrot* by Caspar Netscher had been sold in 1940 by a Jewish family who lived in Hungary. That alone made me take note."

"Why?" Roxy asked.

"That's one of the many methods the Nazis used to disenfranchise the Jews." Colin's jaw tightened. "And also to steal from them. Before all of them were sent to concentration camps, when they were still contained in the ghetto areas of the cities, the Nazis would find out who had valuables in their homes. Then they would tell the family if they sold a masterpiece, a diamond ring or a Stradivarius violin for a few dollars, this family would be protected from ever being sent to concentration camps."

Olivia put the notebook on the table, her lips thin with anger. "Of course they never kept their word. They did give the family the two or three dollars for the painting or whatever, making the sale legit, but that money was useless. The Nazis would come at night, grab the family, take all the money they had in their house and send them off to concentration camps."

"Many masterpieces changed hands like that." Colin's top lip curled. "Legally. All the right paperwork was done. It was all above board."

"But it was still stealing." Olivia crossed her arms. "Six years ago, I helped a family reclaim a Van Gogh that had been taken from their grandmother in Poland. That was the first time I truly realised the vastness of the atrocities the Nazis committed."

"Almost six million Jews, one point eight million non-Jewish Polish civilians, millions of Soviet civilians, about two hundred and fifty thousand disabled people, thousands of homosexuals killed. Slaughtered. Also around two hundred thousand Roma were murdered by the Nazis." Tension caused Colin's voice to sound strained, his lips losing colour. His hand tightened around mine. "Twenty-five museums in Poland alone were destroyed, over half a million individual art works looted. In only one country. Thousands of paintings burnt in public and tens of thousands of artworks taken from their rightful owners. There is a lot of speculation on how many pieces have been recovered, but the most common belief is no more than fifty percent. The rest of that cultural wealth is very possibly lost forever."

Olivia took a deep breath and held it for a few seconds. She exhaled slowly, her facial muscles more relaxed. "So *A Woman Feeding a Parrot* was sold in 1940 to none other than Gyula Koltai."

"Bloody hell!" Manny sat up. "A relative of István?"

"His grandfather." Olivia looked at Andor. "I know István is dead. Do you think it was accidental?"

"No." Andor had been quietly observing Olivia. He narrowed his eyes. "Neither do you."

"Not after the last week I've had." She shook her head. "That was why I wanted to meet with you. I don't know how he died, but the fact that he died so soon after I spoke to him is extremely suspicious."

"What did you talk about?"

Her laugh held no humour. "Nothing. He was very polite, but didn't answer any of my questions. He was curious why a lawyer from the US would want to see him. The moment I mentioned the painting bought by his grandfather, he went as white as a sheet and refused to say anything else. I had looked a bit into his grandfather, but didn't find much. On a whim I asked him if his grandfather bought many such paintings. Again he didn't answer me, but the panic on his face was enough of an answer for me. I think his grandfather dealt in Nazi-looted art."

"Hell. This is getting worse." Manny rubbed his hands hard over his face.

"I don't know what this is yet." Olivia picked up her notebook again. "He did give me one thing though. I think it was just to get rid of me. He told me that if I wanted answers I should speak to King."

"Who's King?" Colin frowned. "Is it a pseudonym?"

Andor shook his head. "Huh. King? Did he say anything else about King?"

"No." Olivia opened her notebook. "I wrote it down exactly as he said. And it was just to find out more about King. I didn't know who or what that was, so I decided to look more into István's grandfather." She looked at Francine. "I bought a new smartphone, one of the pay-as-you-go numbers, made sure I bought a lot of data and did all my research on that. I found out that old Gyula was quite the businessman and, as it appears, an art dealer. I found three articles that mentioned him as the person who had brokered a deal for a masterpiece. He never named the original owner, but I have my suspicions that he'd owned those artworks.

"Again I followed up on all the names mentioned in those articles. And that's when I came across a Franz Szabo and a Lajos Szell. I did as much as possible digging and that's when I discovered that those men had been friends with good ol' Gyula. And that Szabo's grandson Gabor and Szell's grandson Ferenc both had recently died. From natural causes. Just like István."

"Motherbleeper!" Andor slammed his fist against his thigh. "That's it. This is the connection I need to make my case that a serial killer is responsible for their deaths."

For a few seconds it was quiet around the table. Only Vinnie reacted to Andor's exclamation with an exasperated sigh. I used the silence to consider everything that Olivia had revealed. I had many questions and thought about where to start. I looked at Andor. "Do you know who or what this king is?"

"I think István was talking about the Roma leader whom everyone calls King. His real name is Stefan Bílá, but I don't think anyone uses it. He's one of the few Roma leaders who does everything he can for his people, not for his own pocket. Like a benevolent king. He's sixty-something years old and has been doing everything he can to get his people the highest education possible, to get the best government support possible and to push his people to achieve their dreams. He's also turned out to be a very good businessman. He's got a lot of his community involved in his business."

"What business?" Colin asked.

"Restoration." Andor thought about this for a few seconds. "Huh. I wonder if they have ever restored valuable artworks. They've built up a strong reputation in Europe for restoring antique furniture and even jewellery. Hmm."

"Why would István send us to King?" Colin leaned back and looked at the ceiling. "There must be some connection between him and these men. Or at least their grandfathers." He straightened, a frown pulling his brow low. "But he's too young to have been a peer."

"And as a Roma, he would never have moved in their circles." The corners of Andor's mouth turned down. "You have to keep in mind that discrimination against the Roma was in full force those years. It's much better now, but it's still an awful reality here in Hungary."

"We need to speak to him." Not only did I have a lot of questions for this man, I was also curious to meet the person who demanded such respect from Andor.

"I'll set it up." Andor got up and took his phone from his trouser pocket.

I took note of the fear flashing across Olivia's face before she pulled her shoulders back. "I'm going with."

That resulted in an argument in which Manny insisted that she stay out of our way while we investigated. Vinnie was fretting about keeping all of us safe, Francine was tapping away on her tablet screen and Roxy was watching all this with amusement.

Colin was the only one not taking part in the chaos around the table. We'd had numerous conversation about the depth of his hatred for what the Nazis had done in Europe. Only once had he talked about the deaths of almost one million people in the Treblinka extermination camp. The strength of his emotions had made his voice sound strangled as he'd explained his deep-seated loathing for that part of history. That conversation had given me a lot of insight into what was driving him.

It also helped me understand why this case was affecting him so deeply. It wasn't only because of Olivia's unexpected involvement, but also because of the possible Nazi connection.

We definitely needed to speak to this King so we could solve this as quickly as possible. I was relieved when Andor managed to reason with Olivia and even convince Vinnie that it would be best if only Manny, Colin and I accompanied him. I was already thinking of the many questions I had for this Roma leader.

Chapter NINE

"AND THIS IS my pride and joy." Stefan Bílá, or King as he had introduced himself with a self-deprecating laugh, pointed at the nineteenth-century coffee table next to a modern and very comfortable-looking sofa in his home office. A small smile lifted his cheeks and caused wrinkling in the corners of his eyes. "This was the very first piece I ever restored. I wouldn't allow my dad to help me and really made a mess of one of the legs." He laughed softly. "My dad fixed that leg. It was far beyond my abilities."

"You've been doing this for a very long time." The admiration in Colin's voice was genuine. He'd been in awe of every piece of restored furniture King had been showing us for the last fifteen minutes. Manny was not that interested in the furniture. He'd been taking note of the security cameras and other security features in the mansion.

Andor had joined Colin in asking questions about the furniture and the restoration process. I was observing everyone. King was an interesting man. He'd welcomed us at the door of his enormous house and had not once exhibited insincere nonverbal cues. His welcome had been genuine, as well as the pride he took in all the meticulously restored pieces.

King's house was on the Pest side of Budapest, just outside the city borders. On the way here, Andor had pointed out numerous noteworthy sights and had joked about being a tour guide. We'd driven past the majestic Parliament buildings and yet again I'd been impressed by the beauty of the architecture.

Colin had talked about it being a magnificent example of Neo-Gothic architecture and Andor had boasted that it was the third largest Parliament building in the world. He'd offered to take us on a tour. I'd declined. I wanted to solve this case and return to my home and my routine.

One thing Andor had mentioned that I'd found interesting was that King had bought most of the properties in this area over the last fifteen years. He'd turned this neighbourhood into a family-friendly and low-crime zone.

"Sometimes I joke that I was born with woodworking tools in my hands," King said. "I used to sit with my dad for hours watching him restore chairs and tables that the local people brought to him."

I was surprised by the bitterness that accompanied his memory. "Why was that a negative experience?"

"Damn." He waved his hand towards the four wingback chairs arranged around an antique round coffee table. He waited until we were all seated, then looked at me. "Some days I really think I've forgiven everything and everyone and then there are days that it comes back to me and I let it slip. I apologise."

I didn't see a need for him to apologise, but was more interested in something else. "Who and what do you need to forgive?"

His eyebrows rose high on his forehead and he stared at me. He must have seen something to make him realise my question had been sincere. "Sadly, a lot. You see, my dad did all those restorations for people who wouldn't even speak to him. If it hadn't been for our neighbour, old Mister Darabont, my dad would never have had any work. That old man didn't care what people in the village and the area said about him. He spoke to us, sold us eggs and honey from his farm and bought a kilogram of cookies from my mother every week.

"He didn't care that his neighbours and friends were telling him that my family was going to poison him and steal everything from his farm. He didn't care when some of them turned their backs on him because he befriended the horrible, evil, dirty gypsies." Again the bitterness slipped into his tone and showed clearly on his face.

He inhaled deeply, then smiled. "Once he came around to pick up his cookies and saw my dad working on a bookshelf. He was so impressed with the quality of my dad's craftsmanship that he asked my dad if he would be able to restore an antique wall unit. Even though my dad loved making furniture from scratch, restoring something was his true passion. He was so excited about it, he refused to give old Mister Darabont a price.

"Three weeks later, the wall unit was restored, my dad was over the moon to have worked on an eighteenth-century piece of furniture and Mister Darabont started marketing my dad's skills. For almost five years, he was the broker between my dad and the many racist people who wanted their furniture restored, but refused to do business with a gypsy.

"My mom used to say that it was a blessing in disguise. Old Mister Darabont used to charge outrageous amounts for the work my dad did. He was so angry on our behalf that he punished his friends by making them pay for it. He also refused to take more than ten percent of the price. That was his fee and if my dad didn't want to take the rest of the money, he threatened to burn the cash right in front of us."

"He sounds like quite the character," Colin said.

"Oh, he was that and so much more." King looked around the room. "To this day, I believe we have all of this because of him."

"A good man."

"The best." He leaned back in his chair. "After five years, my dad's reputation had gone further than our county. People from all over the country were bringing their furniture to be restored. You have to remember that those were the days of communism. It was really hard to get anything new. So when people had the option of having their grandparents' furniture restored to its original glory, they grabbed it.

"Soon my dad had too much work to cope with on his own. He got my two uncles involved, then a friend and within ten years most of our Roma community was involved in the business in some form."

"I understand your dad died eleven years ago." Andor leaned forward. "It must have been a shocking loss."

"It was." Remembered sadness showed on his face. "But we did expect it. Two years before, my dad had been diagnosed with cancer. The treatments weren't as successful as the doctors had hoped and the last six months were basically just making him comfortable."

"I'm so sorry for your loss." Colin's voice was soft, his expression genuine.

"Thank you." King smiled. "I believe that he is still here with me. In every piece of furniture he restored, in the memories he created with me, the community, my children, but also in everything he taught me. The Romani nation is stereotyped as people waiting for a handout. Sadly, there is some truth to it. My father never allowed us to think for one second about asking for anything we didn't work for. He instilled in me and my sister a strong work ethic and later passed it on to everyone who worked with and for him."

My knowledge of the history of the Roma people was basic at best. I knew that they also went by Romani, Sinti or Kale people. They had originated in the northwest parts of the Indian subcontinent and migrated, voluntarily and at times involuntarily, to Europe sometime after the sixth century. Their identity had never been based on a homeland, but rather in their nomadic lifestyles and freedom of movement.

From more recent articles I'd read, I knew that most of the Roma people were indeed perceived as uneducated, lazy and with no ambition to better themselves. The wealth surrounding us in this room and house was evidence that King and his people were the exceptions to that rule.

"I've been talking non-stop since you arrived." He shook his head. "My wife always says I talk too much. I know you didn't come here for my life story, but I still don't know what I can do for you. When your Captain Palya phoned, I was more than happy to help in any way I can with a case that involves my people. I want us to have a reputation for cooperation, not for obstructing justice." He chuckled. "I've always wanted to use that term. Obstructing justice. I've seen it so many times on American TV shows and thought it sounded so professional. I don't get many opportunities to practice my English… No, no, I'm lying. I talk at least once a day with someone from abroad who needs restoration done. It's just that I love English. It falls softly on the ear. But that's me talking too much again." His smile was wide and genuine. "What can I do for you?"

Andor responded with an equally genuine smile. It was clear he was enjoying King's verbosity. "We're investigating a case that so far has not yet led us to any Roma connections. But your name came up."

"My name?" He blinked a few times. "Really?"

"Yes. Someone we interviewed didn't want to give us any information for whatever reason, but they told us to speak to you."

King leaned back in his chair, a deep frown furrowing his brow. "I really can't imagine anything that would attract the police's attention that would involve me."

Manny looked at me and I nodded. King was telling the truth.

"Do you know Franz Szabo?" Andor searched King's face for a reaction as he mentioned the man Olivia had found was connected with István Koltai's grandfather.

King frowned and took a moment to answer. "No."

"Gyula Koltai?"

"No."

"Lajos Szell?" Ferenc's grandfather.

"No." As soon as he answered, he started shaking his head. "No, wait. I've heard that name before. Szell? Hmm. Let me think." He scratched his chin. "Wasn't he the one who became the first multi-millionaire in Hungary after the fall of communism? It was a topic of discussion around the dinner table for weeks."

I didn't know enough about the Szell, Szabo and Koltai grandfathers yet. I most definitely didn't know enough about Szell's financial success. I hoped Francine could give us complete information on these three men as well as any possible connections.

"Are you sure you don't know any of these men?" Manny asked. "Maybe you restored something for them and you don't remember."

"That is a possibility. I can check if you want."

"Please," Andor said.

King immediately got up and walked to his desk. We listened to the one-sided conversation of him asking his assistant to check all their records for orders from the three men. It interested me that he was speaking English to his assistant. A minute later, he was seated again. "It won't take long. My niece is a genius when it comes to the computer stuff. She started working in the office during her summer holidays for extra cash. When she was sixteen, she single-handedly computerised our archives. At first I thought it was busy-work, but having that kind of data has proven to be very useful." He shook his head. "Again, I talk too much. Please forgive me."

An uncomfortable silence settled in the room. Manny

looked at me and raised his eyebrows in a question I'd come to recognise. "He's been truthful the whole time."

Manny huffed. "You could've just nodded."

"I have no reason to lie." King didn't appear offended at all. "Like I said before, I take pride in the honesty of my business dealings and my cooperation with the authorities." He hesitated. "This is not the first time I've received a visit from you guys, so I know how it works. You ask questions and answer none. But is there anything at all you can tell me? I would really like to know what this is about."

Andor inhaled to speak, but Manny was quicker. "Not at the moment."

Colin glared at Manny, then turned to King. "We are at the very beginning of this investigation and our visit here is simply to cover our bases. We have nothing indicating that you are involved in any criminal activity, but needed to find out why your name came up."

"That is really a mystery to me." King held out his hands in a helpless gesture. "I keep a close eye on my people and I'm pretty confident that I would know if anyone got into something they shouldn't."

This was frustrating. I needed more information, more data. With only a mention of King's name and his genuine denial of wrongdoing, this was beginning to feel like a waste of precious time. King was talking about the numerous Roma charity organisations his business supported. That gave me an idea. "Tell me more about your community." I realised my question was too general and held up my index finger while I thought of a better question. "You mentioned earlier that you are very proud of your people, of their individual accomplishments. Tell me more about that. Who accomplished what?"

King's muscles around his eyes and mouth relaxed, his smile proud. "Where do I begin? Well, there's Damian Varga, who was the very first one in our community to ever graduate from university. That was in 1976. I was in high school then and my dad's business had grown quite a lot. Damian's father was helping mine in the workshop and his mother was helping with the upholstery side of the restoration. She had an amazing skill for the finer work needed with the silk covers for the nineteenth-century chairs.

"My dad had pushed them both to let Damian go to university instead of joining the business after school. He'd seen Damian's interest in architecture and had told the parents that they would be holding their son back if they didn't give him the opportunity." His chest puffed. "In the 1990s he won three awards for his designs. One of those was the Pritzker Architecture Prize."

A woman in her late twenties to early thirties walked into the room and stopped next to King. "Hi, everyone. Don't worry about me. I'm just popping in to say that none of those names are in any of our documents, Uncle Stef."

"Thanks, Erika."

Her smile lifted her cheeks and crinkled the corners of her eyes. The genuineness of her expression made her look younger. She kissed her uncle's cheek and left the room. King nodded towards the door. "She's another success story. When she started high school, her grades started plummeting. My brother and his wife didn't know what to do. The teacher said that Erika was lazy and never did her homework, didn't pay attention in class and was belligerent. We didn't believe that. Erika was hardworking and respectful. But every time we asked her, she closed down and wouldn't tell us why she wasn't doing well.

"It took her father and I putting a spy camera in her rucksack to find out what was going on. Her whole class and the home teacher who insulted my niece were caught on camera abusing that child so badly it made my hair stand on end. It wasn't physical, but the vitriol they spat at her was worse than punches. The school begged us to settle this without going public.

"We took Erika out of the school and accepted the resignation of the teacher and the apologies from the children and their parents. Some of the parents were very ashamed of their children bullying Erika because she was Roma. With the exception of a few idiots, most were incredibly grateful that we didn't take this to the media."

If it weren't for my expertise, I might have missed his micro-expressions of regret and anger. "What did you just remember?"

"Another success story. But one that came with a price." His eyebrows drew together, the corners of his mouth turning down. "Lila was such a bright young girl. She had very few problems at school, mostly because she didn't look very Romani. Her skin is lighter than most of us, which made most people forget where she came from. Only a few times did we have to deal with mild racist situations, but her school years were quite uneventful. Except of course for her amazing grades. Such an intelligent young girl.

"The problems started at university. She insisted on staying in the city and not commuting every day from home. That's why we never knew about the horrid abuse she suffered from a few of her classmates. It broke her. She dropped out of university and completely withdrew from us for a few years. During that time she managed to drag herself back up and started an extremely successful tech company."

Some of the sadness left his face. "Despite being a woman in a male-dominated field, she's highly respected. And she comes to visit us more often now. She even drives a nifty SUV crossover. We are so proud of her."

He told us the stories of another three people, but I'd heard and observed enough. His was a community that had broken away from the mindset that appeared to hold back so many Roma communities. But I could no longer sit and listen to anecdotes when I knew how much research I had to do. I also wanted to find out what Francine had discovered.

The ringing of Andor's phone interrupted my impatient thoughts. I watched his face as he listened to the person on the other side of the call. His *corrugator supercilii* muscles pulled his brows together and down, then his face lost colour. I thought of pointing out to him that nodding was not effective during a phone conversation, but the despondency on his face stopped me. He closed his eyes tightly. "We'll be there in twenty minutes."

"What happened?" Manny was already sitting on the edge of his seat, his hands pressed on his knees to push him up.

"Another murder."

"Murder?" King gasped, his eyes wide. "My name was mentioned in a murder investigation? Oh, my goodness."

Colin leaned forward to catch King's attention. "You're not a suspect or a person of interest."

"But murder." King swallowed a few times. "That's just awful. That poor person's family. Please let me help. You have my word that anything you share with me will be kept in the strictest confidence. My door is open. Any time."

We all stood and Manny reached out to shake King's hand. "We'll let you know if there's anything you can do."

"Please." King looked at me. "Please. I want to help in any way I can."

I nodded, not knowing what else to say. King's concern over being connected to a murder was genuine and so strong it affected me.

Andor took King's hand in both of his, regret clearly visible on his face. "This is my mistake. I should've waited to tell my colleagues what the call was about. I didn't mean to upset you at all. Thank you so much for your time and your generous help."

"Anything I can do. Anything we as a community can do." King shook Andor's hand, then Colin's and walked us to the front door.

The moment we were in Colin's SUV and the door's closed, Andor apologised again. And again. I stopped listening. We were on our way to a crime scene and my brain wasn't prepared for this. I looked out the window and watched the congested streets of Budapest as I pushed Mozart's Flute Quartet No. 1 in D major into my mind. Mentally playing it wasn't enough, so I started mentally writing the quartet, hoping that it would be enough to keep a shutdown at bay.

Chapter TEN

"THAT BASTARD WAS livestreaming this!" Francine stood in the entrance hall to the three-story house we had just entered. Her fists were resting on her hips, her red lips compressed in a tight line. "It's just sick that someone wants to watch a person die."

"What took you so long? It took us twenty minutes from the villa to get here." Vinnie pushed Francine out of the way and looked down at Manny. "Did you drive?"

"I didn't drive, you degenerate." Manny's shoulders slumped and he nodded towards Colin. "He did."

"We got a lot of traffic on the road next to the river." Colin had tried to drive as fast as possible, but there had been an accident on the main road going to the north of Budapest. He'd decided to take another route, but that had proven to be just as congested. Very congested. No matter how hard he'd tried, he hadn't been able to maintain a constant distance between our car and the cars in front of us. Eventually, I'd closed my eyes and focused solely on mentally writing Mozart's Flute Quartet.

"Ah." Vinnie raised an eyebrow. "Did you learn anything interesting from the king dude?"

Colin shook his head. "Nothing concrete."

"Well, that doesn't matter now." Francine grabbed Manny's hand and pulled him into the house. "Come on. You need to see the crime scene."

Manny allowed Francine to only pull him a few steps before he stopped. "Hold on there for a second. First tell me how you know there was livestreaming."

"Well, duh." Francine rolled her eyes. "I checked the data flow from this IP address."

Andor cleared his throat. He'd been talking to a uniformed police officer in the driveway. I hadn't heard him join us. His eyebrows were raised high on his forehead. "Please tell me that you accessed that information legally."

"I accessed that information legally," Francine answered immediately.

I frowned. "Why are you lying?"

"Oh, bleep." Andor's shoulders dropped.

"He asked me to tell him that." Francine's tone implied innocence. It was fake.

"I don't think I want to know how you do things." Andor looked past Francine and Vinnie into the house. "Is the crime scene at least preserved?"

"Yup." Vinnie stepped aside, allowing Andor to enter the room to the right of the entrance hall. "His daughter found him. He didn't show up for their brunch appointment and she got worried so she came to check on him. By that time he was already cold, so she knew there was nothing she could do to save him. She said she just ran from the room, phoned the emergency services and waited in that room." He pointed towards the back of the house.

"She's still there?" Manny asked.

"Yup." He closed his eyes for a second. "She's devastated. I… I didn't know what to say to her, so I left a female officer with her."

"We'll talk to her later." Manny looked at me. "You ready for this, Doc?"

I wasn't ready. I'd had forty minutes to prepare in the car. Even though I'd finished mentally writing the Allegro and Adagio of the flute quartet, I truly didn't want to see a dead body.

"Jenny?" Colin squeezed my hand. "We can take photos and you can study those."

"No." Photos never gave the same impression as being there in person. I inhaled deeply, then nodded. "Let's go."

Manny nodded once, then walked into the room to the right.

It was very clear that this house belonged to a person of wealth. From the wrought-iron gates to the manicured lawn and circular driveway leading past the heavy wooden front door, there was no mistaking the affluence this property represented.

The entrance was large enough to qualify as a room, the dark wooden floors polished to a shine. A large porcelain vase on a modern glass table held a bunch of fresh white roses. I counted. There were thirty roses.

I sighed at the distractions I surrendered to as a means to postpone entering the crime scene. I pulled my hand from Colin's and wiped both my hands on my thighs. With a final deep inhale, I walked into the room. And frowned.

It was surprisingly homely and warm. The outside of the house and the entrance had led me to expect a modern and richly decorated space. Instead I was standing in a welcoming room. Unlike the entrance, this room was carpeted, the thick covering and the large, comfortable furniture muting the sounds of Manny and Andor's conversation.

Blue and green patterned curtains were drawn open to reveal the windows overlooking the front garden. The wall opposite the door was painted the same deep green as the curtains and had only a large flat screen television mounted against it as if it was a work of art.

The other walls were painted a lighter green, preventing the room from being too dark. Both the remaining walls had only one painting each. There was nothing pretentious about the decor. Facing the television was a sofa upholstered in material matching the colours of the curtains and the dark green wall. Two matching chairs flanked the sofa and two small stacks of magazines were on the low dark wooden coffee table between the seats.

Manny and Andor were standing in front of the television, looking at the sofa. From where I was standing, I couldn't see what they were looking at. I walked closer.

Lying on the sofa was a man who appeared to be in his fifties. If his eyes hadn't been wide open, it would've been easy to assume he had fallen asleep while watching television. His left hand was trailing on the carpet, his body shifted as if he was reaching for something.

"When Vin and I got here, the TV was still on." Francine pointed at the television. "And it was where the livestreaming came from."

I narrowed my eyes and inspected the dark frame around the screen. "I can't see a camera."

"It's here." Francine pointed at the top centre of the frame. "It's so well designed that it blends in completely with the frame."

Andor turned around and looked at the small glass-covered circle in the frame. "I didn't know they made TVs with cameras."

"Of course they do." Francine blew through her lips in a rude sound. "If people aren't constantly on their smartphones, they're running everything through their televisions."

"I don't." Manny stepped closer to the sofa, closer to the body.

"You also use your smartphone only to make and receive calls and texts." Francine rolled her eyes and looked at me. "I keep telling him it's a small computer. He should use it to search for stuff, check his email and use the apps I downloaded. But no, Mister Anti-Technology only uses it to send me SMSes full of typos."

Manny ignored Francine and looked at Andor. "Tell me more about him."

"His name is Antal Udvaros." Andor looked at his phone, then smiled at Francine. "I use my phone to do research."

"See!" Francine pointed at Andor, but looked at Manny. "Learn from the younger people."

Andor's eyes widened and he looked apologetically at Manny. His arms moved closer to his torso when he registered Manny's irate expression and he swallowed, turning his attention back to his smartphone. "Um, yeah. As I was saying, Mr Udvaros was the owner of a chain of boutique hotels in Hungary. Well, maybe a chain is too big a word. He owned seven boutique hotels around the country."

"Is this how the body was found?" Manny asked.

"The daughter said she didn't move him." Vinnie walked to the far corner of the room, winked at me and leaned against the wall. I was grateful that he knew how quickly I felt claustrophobic. He nodded towards the outside of the house. "I asked the paramedics who arrived, but they said they immediately knew he was beyond saving, so they didn't move him either."

"And the officers told me that they also didn't move anything," Andor added.

"Huh." Manny lowered himself on his haunches and tilted his head to see under the sofa. "I'm willing to bet that either he was trying to reach the phone or it fell from his hand."

"There's a phone down there?" Andor took a pair of black latex gloves from his pocket and put them on. He knelt down next to Manny and carefully reached under the sofa. He straightened and lifted a gold-coloured smartphone.

"I'll take that, thank you very much." Francine held out her hand.

Andor hesitated for a second, pulling the device closer to his chest. Francine raised one eyebrow and wiggled her fingers. Manny scowled and snapped his fingers. "Give her the bloody phone."

"It's not that I don't want Francine to look at the phone, I'm just thinking about evidence protocol." Andor looked at Francine's hand. "You should wear gloves. We might be able to get some foreign prints from the phone."

"Hmm. That makes sense." Francine wiggled her fingers again. "Gimme gloves then."

Andor chuckled. He left the room, but came back almost

immediately with a box of disposable gloves. He offered it to Francine first. "If anyone else wants to touch something, grab some gloves first."

I wasn't planning on touching anything and tucked my hands under my arms for good measure.

Francine took the phone, then looked at the television. "I will need to take all the devices."

"Do you need the hardware or can you download what's on it and work with that?" Andor asked.

"I suppose I can download everything." She thought about this. "But I still think it would be best if I have the hardware. You never know if someone managed to add something to the devices that looks like it's part of the design."

Andor nodded. "I won't have problems pushing all of this to the front of the line. I'll get them to process all the devices as soon as possible."

"How did you know the television was being used to livestream?" I asked.

"I will answer in a sec." She looked at Andor. "I have a question for you first. Why are we here? How did you know that this might be the same killer?"

"I put out an alert for any rich, powerful or influential people who died of seemingly natural causes. I asked to be informed the moment such a death was reported. I also asked that no one touch the scene, unless the paramedics can revive the victim. If not, then everything must be preserved until I get here."

"Smart man." Francine turned to me. "When we got here, the television was still on. The first responders said that the daughter was waiting outside for them. She refused to come back into the room and said that she ran out the moment she felt how cold he was. The two officers arrived at the same time as the paramedics and the one officer said he remembered about the alert. That's why he told everyone to leave things untouched.

"Since there's no computer in this room and I didn't see his smartphone, I assumed that the livestreaming was coming from the television." She took her tablet from her oversized red handbag. "I checked the data transfer from the IP address, then connected to the television. Whoever was streaming noticed my presence and disconnected before I could trace him."

"Why are you so concerned?" I stared at the deep frown pulling her brows in and down.

"This person is good. Like scary good." She glanced at the television with wide eyes. "Good enough that I'm wondering if we've crossed paths in the cybersphere."

"Which means you really have your work cut out for you," Colin said. "Can you trace this person?"

Francine shook her head. "He was using a gazillion proxies. I would need to keep him online for a while to follow that thread and most likely won't catch him then either. But fear not." She lifted a manicured index finger in the air. "I'm still known in cyberspace as 'that bitch who can destroy us all'. I'll get him."

"Or her." Andor's *zygomaticus major* muscle lifted the left corner of his mouth.

"Ladies and gentlemen, we have a bona fide equal-opportunity, open-minded young man here." Francine winked at him. "Don't you worry your sexy little head about this psychopath's gender. Just give me all the devices. I'll perform devicetopsies and will find even the smallest breadcrumb left behind."

"Why are you talking like that?" My top lip rose in disgust. "What is a devicetopsy and why would you waste time with breadcrumbs?"

"Autopsy on devices, girlfriend. And don't you tell me that isn't a word. I'm making it a word." She waved her hand as if spreading something on the carpet. "And breadcrumbs. You know? Clues."

I turned my back on her. Intellectually I understood that people made jokes when dealing with challenging situations, but the prone body of Antal Udvaros was causing me great unease. My eyes narrowed as I looked at the colourful painting against the wall. I stepped closer to confirm my suspicions. "Is this an original Jackson Pollock?"

"I doubt it." Colin joined me and stepped closer to inspect the large rectangular painting. His body jerked and he leaned even closer to the artwork. For almost a minute he inspected the painting from numerous angles and distances.

Andor and Manny were discussing the medical examiner's preliminary opinion. Andor assured Manny that a full autopsy would be done and instructed the crime scene investigators to test the tumbler on the small table next to the sofa, all the bottles of alcohol found in the room as well as any food and dishes in the kitchen.

I was only partly paying attention to the discussion about the dead man. The tension in Colin's body concerned me.

"What are you seeing, Frey?" Manny walked around the

sofa and joined us. "Please tell me you see more than just paint splatters."

Colin glared over his shoulder before leaning closer to the signature in the corner. He straightened, his eyes wide. "This painting is worth around fifteen million dollars."

"Holy hell." Manny took a step back. "For splatters?"

"For an original Jackson Pollock." Colin turned from the painting to face Manny, his smile mocking. "I know you know who Pollock is and how much his work is worth. We talked about it four months ago when Francine bought the spring coat that I said looked like a Pollock painting."

"Ooh, my favouritest coat." The smile pulling at Francine's lips always indicated she was either teasing or stirring up trouble. She blinked innocently at Manny. "You still told me how sexy I looked in that coat and then agreed to buy me a Pollock painting. And Prada shoes. And Jimmy Choo shoes."

"I agreed to no such thing." Manny looked hard at the painting, then at Colin. "You're sure this is real splatter?"

Colin's sigh was tired. "You are such an uncultured philistine."

"So? Is it?"

Colin turned back to the painting. "This is an authentic Jackson Pollock. I will stake my reputation on it."

"Then we'll take all the artwork with us." Manny looked at Andor. "Your Captain Palya wanted us to work from his office, so he's going to have to deal with the art being there as well."

Andor laughed. "He's going to be so pissed off."

"You look happy about it." I didn't understand.

"Let's just say he's not a big art fan." Andor looked at Colin. "Forgive my ignorance, but is it possible that this painting was also looted by Nazis?"

"It's highly unlikely." Colin stared at the painting for a few seconds, then shook his head. "No, this is from his drip period. He created his most famous paintings during this period and it was from 1947. After the Second World War ended."

While Colin talked more about the many mental health issues Jackson Pollock battled as well as his alcoholism, I looked around the room again. I avoided the sofa and the body on it, trying to register as many small details as possible.

I liked that the room was not cluttered with numerous ornaments. There was no evidence of a struggle or a search. The magazines on the coffee table didn't look disturbed, the furniture didn't appear to have been moved. A light caught my eye and I walked closer to a wooden cabinet that held a display of high-end liqueurs, whiskeys and brandies.

"That's a signal booster." Francine joined me and looked at the small black device with two antennae raised on its side.

"For wifi?" I asked.

She leaned closer, then straightened. "Hmm-mm. This is one of the best brands when it comes to boosting wifi signals so you have good reception throughout a house."

"It would make sense to have a booster in a house this size," Andor said. "I have one in my two-bedroom flat and can only imagine how weak the signal would be if it had to travel through these walls or floors."

"How strong is the security on these boosters?"

"The same as any other device." Francine shrugged. "All

these devices come with a preset password. If you don't change the password and don't update the software, your chance of being hacked becomes much bigger." She nodded at the television. "Even that can be easily hacked if the owners don't have proper password protection."

Andor looked closer at the wifi booster, then nodded. "This is a very high-end brand. Most Hungarians can't afford the device and the membership fee."

"There's a membership fee?" Francine frowned. "That's strange. Usually you just plug one of these babies in and voila! You have a stronger wifi signal."

"Well, yes." Andor looked at the booster. "It does that. But if you want all the extras, it will set you back around sixty euros per month."

"For what?" Francine's tone rose a pitch in outrage.

"For the monthly software updates, the increased security, the proactive customer service. These guys will contact you before you even know there's something wrong with your internet." He pointed at the device. "Buying this gives you top-notch internet security and virus detection."

"Huh." Francine took a step back. "That means that this device gives the company access to your computer, your data, your browsing history, the works."

I knew Francine would inspect the booster for any malware as well, so I didn't mention it. I glanced around the room one more time and took a step closer to the door. The oppression of the scene was getting too much for me. Already I'd spent too much time in the same room as the dead person.

Without another word, I left the room. I walked through

the downstairs bedroom and bathroom, but avoided the kitchen when I heard soft crying. I wasn't yet ready to deal with the emotional turmoil of the woman who'd found her father's body.

On the first floor were three large bedrooms, all with ensuite bathrooms. The top floor was one large room that was roughly divided into two parts. A fully equipped home gym took up one half of the room, a wooden bar and pool table the other half. There were no bottles in the bar, just a thin layer of dust on the glass shelves. The pool cues and table looked well-used though.

I made a note of the art on the walls, but there was nothing else of interest. At least, nothing that I thought was pertinent at the moment. When I reached the ground floor, Colin and the others were standing outside, talking. I was grateful to leave the house.

"Oh, goodie, you're here!" Francine shook her index finger at Manny. "Tell this man why I'm not going to the police station."

I took a step back. A few times Francine had tried to involve me in an argument she'd had with Manny. Each time I'd refused to be drawn in. This was no different. "No."

"You're the worst bestest bestie ever." She turned back to Manny. "It's a police station, handsome. Why on earth would I want to be using my skills in a place where there are people who would just love to lock me up and throw away the key?"

"I'm tempted to lock you up." Manny's lips thinned when Francine's eyes widened.

Immediately, she fluttered her eyelids and attempted to look flustered. She was not successful. "Don't talk sexy like that to me in public. Those things are for the bedroom."

Manny turned his back on her and looked at Vinnie. "You also going to give me hell?"

"What's going on?" I quietly asked Colin.

Colin chuckled. "Andor has been speaking with Captain Palya, who insists that we go the station as soon as possible. He's also insisting that everyone works from his office."

"It's not an office in the traditional sense." In my mind an office needed a desk and that room only had a conference table.

"Hmm." Colin nodded towards Vinnie and Francine arguing with Manny. "They're being difficult about working from the police station."

It took less than five seconds to determine that neither Vinnie nor Francine showed genuine signs of anxiety. This annoyed me. I took a step closer. "Why are you wasting time? If this is your attempt to make a point that you don't want to be associated with law enforcement, it's inane. You've been working with GIPN, Interpol, Europol and the French police for the last five years. We have a lot of research to do, a lot of data to gather so that we can stop the person who is killing these people."

It was silent in the garden. Even the officers who were guarding the gate had stopped talking. Francine and Vinnie looked chagrined and Manny's eyebrows were raised. He smirked. "You heard Doc. Let's get to the station so we can get to work."

Chapter ELEVEN

"WHAT ARE YOU complaining about? Chantelle is a perfectly fine name." Vinnie's nostrils flared as he looked away from Francine and shook his ID badge at Andor. "I'm Rick. Rick! Do I looked like a Rick to you?"

"Take that up with Captain Palya." Andor didn't even try to hide his amusement. "He's the one who issued your security clearance and ID badges."

"But Rick!" The utter disgust on Vinnie's face made everyone laugh. Except me. I didn't understand Vinnie's objection to the alias Captain Palya had given him. "Tell them I'm not a Rick, Jen-girl."

I didn't respond. This was a pointless discussion.

"Oh, keep your panties on." Francine put the lanyard over her head and lifted her hair so it settled against her neck. "No good hacker was ever called Chantelle."

"Which makes it a perfect cover." Colin shook his head, took my hand and walked towards Captain Palya's office. It had only taken seven minutes for both Vinnie and Francine to be issued their temporary badges and pass through security to enter the non-public area of the police station.

"Says Henry Vaughan." Francine shook her index finger at the ID badge hanging around Colin's neck. "You always have cool names."

"Henry Vaughan was a poet, author, translator and physician. He had a twin who was a philosopher and alchemist." An uncommon sadness entered Colin's expression. He shook his head and forced his lips into a smile. "Henry was the one with the cool name. I'm just borrowing it."

"At least you're not Rick." Vinnie's huff turned into a growling sound when Andor chuckled. "Laugh it up, dude. I'll find a way to get back at you."

Andor raised both hands. "Hey, I didn't issue the badges. I'm not to blame."

Their arguing continued all the way to Captain Palya's conference room-office. Manny had given Vinnie only one glare and then marched ahead of us. He opened the door and jerked before he entered the room. "What the hell happened here?"

"She did." Captain Palya's booming voice greeted me as I walked into the office. He was shaking his index finger at Olivia.

The conference room was nothing like the space we had left yesterday. The dividing walls had been removed to create a space that could easily house fifty people. The conference table had not been moved and Captain Palya's computer and papers were still taking up the far end of the table.

It was the rest of the conference room that delighted me. I felt absolutely no anxiety when Francine, Colin and Andor also entered the room. Vinnie followed them in, then leaned against the wall next to the door, looking around the room—no doubt analysing the security. There was a lot of open space and the natural light coming from the large windows was an added bonus.

"I didn't really do that much. I only created work stations." Olivia was standing on the other side of the room next to an extremely large electronic whiteboard. Two months ago, Francine had spent an hour explaining all its many uses when she'd tried to get Manny to buy one for our team room. He'd told her he would think about it.

The sound Francine made when she saw the whiteboard could only be described as a squeal. "Ooh. I want one. I've been wanting one since forever. But certain people wouldn't give it to me. Ooh! Now I can work on it."

"It's great." Olivia turned it on. An orange triangle moved clockwise on a dark blue background for three seconds before the screen changed and revealed numerous newspaper article clippings neatly arranged in three rows. "We got one of these for each of our conference rooms last year. It takes a bit of learning to know and use all its functions, but it's really magical when I need to brainstorm. I've requisitioned one a few times for my office when a large sheet of paper was not big or good enough for the different elements of a case."

"These stupid things should come with a pilot's licence." Captain Palya sat down in his chair and shuffled a few papers around. "So far I'm the only one outside of the IT department who knows how to work it. Three other officers tried and failed miserably when they went through the training."

"It's not that hard." Olivia tapped on the board. It appeared to react in a similar manner as the touch screen of a computer. "It took me about ten minutes to put my findings on the system and to organise them so it's easy to sort through."

"What findings?" Even though the technology interested me, any new data would be much more important.

"Francine and I were searching the internet for articles on Grandpa Szabo and Grandpa Koltai when you guys phoned." She turned to the board. "So when Francine left to join you at the crime scene, I continued searching as many databases as I could, looking for anything and everything that mentioned people by those names. I found quite a few articles. Unfortunately, none of it gives us actionable information, but I reckon that there might be some little clue in there that might send us in the right direction."

I was impressed. Olivia's logical thinking would be an asset to our investigation. I walked closer to the board and looked at the top left article. "When was this published?"

"That's what's really cool." Olivia's voice rose a pitch in excitement. "I found this online library that had scanned and uploaded all the newspapers as far back as 1900. I don't need to go to the archives now. Unfortunately, the articles are all in Hungarian, so it doesn't really help me, but—"

"We'll translate." Andor walked past me, closer to the board.

"It might be a good idea to first scan the articles to see if they are relevant." Olivia looked at me. "I did a search for any and all mentions of Grandpa Szabo and Grandpa Koltai. The first seven articles are from that search. All the others come from internet searches I've done."

"Give us a minute." Captain Palya got up and joined Andor at the board. I took a few steps back as the captain waved his arm to the left. "Garas, take that side and look for anything that could be useful. I'll take the right and we'll meet in the middle."

I didn't like this. Usually, I was the one who not only found such articles, but also searched them for relevant information. How could I trust that Captain Palya and Andor would know what could be relevant or not? The more I thought about the high probability of them missing some key information, the more agitated I became. My breathing increased, as did my blinking.

It was only when Colin took my hand in his that I realised I'd been scratching my thigh nonstop. My skin was burning, but it didn't feel broken. He pulled me to face him, concern pulling his brows together. "What's wrong?"

"I don't trust them." The words fell from my lips before I had time to properly organise my thoughts. I shook my head and raised one hand when both Andor and Captain Palya turned to face me, their expressions communicating their displeasure. I closed my eyes, took a few deep breaths and mentally wrote the first five bars of Mozart's Piano Concerto No. 20 in D minor before I looked at them. "I don't know you. I don't know how your minds perceive and process information. Therefore I'm uncertain that you will notice key information that could be easily overlooked."

Captain Palya's nostrils flared and his lips thinned as he inhaled to speak, but Andor stepped forward with both his hands palm down in a placating gesture. "And I don't know you. But I took a leap of faith when I researched your reputation. You know my reputation. You know that I'm one of the best investigators in Budapest, if not Hungary. Captain Palya is not heading this department because of his handsome moustache. He got here because he is exceptionally good at leading as well as investigating. Trust us. If there's a clue in here, we will find it."

I couldn't. The fallibility of the human mind was far too prevalent for me to trust as openly and easily as Andor. I bit down on my bottom lip to strengthen my focus not to say something that would offend.

Colin took a step closer to Andor and Captain Palya. "We're used to working as a closed unit, so this is new for us. We trust that you will be thorough."

Nobody from our team agreed with Colin, but also no one contradicted him. It was clear on the faces of the others that they also found it difficult to blindly trust someone we'd never cooperated with before.

Francine shivered as if to shake something off her shoulders and turned to the desks arranged against the wall closest to her. "Ooh, computers."

Olivia smiled. "Captain Palya got their IT department to bring us two laptops. They said they didn't have any more, but"—she lowered her voice to a loud whisper—"I got the feeling that they didn't want to trust us with more."

"Everyone has trust issues." Francine shrugged. "No biggie. I have my laptop which I can guarantee will eat both of theirs and still be hungry."

My confusion lifted when I looked at Francine. She was jesting. She sat down at one of the four desks and put her laptop next to the one already open and running.

Olivia sat down next to her, but looked at me. "These computers are connected to the police network, so we have access to all the case files."

Francine rubbed her palms together, but pouted when she

started typing on the police computer. "Oh. Hmm. This is not good. This computer speaks Hungarian."

"I can imagine all their case files, reports and such will also be in Hungarian." Manny pointed at Francine's computer. "Can't you design some translation program thingymajiggie?"

"Listen to you speak tech jargon." Francine winked at him. "It's very sexy."

Manny lowered his brow and scowled at her. "Can you?"

"In a jiffy." Her attempt to copy Manny's accent was an awful failure, but it made Vinnie laugh. Even Olivia smiled for the first time since we entered the room.

"I think I've got something." Andor was staring at the electronic whiteboard, his head tilted. "Cap, can we access the internet through this thing?"

Captain Palya stepped closer and looked at the article in front of Andor. "Think of this as a big touch screen, Garas. We can do anything on it."

"What are you looking for?" Francine's fingers were hovering above her keyboard.

"Huh." The captain nodded his head slowly as he read the article. "This might be something." He turned to Francine and gave her a website address.

Andor touched the screen and highlighted some text. "This says that there is an archive of photos from 1925-1939. The Ministry of Culture had a project ten years ago where they uploaded as many photos as they could find from that era. There are photos from government events, private functions such as weddings and funerals, as well as gala events where all the who's who of that time gathered."

"Got it." Francine blinked a few times. "Oh, you sweet

young man. How wrong you are. There are not thousands of photos here. There are tens of thousands."

"Are they searchable?" Colin asked.

"Let me… Yes!" She typed on her keyboard, pressed enter and tapped her manicured nails impatiently, staring at the monitor. "Ooh! We've got results."

I walked closer and looked over her shoulder. And squinted. "Can you put that on the whiteboard?"

"Hmm." She typed a few commands. "Done."

I turned to look at the photos. There were seven of them. A cursory glance told me that Francine had searched Franz Szabo's name. He was in all the photos. I walked from the one side of the whiteboard to the other, committing the photos to memory. Then I slowly walked back to confirm my observations. I ignored the speculation and talking around me, and focused on the nonverbal communication of the people in the photos.

"What do you see, Doc?"

I turned around and blinked in surprise. I was the only one standing in front of the whiteboard. Everyone else had moved away. Captain Palya and Manny were seated at the table, Francine, Andor and Olivia at the desks, Vinnie was leaning against the wall, very close to the door, and Colin was standing in front of the windows.

I turned back to the whiteboard and enlarged the third photo. "This photo has all three men in it." I pointed. "Szabo, Szell and Koltai. They are in most of the other photos and always close together. In this photo they are in a serious conversation, but their body language is clear that they know and trust each other. See how open their body language is. Their arms are away from their torsos, they're leaning towards each other, even into each other's personal space. Trust."

"We found more photos." Francine raised an eyebrow and waited until I nodded before she placed those photos on the whiteboard as well.

I inspected them and nodded. "Yes, they were definitely friends. We need more information on them. That will tell us how their connection has led to the deaths of their grandsons. And now Antal Udvaros."

"I did a quick search." Andor nodded at the computer on the desk behind him. "The men in these photos were the elite of those days. They were very successful businessmen between the two world wars. All of them survived World War Two and somehow managed to hold on to their successes, money and power during the Soviet reign. I'll have to do more research to figure out how they managed that without being part of the Communist Party, but when communism ended, they were able to continue their respective businesses without any problems."

"Is it possible that they were part of some secret organisation?" Francine's eyes were wide. "Like a type of Freemason secret society of business owners?"

"Are you serious?" Captain Palya stared at Francine in shock.

She lifted her shoulders as if innocent of creating another conspiracy theory. "I'm just asking."

"Ignore her." Manny turned back to the whiteboard and looked at the photos. "We need to learn more about these men, but especially their businesses."

"I've got something." Andor pulled the laptop closer. "It says here that Ferenc Szell's father founded his business in 1989. His son, Ferenc, was named co-owner of one of the first large corporations started after the fall of communism. The Szells set the gold standard for family businesses to recover after the oppression of communism."

"Communism really did a number on your country." Olivia shook her head. "Two years ago I handled a case that had some links to Slovakia and Estonia. I learned about the suffering that communism brought to this region. We weren't taught these things at school. I don't know about other Western countries, but when I studied history at school, it was very, very basic information about communism."

"The communism we experienced after 1960 in Hungary was a bit different from the other countries." Andor coughed for a few seconds and frowned. "Stupid seasonal allergies. I thought I was done with them. Anyway, from the sixties until the end of communism, we used the term 'goulash communism'. Of course we named it after our national dish. But we used the term because it was a deviation from the Soviet principles from before. We had an improved human rights record and even elements of free market economics. I reckon that is why Szell was able to become a multi-millionaire from a business started during the communist years."

Olivia asked a question and soon Andor and Captain Palya were in full discussion about that era in Hungarian history. As interesting as I found the personal insight into the effects and reign of communism in Hungary and the challenges of post-communism, my attention kept being pulled back to the whiteboard. There were still so many elements of this case that were unknown and it felt like we had too little to work with at the moment.

I turned to Francine. "Are these the only photos with Franz Szabo's name?"

"Uh, yes." She swivelled in her chair to face me.

"Are all the photos in that archive tagged with names of the people in the photos?"

"No. I had a quick look and I guesstimate that only about a third or even fewer of the photos are tagged."

I nodded. This was as I'd suspected. "Are you still working on that advanced facial recognition software program?"

She rolled her eyes and grunted. "Supposed to be top secret, girlfriend. But yes, I am." Her eyebrows shot up. "Oh, my God! Yes, of course. I'll input the faces of Grandpa Szabo, Grandpa Koltai and Grandpa Szell and set a search for them on all the other photos. You're a genius!"

"I know."

"How many photos are in that archive?" Colin asked.

"Thirty-one thousand, eight hundred and ninety-eight," Olivia said. "I think that it might be generous to say one third of the photos are tagged. Many of those photos don't even have any information like who took it, where or when. I think this project needs some help organising those photos into something that would actually be useful."

I watched as Francine searched for the photo with the clearest profile of Franz Szabo, cleaned it up in a photo editing program and uploaded it to her facial recognition program. She typed a few more commands and a small window opened with a bar showing the percentage of images checked for a match. She then did the same with photos of Grandpa Szell and Grandpa Koltai. I looked at the three bars. This was going to take a while.

"Once you have more matches, it might be a good idea to look for other people who are also in those photos," Colin said. "I mean, people who appear more often than anyone else in those photos. If these men were friends, there might be other people in their close circle as well."

"Consider it done." Francine tapped her index finger on her lips for two seconds, then started typing more commands. "This will take a while though. I'm using pupillary distance as well as ear shape to identify similar faces."

"That was astute." The corners of my mouth lifted in a small smile as I looked at Colin. "We should get even more data when we know who these men's friends were."

"Let me help." Olivia moved her chair closer to Francine, her eyes on the computer monitor. "Just tell me what to do."

For a moment, I listened to Francine boasting that her computer program didn't need much help. I quickly grew bored. In Strasbourg, my role was much better defined when we investigated a crime. I usually sat in front of my fifteen monitors to either search for data or watch footage to find even the smallest nonverbal cue that could help us find the criminals.

Here, I felt out of place. Not only was I so far out of my comfort zone that the blackness in my peripheral vision threatening a complete shutdown was becoming the norm, I also felt redundant. Andor was proving himself to be a very competent investigator. Our presence would no doubt hasten the discovery of this serial killer, but after observing him for the last three days, I was certain he would've solved these horrid crimes in time.

But that was the key. We didn't have that much time. I looked again at the three bars on Francine's computer. The first one was only at twenty-three percent, the other two much lower. I couldn't just stand here and wait for results. I needed to do something. I looked at the whiteboard and allowed Mozart's Prague Symphony to fill my mind with its sophisticated introduction.

A thought came to me and I turned to Andor. "I need to see more photos."

Chapter TWELVE

"WHAT PHOTOS?" ANDOR turned away from the conversation with Captain Palya and Manny, and faced the laptop in front of him.

"Crime scene photos of the deaths of Gabor Szabo, Ferenc Szell and István Koltai…" I slowed down at the mention of the last name when I noticed Captain Palya's expression. "Why are you angry?"

"He's always angry." Francine didn't even turn around when she said this. "I bet he's staring daggers at my back now."

Manny took two steps to his left to hide Francine from the captain's view. He raised one eyebrow. "Are you angry?"

"Of course I'm pissed off." Captain Palya put his hands on his hips, his thumbs facing back—a typical pose when someone became aggressive or argumentative. "We don't have any crime scene photos. There was no reason to send the crime scene investigators to those scenes. All three of those men died of natural causes, remember?"

Andor shifted in his chair. I stared at his back. His neck muscles were tense, his shoulders slightly raised and his arms had moved closer to his body. He was not facing us. I leaned to the side, but still couldn't see his face. "Andor?"

He turned around, saw my interest and dropped his head with a grunt. "Bleep it, Genevieve."

Captain Palya looked from Andor to me and back. He pushed his glasses up the bridge of his nose. "Garas! What the fuck have you done now?"

Andor immediately raised both hands as he looked at the captain. "Nothing illegal, I swear. I might have coloured just a little outside the lines."

Vinnie's chuckle drew everyone's attention to where he was still standing by the door. When Captain Palya glowered at him, his chuckle turned into a full laugh.

"What the bleeding hell is wrong with you?" Manny's jaw jutted.

This made Vinnie laugh even harder. I had not often seen him this amused. It interested me and I paid closer attention. He pointed at Manny, then at Captain Palya and shook his head. "You're… oh, hah!"

His laughter boomed through the room. Francine was now also laughing in response to Vinnie, and Andor also chuckled.

Vinnie looked at me, wiping tears from his cheeks. "Help me out here, Jen-girl."

Now everyone's attention turned to me. I leaned back.

"What's the big guy on about, missy?" Manny only called me that when he was truly vexed.

"Is it about the similarities?" No sooner had I asked Vinnie than he doubled over laughing. I closed my eyes and reached for patience. This was wasting our time.

"What similarities?" Andor asked.

"Vinnie must have noticed how similar in character Manny is to Captain Palya."

"Holy hell!" Manny slumped and leaned away from Captain Palya. "We're nothing alike."

"Actually"—Colin scratched his chin and smiled—"you are."

"Well, I don't fucking care." Captain Palya was now even more irate as he pointed his index finger at Andor and shook it with each word. "When will you learn that I need to know what you're up to so I can protect you? Tell me everything. Now."

Andor glanced at Vinnie, who uttered an amused snort, and raised one shoulder, his smile apologetic. "I took photos of those three scenes."

"You're going to get yourself fired, you idiot!"

"I don't really see how, Cap." Andor no longer looked apologetic. "I had permission from the families to enter their houses and take photos. I revealed nothing of my intentions or my suspicions. There is no reason to question my conduct."

"You got them to sign a release form?"

"I did."

Captain Palya exhaled loudly. "Well? What are you waiting for? Get those photos up on the whiteboard."

"Give me a sec to get them from my cloud account." Andor swiped and tapped the screen of his phone for a few seconds, then turned to the computer in front of him. "The first set is of Gabor Szabo's house. By the time I started thinking there was something suspicious about these deaths, he'd already been dead for seven weeks. His family had sent in specialised cleaners to disinfect the house from top to bottom."

I took a step closer to the whiteboard when the photos appeared. There were four rows with eight photos in each.

"I took photos of every room, but I focused on the room where Szabo died." He got up and pointed at the photos in the bottom row. "These are all of his bedroom."

"Tell me more about Gabor Szabo." This case, Olivia and everything else had happened so fast that there had been no time for me to look into the history of the victims. "In serial killer cases, victimology can tell us a lot about the killer."

"Huh. Okay." Andor tapped on his phone again and read from the screen. "Well, Gabor Szabo was fifty-three when he died. He was a well-respected psychologist who specialised in PTSD. He left behind his second wife of ten years and two adult children. His first wife died from breast cancer seventeen years ago when his children were still very young. He raised them as a single parent. He got married to wife number two when the first child went to university." He looked up from his phone. "His children loved his second wife and their sadness was difficult for me to see."

I nodded and turned my attention back to the photos. "How did he die?"

"In his sleep." Andor's tone indicated his scepticism. "At least, that's what his death certificate says. There wasn't even an autopsy. Szabo had been suffering from high blood pressure, so when his wife woke up next to his dead body, no one seemed too surprised that he'd had a heart attack."

"And Ferenc Szell? What was his background?" Colin asked.

Andor tapped his smartphone screen a few times. "He was forty-nine when he died two weeks ago. It would've been his birthday next month. He was married, but had no children. He was an architect and together with his wife, who was also an architect, started an architectural firm eighteen years ago. They are quite well-known in Hungary for designing houses and doing interior decorating for the rich and the famous." He looked at his phone again. "You know the basics about István Koltai and we just met Antal Udvaros."

"I can do research on all four men with as much detail as possible." Olivia looked at me. "I'm really good at finding small details and catching anything questionable."

I nodded. "The more data we have the better." I turned back to the whiteboard and studied the photos of Gabor Szabo's bedroom.

"Do you want to see the photos I took of Ferenc Szell's office?"

I raised an eyebrow when I turned to him. "He died in his office?"

"Yes. His wife said that he would often work until the early morning hours. She didn't like being alone at home, so he'd work in his home office. She found him there when she went downstairs in the middle of the night to get a glass of water. He'd had flu two weeks before his death and the medical examiner said that combined with his lack of sleep most likely contributed to his heart giving out."

"The photos?" It was not uncommon for people, especially men, in high-stress careers to develop hypertension and suffer heart attacks at an early age. Often a healthy diet and exercise didn't negate the effects of stress and sleep deprivation.

I turned my attention to the whiteboard when a new set of photos appeared. I took a step back. How anyone could work in such a cluttered environment was beyond me. Just looking at it in these photos was causing my breathing and heart rate to increase. I pushed Mozart's Prague Symphony back into my mind and leaned closer to the board.

It took immense concentration for me to see past the stacks of papers, magazines and books placed all over the office on every available surface. Only when I reached the Andante did I manage to take note of everything that was not clutter. I took my time registering everything that could be of possible importance.

"István Koltai's photos?" I barely glanced at Andor, my eyes not leaving the board while I waited for the next set of photos.

I inspected every photo for any and all details. When I didn't find anything that stood out, I nodded and was pleased when photos of the scene we'd left earlier appeared on the board. It was just as I'd thought. I rubbed my arms and took a step back. "I want to organise the sets of photos."

Captain Palya appeared next to me and swiped the side of the board. An option menu appeared. "From here it's just like a computer. You can toggle between boards and windows, copy photos and create a new board where you can display those."

I stared at the board. "I don't want to touch this. I don't know how clean it is."

"Then don't touch it." Captain Palya's voice rose and he exhaled noisily. "Or use gloves if you're so scared you're going to catch a disease."

I looked at him in surprise. His lowered brow and flared nostrils confirmed that I'd offended him with my statements. He stomped back to his seat, muttering under his breath in

Hungarian. Andor chuckled and offered me a latex glove he'd pulled from his trouser pocket. I shuddered and shook my head.

"I have my own." I took the individually sealed gloves from my handbag and soon worked the touchscreen of the whiteboard.

One by one I dismissed possible connections while I constantly rearranged the photos. The conversations, speculations and arguments of the others in the room became dull background noise while I got lost in my work. I found the photos that revealed most of each of the rooms the victims had died in and placed them in order.

Oftentimes, my brain would register something of great importance, but it wouldn't immediately filter through to my cerebral cortex—my thinking brain. I now stood in front of the whiteboard, staring at photos of the four rooms, waiting for that connection to come.

When it did, I jerked and gasped.

"Jenny?" Colin hurried to my side. "What did you find?"

I pointed at the black box under the bedside table in Gabor Szabo's bedroom. "All of them had wifi boosters from the same company."

"A lot of people use boosters when they live in larger houses or apartments." Andor walked closer, frowned and scratched his forehead. "Huh. Well, it's going to be very hard to believe this is a coincidence."

"Why?" Colin asked.

"See the broken triangle?" Andor pointed at the logo that had caught my eye at first. The red triangle had rounded corners, of which the bottom right corner didn't close completely. Andor pointed at the logos on each photo. "Három is a very high-end company. It has the best boosters on the market, but like I told you guys at Antal Udvaros' house, only the well-off in Hungary can afford that monthly subscription fee. Most people buy boosters that cost a tenth of Három's price and they do a good enough job."

Captain Palya cleared his throat. He was looking at an open magazine, the corners of the pages curled from being read a lot. "Here are some stats about Három: They have a thirteen percent market share as opposed to the biggest brand who has seventy-nine percent."

"Három is the Hungarian word for three." Andor stared at the magazine in Captain Palya's hand until the older man jerked it off the table and put it on the floor under his chair.

"Do you have something to say, Garas?"

"Uh, no, sir. I suppose I shouldn't be surprised that you're reading tech magazines." He nodded at the whiteboard. "You were the only one in the department who volunteered for training on this thing."

Francine joined in the discussion about technology, wifi boosters and other things that were not going to help us find the person who'd already killed four men. I thought about this some more. We only know about these four men because Andor had considered these deaths suspicious.

What if there were more people? More victims whose deaths had been made to look natural? More victims who had been watched as they'd died?

I looked at Captain Palya. "What do you know about Három's business practices?"

"Not much."

"Uh." Andor raised his hand as if he was a student wanting to ask a question. "I was at school with the owner's son. We're still pretty tight."

"What does that mean?"

"They're still good friends, love." Colin took my hand and squeezed it.

This was most fortuitous. "Do you know if their customers have to register the boosters?"

"Yes." Andor nodded. "I bought one and had to register online. Even without the top-tiered monthly subscription, all users have to register. It automatically updates the software of the booster and gave me all those security features I mentioned before. It has great antivirus software."

"Ooh!" Francine clapped her hands. "I know where you're going with this, girlfriend."

I ignored her. "We need to compare the list of Három's clients to all deaths by natural causes in the last five years at least." I thought about this. "No. Make it ten years."

Francine pointed at herself and nodded. "I knew it! I knew you were going to say that."

Manny looked at Andor. "Can you get that client list for us?"

"Yes." He swiped the screen of his smartphone. "Give me a minute."

We watched as he left. Colin let go of my hand and walked to Francine's desk. "How much longer for the photos?"

"I reckon another three to five hours." She jutted her chin. "I'm going to tweak this program. This is taking far too long. I think it's using pupillary distance as well as ear shape that's slowing it down."

"Bloody hell." Manny pushed his hands into his trouser pockets. "We might as well go home and get some rest then."

"And speak to Nikki," Vinnie said from the doorway. "She SMSed me to say they arrived safely and that Pink is already settled in his room. He also wants to be in on the video chat."

I'd become familiar with the emotion that was now tightening my chest. It was a combination of concern, relief, happiness and love. I frequently experienced this with Nikki. Since Eric had joined us, I experienced it even more frequently and with more intensity. Now that Vinnie had mentioned a video call with Nikki, the photos on the whiteboard and the case lost some of their interest.

Andor walked past Vinnie into the room. "I spoke to my friend's dad. He's at the airport in London and will be home later this evening. He said that I'll have the complete list in my inbox before six tomorrow morning."

"Why are you concerned?" It was evident around his eyes and mouth.

Andor shook his head. "I don't think I'll ever get used to you seeing everything." His smile was self-deprecating. "I'm just a bit concerned because my friend's dad told me that he's putting his name and his company's future at risk giving me a list with all their clients' names and information. This kind of data is gold for every company. If clients aren't convinced that their information is safe with a company, especially a tech company, the company will lose their reputation and will also lose customers."

"You're having him send it to a secure email address?" Francine asked.

"Of course."

"And your computer is secure?" She giggled when he glared at her. "I take that as a yes. Well, then you and Három's owner have nothing to worry about. We're only going to use that information to find a serial killer, not to hack them or anything."

"Enough of that." Manny sliced through the air with his hand. "Don't talk about hacking with a smile on your face like that."

Francine laughed. "They don't have anything I want, so I don't need or want to hack them. Yet."

Manny scowled and shook his head. "Let's pack up and go home. We can get back to this in the morning."

It took another six minutes before we left the large room. As much as I wanted to work the case, I knew we needed to wait for the results on the photos as well as the client list. And I had a video call with Nikki to look forward to. The forty-minute drive from Budapest to the villa felt extremely long, so I closed my eyes, mentally finished playing Mozart's Prague Symphony and analysed everything we had discovered so far.

Chapter THIRTEEN

"ARE YOU SURE that you're sure?" Despite the ridiculousness of the question, there was no doubt that Francine was completely serious. She didn't even respond to the flirtatious smile the officer on duty gave her when we showed our ID badges to enter the restricted area of the police station.

I exhaled in irritation and didn't bother to modify my tone. "I told you last night and twice this morning that the nonverbal cues Nikki and Pink displayed last night gave no indication of deceit."

"So when Pink said the physio told him if he continues like this, he would probably run a marathon next year, he wasn't lying?" She raised one eyebrow at Manny when he huffed in annoyance. Vinnie and Colin were behind us in the hallway, discussing the security measures they'd increased at the villa now that Olivia and Roxy were staying there for the day.

I thought back to the video call last night. It had been half an hour later than we'd originally arranged on account of Roxy insisting that everyone joined the conversation. I'd been extremely displeased. I was not flexible. Any change in my schedule caused such disruption in my mind that it was hard to focus on anything except the delay or cancellation.

All that had disappeared when I'd seen Nikki's genuine happiness when the video call had connected. At once, I'd been overwhelmed by a combination of relief and intense longing. Especially when I'd seen Eric snuggling on Pink's lap. Eric had been wearing the super-hacker onesie Francine had bought him and had gurgled happily when he'd heard my voice.

Pink had looked the most relaxed I'd seen him since he'd been injured earlier this year. He'd laughed at Roxy's jokes, kissed Eric's head numerous times and threatened Vinnie with a humiliating loss when they next played Drestia. He'd boasted about the free time he'd put to use practicing his skills at this game.

Everyone had been relieved to see Pink in such a positive frame of mind. Except Francine. That deep worry was evident on her face as she looked at me. I sighed. I felt most inadequate at comforting people. I cleared my throat. "Pink was truthful. As was Nikki when you asked them repeatedly if Pink was okay."

Francine stopped and stared at me for a few seconds, then took a shaky breath. "Okay."

We were about two metres from the entrance to Captain Palya's office. Francine pulled her shoulders back, flipped her hair back and nodded with a determined smile. Manny whispered something in her ear which made her eyes widen. Then she winked at him, her posture much more relaxed, her smile genuine.

"What are we waiting for?" Vinnie raised an eyebrow. "Is the old man having problems keeping up with you gals?"

"Put a sock in it, big guy." Manny grabbed Francine's hand and marched into Captain Palya's office. I followed.

The captain and Andor were standing in front of the

whiteboard, looking at a list. Captain Palya glared at the door and scowled when no one else came in. "Where's Olivia Webster?"

"Well, good morning to you too." Francine winked at Captain Palya and smiled at Andor before she put her laptop on one of the desks.

"I see you got the art from Antal Udvaros' house." Colin walked to the stacked paintings leaning against the wall behind Captain Palya's chair.

"It's cluttering up my workspace." The captain pushed his glasses up the bridge of his nose and muttered something in Hungarian which made Andor snort. "I don't know why we need it here."

"Because it's bloody evidence." Manny lifted his chin towards the paintings, then looked at Colin. "Something interesting there?"

"Give me a moment." Colin tilted the frames one by one, looking at the art. He inhaled sharply when he saw a large impressionist landscape and reacted similarly with two other paintings. He inspected all fifteen paintings, then straightened. "We have a Monet, a Picasso and the Pollock that we saw earlier."

"Bloody hell." Manny pointed at the paintings. "Find out if there's anything iffy about them, Frey."

Colin nodded, his expression telling me he was already thinking about researching these artworks.

"Where is Ms Webster?" Captain Palya looked at me, his expression fierce.

Colin took a step forward, pushing his shoulder half in front of me. "She's at the villa. We had a long discussion last night and decided it is best that she keeps a low profile. We made contact with her husband last night and arranged for a secure video call later today when it's morning in New York."

Francine had helped Olivia last night to phone her husband as well as her boss to let them know that she was unharmed and safe. Neither call lasted longer than thirty seconds. Francine had then used one of the many brand-new smartphones she'd found in Émile's office to set up a video call app that would be secure. In a second call to her husband, Olivia had instructed him to buy a burner phone and upload the same app. That call had also lasted less than thirty seconds.

Roxy had rubbed her hands in glee and giggled while she said it felt like she was in a James Bond movie. I hadn't even attempted to stop myself from informing Roxy how improbable most of the feats in those films were, a few completely impossible. She'd giggled even more and I'd left the room.

"I was the one insisting she stay out of sight," Francine said over her shoulder as she typed commands into her laptop. "I've been thinking about this killer and the way he cyberstalked Olivia. He's good. Really good. I wouldn't put it past him to find a way to access city cameras and run a facial recognition program to find her. As it is, he knows she's in Hungary. I think it's better if she stays out of sight for a while."

"Makes sense." Captain Palya lifted his chin towards Francine's computer. "Talking about facial recognition software, do you have results on your search?"

"Oh, do I ever." She typed a command and the list on the

whiteboard was replaced with eight photos. "Grandpas Szabo, Szell and Koltai were quite the party animals, I'll have you know. They were in"—she looked at her laptop monitor—"three hundred and fifty-two photos. All three of them. At the same time."

"Anyone else?"

"Two others." She got up and pointed at a short man with wire-rim glasses and fine features. "This is Grandpa Udvaros. He is in three hundred and twenty-one of the photos with the first three." She pointed at an overweight man with a thin moustache and ruddy cheeks. "This is János Nagy. He's in three hundred and eleven photos with the first three. All five of them were in three hundred and seven photos together. Then there are other combinations of these men, but no one else appears as frequently together as these five."

I stepped closer and looked at their nonverbal cues. "They're friends. Good friends. There is a lot of trust between them."

"What do we have on their backgrounds?" Manny asked.

"I got Olivia to compile everything she could from archives," Francine said. "She also found a few more articles on these men. I went a bit deeper, but couldn't find much more than whatever was recorded in government databases. Olivia created a spreadsheet with this information. I sent it to everyone just before we came here."

"Huh." Andor narrowed his eyes as he swiped his smartphone's screen. "This is interesting. Out of the five grandpas, only four served in the military. They were enlisted during World War Two, but none of them had been in any direct battles with the Nazis."

"Who was the one who didn't serve?" Manny asked.

"János Nagy."

I wondered if this was significant.

"I asked Olivia to look for anything else that might be suspicious in these men's backgrounds and connections," Colin said. He'd told me last night just after we'd settled in bed that Olivia had become exactly what he'd known she could be. His face had told me he was proud. And relieved. "She promised to do it this morning before she phoned her husband."

"Good," Manny said. "We need to find out what these bloody men had in common and why this killer is going after their grandsons."

"I've got names." Andor tapped the whiteboard until he had the earlier list back up. "I got my friend's dad to send me a list of not only their current client base, but also of all the clients they've ever had. I thought it would be better to have too much data than too little."

I agreed with his reasoning. Plentiful data helped in determining patterns and noticing anomalies.

Captain Palya pointed at the list. "We compared it with all the natural deaths in Hungary in the last ten years and got seventeen cases, including the cases Garas first noticed."

"The first one died nine years ago." Andor enlarged the list to show the first name. "Hanna Taikon passed away from an apparent heart attack. She was only forty-nine."

I held up both hands to stop them from continuing. "How can you be sure that the deaths of Hanna Taikon or any of the other people on this list can be attributed to the same killer? That these weren't genuine natural deaths?"

"Well, we can't be a hundred percent sure." Andor shrugged. "I won't be surprised if not all of these seventeen people were killed by some cyber-stalking serial killer. But we'll have to find a way to eliminate the people who really died from natural causes."

"One of the best ways to find a serial killer is through their victims." I had taken a few semesters of criminal psychology while at university. I'd never expected that information to be as helpful and play as big a role in my life as it currently did. "Serial killers are usually male. Only about fifteen percent of serial killers are women. Most female serial killers fall into two categories—team killers or black widow killers."

"I hate spiders." Francine shuddered. "I suppose these women kill their men after they used them for whatever purpose."

"That would be correct." I'd found the comparison to the spider species apt. "Female serial killers usually use low-profile methods of killing. Poison is their preferred choice."

"How many victims make a serial killer?" Francine asked.

"Usually three. But we need a pattern to classify it as such." Captain Palya looked at the list. "Even if we eliminate half of these people, we definitely have a serial killer on the loose."

"The question is how this person is choosing their victims." Not knowing what drove the killer bothered me.

"Can we assume it's a he?" Andor's expression revealed the genuine nature of his question. "I mean if we go with statistics, it's most probably a he."

"I think we should look for a man." Captain Palya nodded. "In all my years in the force, I've never come across a female serial killer. Not that I've come across many serial killers. But in my experience, most women kill for exactly the same reasons men do, but the way they do it is different. These murders are not quite what I would expect from a female killer. There's a certain logic and patience to it that I can't attribute to the female psyche."

"Oh, my God. You're sounding so sexist right now." Francine's lips were thin, the corners of her mouth turned down. "Not all women are hot messes. Liking pretty things doesn't mean that we can't apply logic and have patience."

Captain Palya took a step back and took a slow breath. "I'm thinking that no matter what I say right now, it's going to sound bad and dig me into a deeper hole, so I think I'll just not get into this argument."

Manny chuckled. "Wise move, old chap."

Colin frowned and took a step closer to the board. "Are these dates correct?"

"Yes." Andor tilted his head and narrowed his eyes as if looking for something on the list. "The first date is the date of birth, the second is the day they died."

"Shit." Colin pushed his hand through his hair and looked at me for a few seconds. After all these years, I knew him well. He'd found something that was disturbing him greatly. He turned his attention back to the whiteboard and stared wide-eyed at the names.

"Are you going to share with us, Frey?" Manny exhaled angrily. "Or are you just going to stand there and stare at the bloody board the whole day?"

Colin ignored him. After a few seconds, Colin tapped on the pen icon, then drew lines through five names. Only twelve remained.

I waited.

"Frey!" Clearly Manny didn't have the patience to allow Colin to process whatever insight he had gleaned.

Colin turned around. "I know when the next murder is going to take place."

"Holy hell." Manny lowered his brow. "Talk. Now."

Colin swallowed and turned back to the board. "The dates of these twelve deaths are all on the same day as the birth of a Romanian artist."

"Romanian or Roma?" There was a difference and I needed to know.

"Romanian and Roma."

"Artists as in…?" Captain Palya didn't finish his question, just lifted one eyebrow.

"Painters." Colin pointed at the first date. "Twentieth March. This death is on the same date as the birthday of Theodor Aman—he was known for his work in Romanticism. And look at the next one. The date is the same as the birthday of Camil Ressu. He was an impressionist painter. And this death on twenty-second October, same as the birthday of Corneliu Michailescu, a cubist painter."

"Okay, okay." Manny pushed his hands in his trouser pockets. "We get the gist. But are you sure about all the dates?"

"I know my artists, Millard." Colin shook his head, then turned to Andor. "There is your extra information for elimination."

"Francine, can you run the names of the Három client list against all deaths as well as the birthdates of all Romanian artists?" I didn't know if we would get any more names than the twelve we currently had, but I needed all the victims if I were to analyse victimology.

"On it." Her fingers were already flying over the keyboard. "Do you want me to go back further than ten years?"

I thought about this. "Yes. Do fifteen."

"Running it now." She typed in a few more commands, then leaned back. "It shouldn't take more than thirty minutes to get results."

Colin was still staring at the list. I deeply despised being interrupted when my brain was busy analysing information, so I left him alone. Then I recalled what he'd just said and could no longer wait. "When will be the next death?"

"Today." He frowned and looked down to his right as if having an inner conversation. "Or not. There's really no way to know."

"If I look at this, I would say you're right." Andor waved at the board. "Look how the last five deaths are clustered. Assuming that there are not dozens more victims, the killer took his time between kills. The second death came sixteen months after the first. Then another waiting period of eleven months, then thirteen months, then eight months. But the last murders have been taking place weeks apart and now days apart. So, yes. I think it might be today."

"We need to stop this arsehole." Captain Palya rested his fists on his hips. "I'm not having a lunatic running around my city killing people. For what?"

That was a good question. Not only did we not have complete victimology, we also had no clue as to what motivated this killer.

We had many disconnected parts of this crime. But each

time we discovered something new, it enabled us to get a step closer to the real crimes and to the killer. I hated the helplessness I experienced at thinking about some person who would fall victim to an unknown killer today. If Colin's prediction was correct and it happened today.

It felt like something heavy was resting on my chest knowing that there was nothing I could do at present to prevent this from happening. Rationally, I knew that I was not responsible in any way, yet an obsessive urge pushed at my mind to find this killer and stop them from taking any more lives.

Having to wait for Francine's results and for more data to come in was most frustrating. Just as I took a step towards her desk to ask her how much longer, the sound of a child laughing came from my handbag. I glared at Colin and took my smartphone from its pocket. I hated it when he changed the ringtones on my phone. It was Roxy. I swiped to answer the call. "Yes?"

"Hey there, gorgeous genius. How's everyone doing?"

"Fine." I loathed small talk. "Why are you phoning?"

"Can't I just phone to chat?"

"No."

She giggled. "Yeah, I know you don't do chatting. Okay, so I phoned to say that I just emailed a spreadsheet with info on the grandsons—Gabor Szabo, Ferenc Szell, István Koltai and Antal Udvaros. Olivia and I got as much on these men as we possibly could, but I'm sure you'll find even more on them in government databases. We compiled everything we got from the internet and social media. It's quite a lot and for now I think this should give you enough to work with."

I remembered to mumble a "Thank you" before I ended the call, took my tablet from my handbag and sat down at the conference table. A few swipes and I had my email opened and was looking at a spreadsheet that was definitely not the creation of Roxy's disorganised mind. It was neatly arranged in a sheet per person with clearly laid out information about each man. I started reading.

"Doc!" Manny knocked on the table right next to my tablet. I looked up into a deep frown pulling his brows in and down. "Who was that and what are you doing?"

"Roxy." I looked at my tablet. "She sent information about the victims."

"Anything useful?"

"I don't know yet. I've just started reading through it."

"Well, read faster." He straightened. "What are you thinking so hard, Frey?"

I didn't hear Colin's answer. I was focused on the details about the victims. If they had been murdered by a serial killer like we believed, I wondered if there was anything else connecting them. Aside from their grandfathers appearing together in many photos. Roxy and Olivia had given the same information we already knew, but had added a lot more about the men's professional lives as well as their online presence.

I finished reading and pushed the tablet away from me. There wasn't anything here that connected these men in a manner that would not be wildly speculative or circumstantial. Either we needed to look deeper into their personal lives or we needed to widen the search in their lives to the people close to them. That might be the key to finding the killer.

"Got it!" Francine shifted in her chair and drummed on the desk as if to announce something. "I got the twelve names we already have and two more. I'll add the new ones to your list, Andor."

He nodded. "Are those two deaths earlier than the ones we already have?"

"Nope." She tapped the enter key and swivelled in her chair to face the whiteboard. "See? They fit in the middle somewhere. From what I've found, the death nine years ago was indeed the first one."

"Then I need more information on this person." I flinched when everyone turned to look at me. "If this was the killer's first victim, it would tell us a lot about the killer. The first victim usually has great significance to a serial killer. It is not always the case, but it would be wise to look into this. Thoroughly."

"Then we have our work cut out for us." Manny sat down next to Francine. "Do your thing."

"Ooh, talking sexy to me again, handsome?" She winked at him and started typing on her computer.

I longed for my viewing room with my computer, my keyboard and the fifteen monitors where I could distribute findings and peruse at my own leisure. This was the first time we'd worked outside of our office and I vowed to fight against ever doing this again.

Since it would be unproductive to spend any more time being annoyed at the current working situation, I pulled out a large notebook from my handbag and settled down to lay out my thoughts on our findings so far. Around me, Colin, Andor and Captain Palya discussed the Romanian artists.

Vinnie didn't move from where he was leaning against the door, but frequently commented on something Manny had said to Francine, in an obvious attempt to irritate the older man.

I allowed these sounds to wash over me while I called up one of Mozart's earlier sonatas to mentally play in my mind. I needed clear focus if I were to see some connection that we'd overlooked so far. I inhaled deeply and started writing.

Chapter FOURTEEN

"COME ON, JEN-GIRL. You need to eat." Vinnie grabbed the back of my chair and lightly shook it. "Up and at it. Food, food, food."

I looked away from Francine's laptop monitor towards the conference room table. I'd been completely absorbed with the research Francine and I were doing. I hadn't heard the table being set or the food being brought in. Only now that I was looking at the table did I smell the food.

"You'd better grab a chair or there will be nothing left, Doc." Manny emptied a heaped spoon of what looked like a pasta salad onto his plate. "I'm already on my second helping and Garas is eating like a teenager."

"It's because this food is really good." Andor took another bread roll and used it to soak up the sauce left on his plate.

"One of the few things we agree on, Garas." Captain Palya looked at the large portions on his plate.

"You don't have to invite me twice." Francine winked at me, then got up. A pleased expression replaced the concentration that had been evident on her face for the last five hours. "Spaghetti! Ooh, just what I need. A serious pasta infusion. And potato salad. Vin! Did you do all of this?"

"Nope." Vinnie shook my chair again and smiled when I got up. He nodded towards the table. "Cook did it all. He promised me that the food was prepared exactly the way you preferred it, with all the cleaning and sterilising and stuff."

I searched his face, but saw no sarcasm. Only honesty. "Thank you."

Colin was sitting next to Andor, a large helping of the potato salad all that was left on his plate. He smiled when I sat down across from him. "We need to get this potato salad recipe. It's really, really good."

"That's why he made two large bowls of the stuff." Vinnie pointed at a sealed plastic container. He waved at the plentiful food. "Where do you want to start, Jen-girl?"

I had been so engrossed with the work Francine and I'd been doing that it had bordered on the point of hyperfocus. When that had happened in the past, days would go by when I would forget to eat, sleep, bathe, even drink water. That was why hunger now suddenly overwhelmed my senses. I hadn't registered any of my body's needs.

"I'll have the pasta salad." I'd had that on the first day when I'd still been very sceptical of the skills Émile had boasted his cook had. The salad had been light, yet filling and flavourful. Vinnie had threatened the cook with a painful death if he didn't share the recipe. Cook had failed to hide his pleasure.

"After the salad, you must try the spaghetti." Vinnie pulled the large serving dish closer to his plate. "I swear it's even tastier than last Thursday."

I looked at the dishes and tilted my head. "These are all dishes we've had before."

"Yup." Vinnie heaped another spoon of pasta onto his plate. "I thought it would be safer to ask Cook to make food we've already had and liked. That way I know everyone will eat."

Even though Vinnie hadn't prepared our food like he usually did, I could see that it had been important to him to be in control of what we ate. I thought about the earlier discussion I'd had with Roxy and Francine and realised that Vinnie also never asked for appreciation. I cleared my throat. "Thank you."

"Huh?" Vinnie stopped chewing and looked at me in surprise. Then his cheeks lifted and the corners of his eyes crinkled in a warm smile when he swallowed. "You're most welcome."

It was quiet around the table for a few minutes. I finished the pasta salad, then followed Vinnie's advice and helped myself to some spaghetti. The trust I had in Vinnie was evident in my immediate acceptance of his advice. I hadn't once questioned the cleanliness of the food preparation, the plates and eating utensils. I'd just taken it for granted that Vinnie would never have offered me food that had not been prepared to standards that passed his approval. That included the taste. The spaghetti once again didn't disappoint.

"Doc!" Manny knocked on the table, his scowl telling me he'd been trying to get my attention for a while.

"Yes?"

"Are you listening?"

"Yes."

"Well then, I suppose I can continue." Captain Palya's expression warned me that he was irritated. He pushed his glasses up the bridge of his nose. "I got full background on Hanna Taikon."

"The killer's first victim," Andor said.

"The first we could find." The captain paused. "Well, I did an even deeper search and couldn't find anyone else who matched our victimology. So I'm pretty sure this is the first victim."

"Palya says she was a teacher." Manny's interruption indicated his impatience.

"That she was." Captain Palya took a sip of water and carefully placed the glass in front of his plate. "She was born in Budapest, studied here and worked in three different schools during her career. She left the first school after only a year and a half, the second after three years, but then stayed with the third school for more than twenty years."

"What was wrong with her?" I asked.

"She was quite the racist." He pushed down on his top lip when his *levator labii superioris* muscle raised it in disgust. "She was fired from her first school because she refused to touch an African child when the kid fell on the playground. She left the second school voluntarily when they privatised and actively started marketing to include foreigners. It seems like she was luckier in her third school. Despite the numerous complaints against her, she never received any reprimands. When I spoke to the current director of the school, she said that the previous director told her that Ms Taikon was one of the best teachers they had."

"She wasn't," Andor said as if he knew the answer.

"No, she was not. The new director told me that this Taikon woman only spoke to white, Christian, Hungarian children in her classes. If you were anything but that, she wouldn't answer your questions or address you in any way."

"God, people can be awful." Francine pressed her lips

tightly together and shook her head. "We're all humans, regardless of race, gender, religion, anything. And to do that to children? Awful."

"That's why the new director asked Ms Taikon to resign." His moustache twitched in an almost-smile that held no humour. "She died before they could reach an agreement. There was even a small protest at her funeral. That's how not loved she was."

"I don't get why people are like that." Francine's hold on her knife and fork tightened. "I mean intellectually I get it, but I really don't understand how anyone can think that they are superior to others."

"Says the computer snob." Vinnie raised an eyebrow.

"Don't say that." Francine shook her head. "Being a snob when it comes to using technology and software does not put me in the same category as these people."

"You're right, Franny." The contrition on Vinnie's face was sincere. "I'm sorry."

"Okay, so we know that the first victim was a horrid racist." Manny looked at Andor. "What about the other victims?"

Andor's brows pulled together as he looked down at the printed pages in front of him. "I didn't find anything like that in the backgrounds I've been able to build on the other victims. Doesn't mean that it isn't there though. I just haven't found any mention of racism like that."

"What did you find?" Captain Palya asked.

"Nothing substantial connecting them." Andor smiled when his captain said something in Hungarian. I didn't understand the words, but the captain's expression alerted me to his annoyance. Andor controlled his smile and tapped on the papers in front of him. "I looked at their histories as far back as I could track them digitally. A few went to the same university, but at different times or at different faculties. Another three went to the same high school, but also different years. There is no one thing or one place that connects them all."

"But there is something." Captain Palya leaned forward. "Stop working up to it, Garas."

"The boosters," Andor said. "All of them had Három wifi boosters and they were registered."

"That's how we found these names in the first place," Colin said. "We need something else that connects them."

"There is one more thing." Andor glanced at his phone lying next to the papers. "I confirmed it with my friend's dad. All fourteen people had received their boosters as a prize or a gift or as some marketing gimmick. With it they also received a lifetime membership to the highest tier of service."

"Who gave them the boosters?" I needed that name. This could be the killer.

"Huh. I didn't ask." He reached for his phone. "I'll do that now."

"Hold your horses," Manny said. "Let's first get all the data. Maybe we have a few more questions for this man."

Andor nodded and put his phone down on the table.

"I've been speaking to Rox." Vinnie's smile was gentle. "She's been looking at the medical records of the victims. Well, not all the victims, only those Andor was able to send to her. And Rox says that all those deaths are completely viable. With the medical histories, she wasn't surprised that doctors didn't suspect foul play. For example, she said that the third victim died of kidney failure. This guy was in hospital with kidney stones twice."

Vinnie stopped when Andor coughed and took almost a minute to ease his breathing. Vinnie pointed at him. "Like that. I think Rox said it was victim seven had a history of asthma and died from an asthma attack."

"I don't have asthma." Andor inhaled deeply and pulled his shoulders back. "This is just bleeping seasonal allergies. This year has been particularly bad."

"Just sayin', dude." The corner of Vinnie's mouth lifted, causing Andor to laugh. I never understood the need for macabre jokes. Vinnie sobered when he looked at me. "Rox said that she wished she could help more, but without an autopsy, she wouldn't be able to tell if there had been foul play or not."

"Well, I think Genevieve and I found the smoking gun." Francine shook her shoulders like she usually did when she was boasting.

I frowned. "We didn't find any weapons."

"Oh, but we did." She winked at me, then looked at the men. "Our genius friend here got me to delve into the victims' families. We first checked into their parents, but found nothing that connected them. We knew the grandfathers are connected from the photos, so we looked for more connections than just their pretty pictures."

"Did you check just the Szabo, Szell, Koltai and Udvaros grandpas, or did you check the fifth grandpa too?" Andor asked.

"Oh, we checked all five of them, Grandpa János Nagy included. And guess what?" She looked around the table waiting for a response. Manny's scowl brought a bright smile to her face. "We found that four of the naughty old men had a business registered in their names. Grandpa János Nagy had his own leather business and wasn't part of the other business."

"Holy hell." Manny leaned back in his chair. "What business?"

Francine paused. She was being melodramatic and it annoyed me. I put my knife and fork down. "An art dealership."

"No!" Francine's wail made me jerk back. She slammed her hands on the table. "I was going to present it. With a picture."

"Doc was faster." Manny only lifted an eyebrow when Francine turned slowly and gave him a faux-aggressive look.

"Shit." Colin turned to look at me. "That's… that's quite a connection. What's the name of this dealership?"

"Rubique Art."

"No. Can't be." Some colour left Colin's face and he blinked a few times. "I did two authentications for them many years ago. I thought they were a French company."

"They are," Francine said. "These photos were taken between the two world wars. In that time the grandfathers registered their business in France. I have a few theories about why they did that, but Genevieve won't indulge me by entertaining them."

"Then please don't tell us." Manny sounded bored.

"And what if I'm right?"

Manny looked at me. "Is there any viability to her theories?"

"They are comparable to her theories about alien abductions." I'd been most irritated when Francine had wasted time spouting one such theory after the other.

"You are all cold-hearted unbelievers." She flicked her hair over her shoulder. "Anyhoo… the four grandpas started their business in 1936. The records we managed to dig up showed two to three transactions a month. Between 1936 and 1940 they seemed to have done legitimate art deals. Roxy and Olivia found newspaper articles in the archives about their business. The translation program is mostly correct, so I feel safe to say that the journalist was highly impressed by these men and their flawless reputation."

"What happened during the Second World War?" Colin asked.

"Their business dealings increased exponentially. They expanded their client base to America, Canada and China. They sold a lot of masterpieces to extremely rich people in those countries."

"Shit." Colin's *masseter* muscles bulged as he clenched his jaw. "I just know where this is going."

"We haven't had enough time to confirm our suspicions yet." And I hated speculating. "But in this case, I agree with Francine's theory that this art dealership sold Nazi-looted art."

"Holy bloody hell, Doc!" Manny rubbed his hands hard over his face. "How did no-one see this before?"

"Because there were just too many artworks stolen from people whose entire families had been killed by the Nazis." Colin was no longer the suave poet. His anger made his voice hard, his lips pulled in a thin line. "In many cases no one even knows these artworks were taken by the Nazis, because there was no one to report it. Only in accidental cases did someone do a bit more homework while authenticating a piece or checking its provenance and find red flags. There are still an estimated hundred thousand works of art missing, of which we have no idea how many are lost forever."

"Such awful destruction." The corners of Andor's mouth were turned down. "Even though I learned about this in school and my grandparents told me stories, I'm still horrified every time I hear about this."

"Was your family affected by the Holocaust?" Francine asked.

"No." Sadness pulled at his eyes. "But my grandmother always talks about her best friend who lived next door to them. The friend and her husband were Jewish and they were rounded up quite early in the war. My granny never saw or heard from her friend. Apparently they'd been like sisters."

A grave silence settled at the table. I never allowed myself to analyse the actions of the Nazis too closely. Unlike my studies into abnormal and criminal psychology, merely thinking about the atrocities the Nazis committed brought a feeling to my chest that I had come to recognise as dark horror. This would morph into panic which would send me into a lengthy shutdown.

It was for this reason that I redirected my thoughts back to the case. I thought about everything Andor had revealed about the victims and their memberships of the wifi booster company. Then I analysed the information Captain Palya had uncovered about the first victim. I reached for my tablet and started looking at the details we'd been able to find about the other victims. A few things caught my attention and once again I wished for the fifteen monitors in my viewing room.

In lieu of that, I pulled my notebook closer and started making new notes. Soon I lost myself in this new line of thought. When I looked up, I was surprised to see that I'd been making notes for almost an hour. And I'd filled eight pages with graphs, tables and mind maps.

Colin was still next to me, busy on his tablet. Vinnie was standing by the door, speaking quietly on his phone. His expression told me he was speaking to Roxy. Francine was furiously working on her laptop, Andor sitting next to her, whispering something every now and then. Manny and Captain Palya were looking at something on the captain's computer monitor.

"The…" My voice came out hoarse and I cleared my throat. "The killer is in his or her late twenties or early thirties."

Manny's head jerked up. "What the hell, Doc?"

"Start explaining." Captain Palya moved his laptop to the side, his attention fully on me.

I took a moment to organise my thoughts and took one sheet of notes. I laid that on the table. "I looked at the victims' lives. We know that Hanna Taikon, the first victim, taught at schools. We also know the exact years she was there. So I started looking at how these victims could form a timeline. Well, when victim two was a student at university, victim four was a professor at the same university. Victim three was working at a shop that made photocopies for students. He worked there at the same time victim two was a student and victim four was a professor.

"Victims seven and nine were at the same school where

Hanna Taikon taught. At the same time she was a teacher there. Victim five was a dance teacher close to that school—at the time when all the others were there. Victim six worked at a recruitment agency during the university time and for two years after that. Victim eight was the human resources manager at a graphic design firm. He was responsible for the hiring of new employees. And then we have the last four victims who we've connected to the photos of their grandfathers."

Colin pulled the sheet closer to him. "So if we take this timeline, the killer was taught by Ms Taikon. Those two victims did something to him at school. Most likely bullied him. The same with the students and the professor. The copy-shop guy pissed him off or gave him bad service. The recruitment agent sent him to bad interviews and the HR guy didn't hire him. And this timeline would put him in the age range Jenny said."

"If the killer is a him." I was beginning to strongly doubt it, but had nothing concrete to support my qualms. "And you're creating scenarios that have no base."

"All hypothetical, love. Just to give an idea of where our killer's motivations come from."

"Well, bleep it." Andor's eyebrows were raised high. "This would definitely be completely screwed up, but would explain that the killer is taking revenge on these people for something they'd done to wrong him. Or her."

I hated speculation. Truly hated it. But I'd come to understand and even value the importance of brainstorming and evaluating numerous possible theories. So I pulled my shoulders back and took a deep breath. "I furthermore posit that the killer is of Roma descent. Knowing what I was looking for made it easier to find information to support my theory. I discovered that both Ms Taikon and the professor had complaints against them for racism. Especially for vicious discrimination against Romani students. Victim eight, the HR manager, was fired because it had come to light that he never hired anyone who wasn't white and Hungarian. And victim seven ran an online forum dedicated to Roma hate."

"Holy hell." Manny slumped in his chair.

"This is going to cause a furore." Andor looked at Captain Palya. "The media is going to go nuts over this."

"Then we'd better get this son of a bitch before they start publishing crap." Captain Palya looked at me. "So? How do we find this man?"

"Or woman," Andor added.

Colin leaned back in his chair and stared at the ceiling. "If this killer is Roma, it would explain why King's name came up." He straightened and looked at me. "Somehow Koltai knew what his grandfather had done, knew who the killer is and how his grandfather is connected to the killer. But how would King help us make that connection when he doesn't know István Koltai? And he doesn't know anything that could help us?"

"Maybe he doesn't know what he knows," Andor said. "We should—"

"Woohoo!" Francine's loud exclamation startled me. She punched both fists in the air, then pointed repeatedly at her laptop monitor. "I got you. Got you, got you, got you."

Manny got up and walked around the conference table. "What have you got?"

"I'm hacking the hacker-killer-man-woman." She swivelled her chair to look at us. "I saw Genevieve looking at the victims and it gave me an idea. I only have access to the online activities of eight of the fourteen victims, but it was enough. I was looking for a footprint the cyber-stalker might have left while hacking and stalking them. And I must say, he-she is good. The footprint was miniscule. But I found it."

"Do you know where this person is?" Captain Palya put his hands on the table as if to push himself up.

"Nope." Francine's frustration was obvious. "But I have a start. If I follow the little breadcrumbs he-she leaves while cyberstalking, I might be able to plant a virus that will then give me access to him-her." She wrinkled her nose. "We need to establish whether the killer is male or female. It's awkward saying him-her the whole time."

I agreed with her. Not for the reason she stated, but because it would influence how we search for this person. Even though I would never make the mistake of approaching this killer as a typical male or typical female who was neurotypical, there were still certain traits that were mostly male or mostly female.

"Why can't you just hack this person?" Captain Palya's hands fisted and he pressed hard against his thighs.

"Because this person is really, really, really good. I've already told you that."

The captain's nostrils flared, but his response was interrupted by the ringing of his phone. He looked at the screen and his eyes immediately closed, blocking whatever or whoever he was about to confront. He swiped the screen and lifted the phone to his ear.

Andor snorted the moment Captain Palya spoke in a gentle tone. I didn't need to understand Hungarian to know that he was guilty of something and most likely speaking to his wife or someone very close to him. There was a moment of quiet while he listened.

When he replied, Andor snorted again and looked at us. "He's in the dog house. He was supposed to take his wife to dinner to celebrate their anniversary. She's at the restaurant and he's not."

"Don't ask about the dog house, Doc." Manny looked at his watch and swore. "It's time for all of us to go home in any case. It's almost eight o'clock."

"We haven't found the killer yet." There was no way I could leave now. We had to find and stop this person.

"We can't do it if we're too tired to think, Doc." Manny reached for Francine's laptop monitor. "Close this down or I'm doing it."

"Get your grubby hands away from my baby." Francine slapped at his hand until he withdrew it. She gave him a hateful look and started typing commands. "I need to get the programs to continue running without me monitoring them. It's going to take a few minutes. Go bother Genevieve."

"No." I didn't want to be bothered.

Colin and Andor laughed and I noticed for the first time how tired both of them looked. Upon closer inspection, I realised everyone showed evidence of fatigue. Manny was right. We would not be as effective in our work if we were exhausted.

Yet a part of me longed to continue my work. I wanted to deepen my analysis of the victims. I was sure there was something else that would connect them. Something else that would lead us to the killer. But when Francine hid a yawn, I carefully gathered my notes. It was time to rest.

Chapter FIFTEEN

"LOSERS!" PINK'S FACE lit up with pleasure and he stared straight into the camera. "I told you I'm better than you, Nix. You too, Vinster."

Vinnie muttered a vicious swearword and pushed his back deeper against the sofa as he continued to move the video game controller thumbsticks. "Don't get too comfortable in your new level, Pink. I'm coming and I'm pissed off."

"You boys are both going to weep like little schoolgirls when I'm done." Nikki's lips were in a thin line, her eyebrows drawn together in concentration.

It was seven minutes past eleven and no one had gone to bed. We'd arrived at the villa to a delicious, but light dinner. Like me, the others had too much internal energy to settle down to sleep. Colin had been the first to excuse himself from the dinner table. He was sitting next to me on the sofa, working on his laptop. He was looking into the art dealership's history. Every now and then I saw a painting on his laptop monitor. He would zoom in on the paintings and then open another tab that he'd told me was one of his ways to check an artwork's provenance.

Manny was slumped in a recliner chair staring at the very large screen television where Vinnie was playing Drestia against Nikki and Pink in Strasbourg. Olivia shared the sofa with Vinnie, settled against the arm, her feet tucked under her. She was reading a mystery novel on her e-reader. She'd started telling me the storyline, but had giggled and told me that fiction was just that when I'd asked a sixth question about the probability of the plot. Roxy was in the bathtub. She'd taken a glass of red wine with her and had declared the need for tub time.

Francine had set up a workstation on the dining room table. She'd confiscated Manny's laptop as well as mine. I had argued hard against her using my device, but she'd rightly countered that finding the IP location of the killer was important. More important than my desire to find out more about the victims. She hadn't been interested in Colin's laptop because his had a slower operating system. I'd relented only after I'd candidly expressed my displeasure at the situation.

She'd winked at me, blown me a kiss and walked away with my laptop. So here I was. Sitting next to Colin on one of the three comfortable sofas, watching Vinnie, Pink and Nikki playing an online game. They'd been at it for two hours and appeared to be two-thirds through the levels.

My initial interest had been to observe Nikki, not the game. Pink had been delighted when Vinnie had Skyped him and told him to get his lazy butt in front of the television. They'd then set up videos and computers so that Pink and Nikki could see Vinnie and vice versa.

Vinnie and Pink had had to wait half an hour for Nikki while she was putting Eric to sleep. She had the baby monitor Francine had bought next to her on the sofa and glanced at it frequently, even though it had been quiet the entire time. It was a top-of-the-range monitor—one that even Vinnie hadn't known about. He'd inspected it, then had called Pink to hear his opinion. Only then had he approved of Francine's gift, which, of course, had then ended in another one of their inane arguments.

Nikki had accepted the gift and used it all the time. I was relieved to see that she was completely relaxed and having fun playing against Vinnie and Pink. The only tension I saw was her concentration as she worked the controller. I'd closely observed her for most of the first level of the game. Then the clues and battles to the next level of Drestia caught my attention.

It was a truly smart multiplayer game. Vinnie's avatar was an old man who looked very much like Colin's disguise when he pretended to be an eighty-year-old poet. Nikki's avatar was a woman who resembled Francine. The animated figure had long dark hair and a lithe body and was dressed in designer outfits. Pink's avatar was a short teenage girl with spiky pink hair and thick black-rimmed glasses. She was dressed completely in black. Even her nails were painted black.

I was fascinated by the care everyone took when they'd created their avatars. There had to have been studies about the psychology behind the decisions people made when choosing how they would be represented in this online world. I made a note to look it up once we returned to Strasbourg and I settled into my usual routine.

"I got it!" Nikki wiggled in her seat, but didn't take her hands off the controller or her eyes off the television monitor. "Eat my dust, you Y-chromosome losers."

Vinnie chuckled and shook his head. "We can't let her get away with this, dude."

"We're not." Pink's pink-haired girl turned the handle on one of the castle's interior doors. The wall disintegrated, revealing a new room. "We're taking a shortcut."

"Huh." Vinnie's old man followed the young girl into the room. It was decorated in an eighteenth-century style. I didn't have the same expertise as Colin when it came to art and historical correctness, but the décor appeared to be true to that period. Including the masterpieces on the walls. I recognised a Turner landscape and two portraits by William Blake and Goya respectively. I was impressed.

"Find the key, Vin." Pink's girl ran to a large wooden wardrobe and stopped in front of the door, staring at the lock. "We need to get in there."

"Hey, dude." Vinnie stretched and kicked Colin's feet. "We need you here."

"Yeah." Pink looked to the side for a moment. I assumed he was looking at the computer monitor streaming the video that showed our living room. "We could do with your expertise, Colin."

"Busy." Colin waved absentmindedly with one hand, then returned to working on his laptop.

"You're going to need more than the unbeatable Master Colin to catch up to me today." Nikki leaned forward on the sofa, her brow furrowed in concentration. "I'm destroying it over here."

"The key, Vin! Look for it on your side. I'm going to the left." Pink's girl turned to her left and walked to the elegant writing table in front of the window. Another thing that amazed me was the quality of the graphics in these games. The avatars' movements were smooth, almost human-like. The detail worked into each room was equally impressive. The view from the window showed extensive grounds, manicured lawns that led to a high wall surrounding the castle.

I looked from the beautiful summer garden back into the room and frowned. Vinnie's old man was opening, then closing all the drawers in a chest. What had caught my eye was the bouquet of white roses in a round red vase. Unlike most of the vases from that era, this one didn't have any detailed painting on it. But the design on it sent a rush of adrenaline through my body. "Lift the red vase."

"Huh?" Vinnie glanced at me, then shrugged and got his old man to lift the red porcelain vase.

The wardrobe doors swung open to reveal an entrance into a room. Vinnie's avatar reached the wardrobe first, but was immediately followed by the pink-haired girl. This room had no windows, yet it was remarkably light inside. The dark red, blue and green striped wallpaper should've made the room even gloomier, yet all the furniture and decorations were clearly visible.

Including the only painting on the opposite wall.

"It's the Netscher." Olivia shook her index finger at the television screen, her voice breathless. Her *frontalis* muscles lifted her eyebrows high on her forehead, her mouth slightly agape. "What's Nathan's painting doing in this game?"

"Shit." Colin put his laptop down and leaned forward, staring at the screen. "It's an exact copy."

"What the hell?" Manny straightened, his expression fierce.

In an ornate frame and illuminated as if spotlights shone on it, Caspar Netscher's *A Woman Feeding a Parrot* hung on the wall. This was the painting that had brought Olivia to Hungary and had been the catalyst for this investigation into a serial killer.

It was beautiful. A young woman wearing a gold-coloured dress was feeding an African Grey parrot sitting on her hand. She was glancing straight at the viewer. Her expression and body language was made to be flirtatious. I could now see what Colin meant when he'd said Netscher had been a master as a portraitist.

"What the fuck is happening?" Vinnie's fingers tightened around the controller, but he didn't move his old man.

"Colin?" Pink moved closer to the screen, which moved him closer to the camera.

"I don't know what this means." Colin pushed his hands through his hair.

"Doc?" Manny looked at me. "Does this game have anything to do with…"

His question was interrupted by the ringtone of his smartphone. With a grunt he removed the phone from his trouser pocket and answered. Another rush of adrenaline entered my system. After his initial greeting, Manny didn't say anything, yet I recognised his expression. I immediately thought of the effect this news was going to have on Colin.

Manny ended the call and sighed heavily. "We have another dead body. Garas is at the victim's house. We'd better get there immediately." He turned towards the dining room. "Francine!"

"Yes, master?"

Manny's lips thinned. "Get in here!"

Francine walked into the room a few seconds later. She was wearing light blue pants and a gauzy top over a white sleeveless t-shirt and sandals. It looked as if she'd just had her morning shower. Her playful expression changed the moment she registered our nonverbal cues. "What's happening?"

Manny shook his index finger at the television. "Is that bloody thing hacked? Is this house hacked?"

"No."

"Are you sure?"

Francine put both hands on her hips and raised one eyebrow. "Want to tell me I'm not good at my job?"

Colin got up and stood between Manny and Francine. "There's something about this game that might connect to the case. Millard is as usual being an arse, but the question is real. Are you very sure no one was able to sneak past your security?"

"Yes." There was no hesitation, no doubt. "When we took out that game the first time, I ran my three best antivirus programs on it. Our internet, our computers and that game are not hacked. But I will double-check. Again."

"Do that later." Manny moved towards the front door. "Get your things. We're going to another crime scene."

"Yoohoo!" Nikki was waving both arms. "What's happening, guys? Are you safe?"

When we'd first connected to Nikki and Pink, she'd told us that she knew we were working a case. I hadn't responded, but she'd pointed at the camera and boasted that she could read Vinnie and Colin's body language and that it had confirmed her suspicions. Then she'd rolled her eyes and muttered what bad liars everyone was.

"We're safe, punk." Vinnie put his controller on the sofa next to him and got up. "But we've got to get to work. Sleep tight, little punk."

She snorted. "No way I'm sleeping now. I'll wait until you check in with me."

"Pink." Francine walked into the camera's range and faced the monitor showing Pink and Nikki. "I'm going to connect you to my system here. Double-check my findings, would ya?"

"Sure thing. Anything you want me to look for?"

"Nope." She shook her head. "Just make sure that I'm right."

"Yes, my queen."

She laughed and blew him a kiss. Then walked over and kissed Manny full on the mouth when he scowled at her exchange with Pink. "Come on, grumpy. Let's go and catch this bloody serial killer."

"I don't talk like that." He wasn't quick enough to hide the slight lifting of the corner of his mouth at Francine's attempt to copy his British accent.

"No, you make it sound much sexier."

Manny took his hand off her back and walked to the front door. "I'll be in the car. We're leaving in five minutes. Doc, you'd better get your butt over here too."

"I'll tell Roxy and help where I can." Olivia got up and walked with us to the front door. "Please be careful."

It took us twenty minutes from the villa to reach the victim's house. The neighbourhood was quiet just before midnight. This suburb was on the northern border of Budapest, the houses large and the cars parked in the driveways expensive.

We stopped in front of a white three-story house with a sloping green roof, a large veranda overlooking the front garden and spacious balconies on each floor. Vinnie drove the SUV into the property and stopped next to Andor's old sedan. Andor was waiting for us.

He spoke as soon as we opened the doors. "Sorry to get you guys out here so late, but I thought it best if you saw it as soon as possible."

"You did the right thing." Colin waited for me to get out and walked to Andor. "Whose house is this?"

"The victim's." Andor nodded at Vinnie, Manny and Francine when they joined us. "Tibor Bokros is... was the Minister of Human Resources. He's only been in that position for the last eighteen months. Before that he was the chairman of the Committee on Budget, Finance and Audit Office. Before that he was in some committee overseeing the registration of national and international businesses."

I liked that Andor was giving information that we could use to better form a history of the killer. I wondered where this victim would fit in the timeline of the killer's experiences. What this victim had done to the killer to have warranted the ultimate revenge.

"Who found him?" Manny followed Andor up the three steps to the veranda.

"His personal assistant." Andor opened the front door and entered after Manny. "The minister was supposed to attend an important function tonight. When he didn't arrive and didn't answer any of his phones, his assistant came here."

"I'm the assistant." A woman was standing in a doorway leading from the entrance. She was wearing an evening dress, her hair elegantly styled. Her professional makeup didn't hide the lack of colour in her face, her mascara lightly smeared under her eyes. "I have a key to his house. I came in and found him on the floor in his room."

"His bedroom?" Manny asked.

"No." She looked up and left. "I think the Americans call it a den? Or is it a man-cave?"

"Ah." Colin turned to me. "Got it?"

I nodded. I'd argued with Vinnie about the terminology once. I maintained that it was ridiculous.

"Does he have a television in that room?" Francine lifted her tablet.

"Let's just go there." Andor walked to the third door leading from the entrance. We walked through a formal sitting room. There was something incomplete in this room, as if the element that was supposed to bind the décor together was missing. I'd seen this before in the homes of people with newly acquired riches. They would hire professional decorators, but would not fully take their advice. In their ambition to appear as if they'd come from old money, they would insist on adding or eliminating certain suggestions. The result would be the room we were about to exit.

The next room we entered had a completely different atmosphere. It reminded me of the previous victim Antal Udvaros' living room. This was even more welcoming, less elegant. A bulky sectional sofa faced a large screen television mounted on the wall. The difference between this and the previous crime scene was that this wall was filled with photos. I stepped closer, then froze.

A man wearing a crime scene protective suit was on his

knees next to the prone body of who I supposed was Minister Tibor Bokros. When the kneeling man noticed us, he got up and spoke to Manny in Hungarian. Andor interrupted him midsentence with a question. He shook his head, then continued to address Andor. While they were talking, I turned my attention back to the minister.

He was lying in an awkward position. It looked like he had tried to get up, then had hit his head on the coffee table when he'd fallen forward. He had landed half on his side, half on his stomach. It looked like he had clutched his chest when he'd gone down. I wondered if the man talking to Andor was a doctor and if his preliminary findings would include a heart attack.

Colin was standing next to the sofa, grief pulling the corners of his mouth down.

"Stop being a ninny, Frey."

Colin's head jerked up. "Excuse me?"

"You heard me." Manny pushed his hands in his trouser pockets, his shoulders slumping forward. "I can see on your ninny face that you're feeling responsible. There was no way you could've predicted that this person was going to be the killer's next target. Stop feeling sorry for yourself."

"My God, Millard. You are an unbelievable bastard."

"I know."

"Thank you." Colin's words were quietly spoken, his expression grateful. I had been correct in expecting Colin to be particularly affected by this murder. He'd been the one to see the pattern in the dates of the murders. Yet he'd also been the one to acknowledge that it was impossible to foresee whether someone else was going to be murdered on the very next birthday of a Romanian artist.

"It was still streaming when we got here." Francine walked into the room, looked at the dead body, shivered and walked to the television. She didn't notice the tension between Colin and Manny. "I've blocked all data flow from this IP address, so the killer doesn't know that we're here and what we're doing."

"I'm sure the killer knows we're here." Colin inhaled deeply, some of the sadness leaving his expression as he walked to the far wall to look at a painting. "He or she would be stupid not to draw that conclusion the moment they were no longer receiving video from here."

"True." Francine joined Vinnie in front of the television. "Well, what do you know."

"That's what I thought as well."

"What are you two on about?" Manny stayed where he was, waiting for Andor to finish his conversation with the other man.

"Look what's on the telly, old chap." Vinnie grinned.

"I don't speak like that." Manny exhaled heavily and looked at the television screen. "Holy hell."

On the large screen was the same castle room that Vinnie's old man and Pink's teenage girl had entered through the wardrobe door. Netscher's *A Woman Feeding a Parrot* was against the wall. I inspected every detail and felt confident that it looked exactly the same as in the game Vinnie, Pink and Nikki had played.

This was clearly leading our investigation into a new direction. But first I needed to find the one element that we'd discovered to connect all previous victims. It didn't take me long. I pointed at the small black box on the low table under the television. "The booster."

"The same as the others." Vinnie went down on his haunches, reached out, but stopped just before touching the logo. "The red triangle. It's another one of Három's customers."

"We've got to stop this." Andor shook his head. "This is now the fifteenth victim we know of and it's fifteen too many."

"What did the crime scene guy say?" Manny lifted his chin towards the door. I hadn't noticed the man leaving.

"He's our medical examiner. He said that he'll have to do a full autopsy to have accurate results, but it looks like a heart attack. He gave us ten minutes in the room. Then he'll be back to deal with the body."

"I want all the devices." Francine waved her arm around. "From the whole house."

"We'll do the same as last time. Download everything you can, but my guys need to look for prints and other evidence before you can have the hardware."

"Fine by me." She took her ringing phone from her large red handbag and swiped the screen. "Hey, you. Tell me I'm right. Tell me I'm the queen of all queens." She laughed then lowered the phone and swiped the screen. "You're on speaker now, Pink."

"Hi, everyone." Pink sounded excited. "I checked Francine's findings as she asked and she was indeed right. I'm sure she's gloating like crazy right now."

"Right about what?" I didn't like feeling as if I'd missed part of a conversation.

"Oh, yes," Francine whispered loudly into the phone. "I haven't told them yet."

Manny took a step closer to Francine, his body language aggressive.

She winked at him. "I was tracking all the internet traffic from the victims' IP addresses. At least I did as much tracking as I possibly could. And it kept leading me to Arany."

"Seriously?" Colin crossed his arms. "The gaming company? The same company that owns Drestia?"

"The game you bunch have been playing non-stop?" Manny rubbed his hand over his face. "Bloody hell."

I cleared my throat. "I hate to speculate."

"Please do, Doc."

I hesitated. "Well, I posit that the killer is connected to Drestia, possibly even the designer of this game."

"How do you figure that, Doc?"

I looked at the booster. "I saw Három's logo on the red vase in the room with the wardrobe."

"Bloody holy hell!"

"That's why I told Vinnie to lift the vase."

"Which unlocked the door to the other room." Colin tilted his head back. "I wasn't watching. What did I miss, Vin?"

"We haven't been in that room before. It was on the floor of the second highest level." Vinnie turned to look at the television for a few moments. "I wonder what we'll find in that room that will lead us to the highest level." He looked at me. "Colin and I have only managed to get to that floor. We haven't been able to reach the tower room so we can get the scroll."

"What scroll?" There was so much I didn't know about this game.

"The scroll that will award the winner his prize."

"I must say I haven't noticed any triangles anywhere else." Pink's voice came from the phone in Francine's hand. "But I haven't looked for any. As a trained GIPN officer, I would feel really stupid if I'd missed it all along."

"You and me both, dude." Vinnie looked at Colin. "Have you noticed it?"

Colin shook his head.

"Wanna know why you all love me so much?" Francine pouted. "Why you all adore me?"

"Tell me, my queen." Pink's answer was the only polite response to Francine's outrageous question. Manny looked like he was about to say something very rude.

"While trying to find the killer through the IP addresses, internet activities and histories of the victims, I noticed a pattern." She blinked a few times. "Okay, so maybe it was Olivia who pointed it out, but I knew how to pursue it. I'm not going to bore you with my genius, but I'm sure the killer has hacked most of the players of Drestia.

"He-she is rerouting his-her internet traffic through these players' IP addresses. In other words, he-she is using the players as proxies. He-she is hiding behind the players. Once I made that connection, I knew how to follow him-her to his-her home IP." She threw her hands in the air. "My God, we have to find out the gender of this stupid killer."

"The home IP?" I didn't care about her awkward feelings. "Is that the one originating from Arany's address?"

"Yup." She flicked her hair over her shoulder. "And that's why I'm queen."

"All hail." Pink's voice came from the phone.

"Give me that bloody thing." Manny grabbed the phone from Francine's hand and spoke into it. "You're irritating me. The others can speak to you later."

"Bu—" Pink's reply was cut off. That resulted in an argument between Manny and Francine.

"Where is this Arany?" Manny held Francine's phone out of her reach, waiting for her answer.

"Their headquarters are here in Budapest. It's actually quite close to King's house." She wiggled her fingers. "Gimme."

"What time do they open?" Manny pulled her phone closer to his chest. "And who's the owner of that place?"

Francine placed both her fists on her hips. "If I get my phone back, I will start looking for that information. Now give me my bloody phone."

"I don't speak like that." Manny started an argument with both Francine and Vinnie for mocking his accent.

I wasn't paying attention. I was processing everything we'd learned. Information about Arany was of utmost importance as well as a visit to their headquarters. But there were still countless missing elements. I turned to Colin. "I need to play the game."

Chapter SIXTEEN

"WHAT THE BLOODY hell is going on here?" Manny stood in the doorway to the living room, his *corrugator supercilii* muscle lowering his brow. "How are we supposed to be at the top of our game when everyone's exhausted? I thought I told you people to go sleep."

"You didn't tell me." Pink's amused answer drew Manny's annoyed look to the same gaming set-up from yesterday.

"You're getting too mouthy, laddie." Manny stepped deeper into the room, into the camera's view.

"And I thought I told you that wearing those slippers make you look like a total wuss." Vinnie tilted his controller at the fluffy teddy bear slippers on Manny's feet. Like everyone in the room, he was wearing his pyjamas.

"Watch it, Mister Muscles." Francine poked Vinnie with her foot. She was sitting next to him on the sofa, leaning against the armrest, and had tucked her feet under his thigh. "I'll buy you a onesie for your birthday. Then you can match"—her top lip curled as she looked past Vinnie—"that barbarism."

"You're just jealous because I make cuddly look sexy." Roxy rubbed her hands down her flannel one-piece outfit. I had no interest in fashion, but even to me her choice of sleepwear was decidedly impractical and unattractive. She was sitting on Vinnie's other side, leaning against his shoulder.

Manny sat down in one of the reclining chairs and looked between us and the television. "So?"

"None of us could stay asleep." Colin had managed to sleep fifteen minutes longer than me. He looked tired. "We decided to get some work done."

"By playing the game?" Manny looked at the paused screen.

We'd stayed at the crime scene for another thirty minutes last night. I'd walked through the whole house, looking for anything that might take us a step closer to finding the identity of the killer. Colin had joined me, but we'd found nothing. By the time we'd returned to the villa, I'd known that I was not going to get much sleep. My mind had been racing with all the information we'd gathered and was trying to find the link between it all.

I'd only slept for three hours. Then my mind had woken me up with the need for data. When Colin had woken fifteen minutes later, we'd agreed that working was better than tossing and turning in the bed. We'd come down to the living room to find Vinnie and Francine already in front of the television, chatting to Pink.

Pink had taken the responsibility of explaining the workings of the game very seriously and had suggested they played until the third level before he went into any detail. As soon as he and Vinnie had defeated the gargantuan soldier with a range of weapons and unnatural strength, the key to the third floor of the castle had appeared and Pink had paused the game.

"I was just about to explain Drestia to Genevieve," Pink said.

"And me." Roxy waved her hand in the air. "I also want to understand this castle world."

Manny nodded. "Explain."

"Who's that?" The open friendliness on Pink's face was gone. It was difficult to gauge where he was looking since he was still looking into the camera. I looked around and saw Andor standing behind the sofa. Vinnie had insisted he return to the villa with us instead of going to his apartment. He'd said Andor looked like crap and needed to sleep soon and a lot. I didn't think Andor had got much sleep. His hair was wet and neatly combed and he was wearing fresh clothes. Yet he appeared exhausted. I looked closer. No, his pallor was that of an ill person.

"I'm Andor Garas." He coughed and shook his head in annoyance. It took him a few seconds to calm his breathing and he walked around the sofa to sit on the other reclining chair. "I'm the detective in Budapest who got your friends involved in this case. You must be the other IT genius."

"Pink." Pink's focus changed to a different part of his monitor. "Genevieve?"

"Yes?"

Pink smiled like he always did when he realised he wasn't being clear with me.

"Garas is fine." Manny slumped into the chair. "Now talk."

Pink didn't. I hated that I couldn't see on what or whom his eyes were focused, but I suspected it was me. I sighed. "Andor can be trusted. He's proven himself."

"Okay then." Pink winked. "Manny, you and Andor missed us playing through the first two levels of the game, so

I'll explain briefly. The purpose of this game is to get to the tower room. It is the seventh level that no one has ever reached. A few people have managed to get to the sixth level, but every time they are defeated before they get the chance to retrieve the scroll."

"What scroll?" Manny asked.

"We don't know." Colin put his control on the armrest next to him. "At first I didn't think much of it, but now that we know the game is strongly connected to the killer, I'm thinking that the scroll might give us valuable information."

"You sound very sure, Frey." Manny narrowed his eyes. "What did you find?"

Colin's lips thinned. "I'm pissed off that I didn't notice it earlier. The game is fast-moving and there isn't a lot of time to appreciate the art in every single room."

"Just spit it out, Frey."

"Last night, I was looking at the artworks that have gone through the hands of Rubique Art over the years." Colin's nostrils flared when he exhaled hard. "Every single one of the paintings I've seen in the first two levels has been sold by Rubique Art."

"And we know that the grandfathers of four of our victims used to own Rubique Art." Francine tucked her feet under her. "Tell them what else you found."

"Rubique Art is no longer operational." Colin pushed his hands through his hair. "The last painting they sold was fifteen years ago. That was five years before the death of Grandpa Udvaros. He'd lived the longest of all the grandpas, he was the last to go. With him the art dealership ceased to exist."

"Nobody inherited it?" Roxy asked. "Isn't that a bit odd?"

"Most definitely, yes," Colin said. "They never made any attempt to sell the business. I wasn't able to find any of their last will and testaments, but from public records, I couldn't find anything indicating that it was bequeathed to anyone. Rubique Art just ceased to exist."

"What about the paintings in their possession when the last grandpa died?" Andor asked.

"There were none. They had finished trading in artworks and had cleared out their inventory as soon as Grandpa Szabo died. He was second to go."

"They wanted to make sure there was nothing for the authorities to look into once they were all gone."

"That's my thinking too." Colin glanced at me. "And I think we can all agree that the Rubique Art paintings showing up in the game is strong enough circumstantial proof to confirm that the game and the killer are connected."

Manny grunted and looked back at Pink's face on the screen. "The game?"

"This is technically an action game, but there are some things that set it apart." Pink counted on his fingers. "Adventure and strategic elements. You don't often find them in action games. Actually, I've never come across a game that so effectively uses all these elements together. Action games are usually very fast, a constant attack. It's usually a war-type game where you have to shoot and run your way out of a situation, pick up some bonus points and extra weapons or ammunition along the way. But the point is to keep moving. And do it fast. The faster the game, the bigger the challenge and the more gamers like it. Winning it means that they were quick on their feet and not intimidated by the onslaught of action around them."

"Drestia is action, but it's also cerebral." Colin enjoyed the game. "You have to know history and art to work your way through each room and each level. Some rooms are not important. Those rooms are easy to spot because of the conflict in décor and art. If everything in the room doesn't hail from the exact same era, that room was designed to waste your time and will cost you points and possibly your life."

"Only in the game." I needed to clarify it. I'd been horrified when Colin had told me that the first time. "Not your real life."

"Kinda debatable, girlfriend." Francine raised both eyebrows. "Maybe not the game, but a lot of people have lost their lives so far."

"True." The corners of Colin's mouth turned down. He looked at Manny. "There are booby traps in each room, false floors, false doors, etcetera. Small clues help you avoid those traps so you can look for the key."

"Those old keys you guys collected in each room?" Roxy asked.

"Yes." Pink leaned closer to the camera. This was the most animated I'd seen him in a long time. Part of it was obviously his enjoyment of the game, but I strongly suspected it was the fact that he was needed in this case that gave him the energy which was now visible in his gestures. "You can't access the next room unless you have the key. Each varies in difficulty as to where the key is hidden. Apart from the traps, there are also soldiers protecting the key. They are dressed in gear from the same era as the room. Colin can tell you more about that."

"It's really quite impressive," Colin said. "Their armour, weapons, everything corresponds exactly to that era. If not, then that room itself is a trap. So in order to find the key, you have to avoid the traps, find a weapon appropriate to the same era and defeat the soldier or soldiers. Doing it alone is doable, but it's easier when we're playing in teams."

"When we're in a team, there are more soldiers and more traps, but we have more to work with," Vinnie said. "When Colin teams up with us, Pink and I do the fighting and he does the searching. That's why we've come so far in this game."

"One thing that I didn't notice—"

"None of us noticed it, Colin." Pink looked decidedly displeased. "It's frigging embarrassing."

"What?" Manny's tone conveyed his impatience.

"We didn't notice Három's logo." Pink looked disgusted. "Once Genevieve pointed it out last night, I now see it every time we look for the key."

"And where the logo is, the key is right under it, next to it or on top of it," Colin said. "Every time."

Roxy patted Vinnie's arm. "In your defence, that logo has been so smartly interwoven in the artwork, furniture and design, I'm not surprised they didn't see it. If Genevieve hadn't pointed a few of those out, I would never have seen them myself."

Roxy was correct. The more I saw of this game, the more impressed I was with its creator. And the more convinced I was that the creator was also the killer. Why else would there be so many connections?

"There is no end to the soldiers. They just keep coming until we find the key," Pink said. "The moment we get the key, the remaining soldiers disappear and we're into the next room or the next level. Some levels have only four rooms, some double that."

"The soldiers make it hard to find and get to the key," Vinnie added. "It can be very distracting when you have to fight three soldiers at the same time and look for the key. That's why we've decided to divide and conquer."

"And conquer we did." Pink turned his gaze which I supposed was towards Manny. "The last battle was epic. Vinnie and I had already killed dozens of soldiers and were pinned down. If it wasn't for Colin killing a few with his great archery skills, we would've been toast and that would've been game over."

"Archery? As in bows and arrows?" Manny stared at the ceiling. "Why do people play these things?"

"Escapism, fun, relaxation, competitiveness, need for winning." Pink shrugged. "Pick one."

Roxy cleared her throat dramatically. "So, I did some research."

"Oh, heavens." Manny slumped even deeper into his chair.

"Shush, you." She dismissed Manny with a single wave and straightened her shoulders. "Did you know that almost a hundred and nine billion dollars in game revenues will be generated this year? Across the globe. How's that for crazy money? And that's from two point two billion gamers."

"Bloody hell!" Manny sat up and looked at Francine. "Are those numbers real?"

"Sure are." She winked at Roxy when the latter fell against Vinnie in offence at Manny's disbelief. "Gamers are also some of the easiest people to hack. Because they are online all the time, they become desensitized to just how vulnerable they are. There is this illusion of community and friendship that makes them let their guards down. I can't tell you how many times gamers discovered that the file they'd been sent to download was actually a virus. They were hoping they'd get shortcuts and extra weapons or ways to get bonus points when they opened the file."

"The gaming industry has their own celebrities," Vinnie said. "They earn thousands of dollars in advertising fees when they play live online. And I tell you, it's really something to watch these guys work. When the best of the best go against each other it's better than watching wrestling or an action movie. These guys are sick."

"Ill, or are you using that word in the same inane manner as Nikki?" I hated that expression.

"The same smart manner as the little punk." Vinnie winced when Roxy pinched him. "Sorry, Jen-girl. Talking about this makes me forget my manners."

Manny's mouth dropped open as he stared at Vinnie, then at Roxy and back at Vinnie. "The end is nigh."

"Shut up, old man." Vinnie put his arm around Roxy's shoulders and pulled her tightly against him. "At least I *have* manners to forget."

"Boys, boys." Francine lifted her tablet. "I've been recording the game this time around. I'm also taking random screenshots that we can study later to see if there's something we've missed."

"I think we'll find plenty." I got up and walked to the television. I leaned forward and looked at the delicate carvings on the legs of the writing table next to the window. This room was from the eighteenth century and the table was a beautiful example of the furniture from that era. "This looks like an emblem."

"Huh." Francine swiped and tapped her tablet screen. "Let me put this into a reverse image searc… Oh, my God. Oh, wow. This is…"

I turned around and walked to her. "What?"

"It's the emblem, logo, shield thingie of the school where Ms Taikon taught."

"The first victim?" Pink asked.

"Yup." She looked up at me. "Think we're going to find more clues like this?"

"We'll have to look."

"That means we'll have to play." Colin took the controller from the armrest next to him and looked at Vinnie. "Ready, Vin?"

"Born ready, dude."

"Hey there." Pink waved at the camera. "We have another guest, guys."

I turned around. Olivia was standing in the doorway, much like Manny had earlier. She was also still wearing her pyjamas. Unlike ours, hers were elegant. The rich burgundy silk long trousers were matched by a fitted short-sleeve night shirt. But like all of us, she looked tired.

She waved at the camera and smiled when Pink waved again. Manny ordered her to sit in the last available chair and she clicked her heels. "Sir, yes, sir!"

Pink laughed. "I like you."

"Everyone does." Olivia sat down crossed-leg on the chair and stared at the television screen. "What can I do?"

Her question gave me an idea. "How much did you retain from helping Francine with the research into the victims?"

"Help?" Olivia's insulted expression was fake. "She helped me. Ask *her* if she remembers anything. I have complete recollection."

Francine laughed and Colin's smile took some of the strain from his expression as he looked at Olivia. "You did have an incredible memory."

"Still do."

There was no deception or boasting in her nonverbal cues. "Good. While Vinnie, Pink and Colin play the game, look for anything that has relevance to the victims."

"Like the school logo."

"Exactly."

She wiggled in her seat and rubbed her hands. "I'm ready."

"I'll pay attention to the artworks." Colin's lips thinned. "I'm sure we'll find more paintings from Rubique Art in each of the next rooms."

"How many more levels?" Manny asked.

"Five." Pink settled back into the sofa. "We've done the first six many times, so it won't take us too long to get to the last level."

"I'm not going to join you guys for this game." Francine opened her laptop and put her tablet on the sofa next to her. "I'm going to keep an eye on what's happening behind the scenes while you're playing."

"Do you think the killer will be active?" Colin asked.

"I don't know. But I'm definitely going to keep a close watch on the data flow from the gaming company's IP."

"Will this require your full attention?" I hoped it wouldn't.

"Nope." Francine buffed her nails on her shoulder. "I can do more than one thing at a time. What do you need?"

"Information about Arany, the gaming company." I needed to be prepared when we visited it later this morning.

"I'll send everything I find to everyone's devices." She raised one hand to stop me. "Not to everyone in the world, just to the devices of everyone on this case. To us."

I nodded.

"What should I look for?" Roxy looked at Manny, then at me. "Anything specific?"

"The only other clue left is Három's triangle," Vinnie said. "Why don't you help Genevieve find them?"

Her laugh was short and genuine. "She'll see it way before me."

"I can't be that certain that I'll notice the logo immediately." I registered her expression and barely contained my impatience. "I'm not placating you. You should know better than to think I would waste time with something so nonsensical. I do, however, believe that together we can find the logos quicker."

"And get the keys quicker," Pink added.

"And go to the next level quicker." Vinnie kissed the top of Roxy's head. "Find us those triangles, Rox."

"Are we going to discuss this to bloody death or are you going to play this stupid game?" Manny crossed his feet, the teddy bear slippers in contrast to the annoyance on his face.

"Sir, yes, sir." Pink winked at the camera. I didn't understand why Olivia tried to hide her laugh with a cough.

I didn't have time to think about that. Pink touched one of the thumbsticks on the controller to start the next level. For the following three hours, the only times we spoke were to point out Három's logos and to take note of Rubique Art paintings and hidden clues directly associated with the victims.

Olivia impressed me. She was quick to notice these clues. One was the birthdate of victim seven in Roman numerals repeatedly carved into a frame of a Rubique Art painting. Another was the name of victim four's business engraved on the spine of a set of encyclopaedias in a nineteenth-century room. The amount of detail the designer of this game had included in each room decimated any doubt we had that this was the work of the serial killer.

I watched in fascination as Vinnie and Pink effectively did most of the fighting, allowing Colin to get hidden caches of weapons, bonus points and extra strength. Because they were playing the game as a team, Colin could share these findings with the other two. Which he did. It made them stronger and more effective in protecting Colin's avatar to rush to the hiding place of the key the moment Roxy or I pointed out Három's logo.

Each level was harder. Not only were the enemy soldiers larger in size, strength and numbers, but it also became harder to locate the logo. The killer had hidden it some places so cleverly that Vinnie and Pink were shouting at us to hurry before they died. I had to remind myself each time that they were talking about their avatars and not themselves. I marvelled at how blurred the lines between the game and reality were becoming.

"Dude!" Vinnie fell back into the sofa from where he'd been sitting on the edge. "That was… insane."

Pink nodded. "We've never reached the second-last level this quickly."

"And none of us have ever finished it." Nikki had joined Pink two levels ago and was staring away from the camera at their television screen. "This was the most beautiful, amazing, epic game I've watched. You guys rock!"

"Team work, punk." Vinnie rested his head on Roxy's shoulder and closed his eyes.

"This is intense." Colin stretched his shoulders and grunted softly. "I need a five-minute break."

"Maybe you guys would like to eat something?" Andor lifted his chin towards the three trays on the low coffee table. "I raided the kitchen."

And none of us had even noticed his disappearance or when he'd brought in the food. Knowing my brain and my character, I'd already decided that I would avoid these types of games from now on. It was simply too easy for me to get lost in a world created to provide non-stop stimulation. My usual obsessive need to see a task to fruition was making it difficult to agree to a break. I wanted us to go through to the last level and complete the mission.

"Ooh! Food!" Francine put her laptop next to her and took a small plate. "Andor, you're the best."

He smiled. "You were all so into the game that I was wondering if my stomach was the only one complaining about being empty."

"Oh, mine has been growling since the little punk gave Pink an energy bar." Vinnie glanced at the monitor with Pink. "Where is she?"

"Gone to make coffee." He rolled his shoulders. "I could also do with a break."

"How're you feeling?" Roxy's expression and tone changed. It was very specific to when she asked questions about someone's physical wellbeing. I wondered if that was the tone she used with her patients.

Pink took his time to answer. When he looked into the camera, there was only sincerity on his face. "The best I've felt in months. It's good to have a purpose."

"You have a purpose, silly." Nikki sat down next to him. "Get better."

"I am better." He took a coffee mug from her with a smile. "I know my body still needs time, but man, I really needed this challenge. I've been going out of my mind."

"An expression, love." Colin smiled at me before he also helped himself to the stacks of sandwiches. I hoped Andor hadn't left chaos behind in the kitchen. Cook would be most displeased. Colin looked back at me. "Want some?"

I looked from the neatly arranged sandwiches to Andor and back. Only now that everyone was eating had I become aware of my own hunger. It took three bars of Mozart's Piano Concerto No. 5 in D major before I could rationalise with myself. I knew how clean the kitchen was. I knew how pedantic Cook was about the freshness of all the products in his kitchen. And I'd come to trust Andor. "I'll have some."

"So, I found something." Francine delicately wiped her mouth and leaned towards her laptop.

"Did you find our killer?" Manny's question appeared flippant, but I observed the seriousness behind it.

"Kinda." She smiled when everyone froze for a second. "I'm now going to call her a 'her'. Why? Because her avatar's name is Lilly."

I took the plate Colin held out to me. "I feel confident that the creator of this game is female. I watched every room, every level with great scrutiny. Working on generalisations, there is enough evidence that leads me to believe this concept was conceived in the mind of a woman. But I need to emphasise that I'm working on generalisations."

"So noted, Doc." Manny looked at Francine. "Where is she?"

"Don't know. And don't get huffy with me. I've been looking for her, following even the smallest trace I could find of her, but she's good."

"Not as good as you," Pink said.

Francine raised both eyebrows, her expression serious. "I'm not so sure about that anymore. The more I learn about her skills, the more I worry."

"Stop worrying and find her." Manny stared at Francine. "You are better than her."

Her smile was instant and filled with affection. "I'll find her bony butt."

"And her real ID," Manny added.

"As soon as I finish this delicious sandwich." She raised the sandwich and smiled at Andor.

He inhaled to say something, but instead coughed. This time was not as strong as before, but it was enough for me to put my uneaten sandwiches back on the coffee table. I knew one couldn't catch a virus from someone with seasonal allergies, but a single sneeze could send a hundred thousand germs into the air. An average cough expelled around three thousand droplets of saliva.

"I'm ready when you are." Pink waved his controller in the air. "I can't wait to see what's waiting for us on the other side of that door."

"Most likely some monster enemy." Vinnie pushed the rest of his sandwich in his mouth and spoke around it. "Ready."

Colin put his plate down. He'd only eaten half his sandwich. He picked up the controller. "I won't be surprised if we're walking into a trap, gentlemen. Keep your eyes open."

Chapter SEVENTEEN

"PINK, AT YOUR six!" Vinnie's avatar didn't hesitate. The old man rushed into the room, his sword raised over his head. Pink's avatar swung around in time to run a dagger through the torso of a soldier twice her size.

The small female avatar's size had counted in her favour numerous times during this and the previous games I'd watched. It was harder for the oversized warriors to aim down at her. She was also faster and frequently killed them by destroying their knees. The weapons Pink had acquired for her with Colin's help were infused with magic and could cut through the usually impenetrable body armour of the soldier now bleeding out on the floor.

Colin's avatar had caused much scorn when Manny had first seen it. Francine had chosen it and had rejected any objections Colin had made. Manny on the other hand had reminded Colin four times that an avatar would never make him a Robin Hood. I'd looked at the avatar's mediaeval outfit always used for the legendary hero and had wondered about Manny's words. The tales of the valiant outlaw who'd stolen from the rich to help the poor in late-mediaeval England indeed had similarities to Colin's life and work.

That avatar now pulled an arrow from the quiver on his back and ran into the room. The well-aimed arrow ripped through the neck of the warrior who had been about to run Vinnie through with his sword. Colin's avatar continued to shoot one arrow after the other, nine out of ten doing permanent if not fatal damage. A few times the avatar stilled while Colin looked around the room, inspecting the era, furniture and art.

This was definitely not the room holding the treasure—the scroll. It was a large ante-room, mediaeval in style. Plain wooden benches lined a stone wall, a fire burning low in the open hearth in the opposite wall. Three chairs were upturned on the edge of a worn carpet in the centre of the room. A chandelier hung low from the ceiling, only five of the nine candles lit.

"I don't see the key." Roxy's voice was strained. "Genevieve?"

I didn't answer. I'd been looking at every painting, every carving to find a triangle with one open corner, but still couldn't see Három's logo.

"Bloody hell." Manny was sitting on the edge of his seat, his hands pressed on his knees, ready to take action. "Trip wire at the right of the carpet."

I looked closer. If any of the three avatars had moved towards the window, they would've stepped on the very thin rope stretched tightly along the edge of the carpet. I didn't see where it led to and had no idea what would happen if that rope was to be touched.

"Booby traps." Vinnie leaned to his left as he got the old man avatar to kill the warrior on his left. "Rox, Jen-girl, find the fucking triangle key."

"Shit!" Colin's avatar rushed to close the door. Nine more warriors had managed to enter the room and Colin closed the door in the faces of dozens more. He turned his avatar back to face the room, nocking an arrow.

The moment he closed the door, I saw it. "There! The logo is on the door handle, the key inside the lock."

Colin's avatar swung around and dropped the bow and arrow. Vinnie, Colin and Pink had thought at first that this was a typical action game where they had to defeat every last enemy before entering the next room or level. Purely by mistake they had discovered that touching the triangle would do that for them. Colin's avatar reached out to the door handle.

"Colin, behind you!" Francine's fists were pressed against her cheeks, her bottom lip caught between her teeth.

Colin's avatar dropped to the floor and turned around in one movement. He threw a dagger at the looming warrior's head. It flipped handle over blade a few times before penetrating the warrior's left eye, blade first. The warrior stumbled backwards, giving Colin time to grab his bow and shoot two arrows at the warrior. One entered his other eye, the other arrow his throat. The warrior slumped to the ground.

Darkness entered the edges of my vision, warning me of an impending shutdown. No matter how hard I tried to remind myself this wasn't real, my brain wasn't capable of distinguishing the difference.

"Dude!" Vinnie's avatar was in the far corner of the room, fighting off four warriors. The old man was holding his sword with his left hand, his right arm completely severed. I swallowed and pushed the rest of the Mozart piano concerto Allegro into my panicked mind.

Pink's young avatar with her pink hair and black-rimmed glasses jumped high in the air, swung her sword over her head and decapitated a warrior. She landed in a crouch, but was not fast enough to avoid the battle axe coming down at her. A millisecond before the axe entered her skull, a bright light flashed and everything froze.

A flimsy curtain in front of the windows moved lazily in the wind. It was completely silent. In the game and in the living room. Then the warriors collapsed. As one they just fell to the floor, their weapons making hollow sounds as they hit the stone floor and carpet.

Colin's avatar was standing, his hand still stretched out to where the door handle had been. The wall and door had disappeared. I gasped.

"Holy, bloody, fucking hell!"

"Motherbleeper."

"Shit." Colin's eyebrows were high on his forehead. He leaned forward, slowly shaking his head.

"What?" Vinnie's muscle tension increased, his eyes searching the television screen for new enemies.

"This is an exact replica of King's office." I was astounded at how precise the duplication was. The modern sofa was there, as was the nineteenth-century coffee table and the four wingback chairs surrounding it, as well as all the art on the walls.

"Oh." Vinnie relaxed slightly. "Is this it then? We've reached the last level?"

"Seems so." Colin's avatar walked to a large tapestry hanging on the wall. "Wow. King had the exact same in his office."

"Which means the killer has a very close connection to King." Olivia was also sitting on the edge of her seat. "There is no way anyone could get all the details right without spending a lot of time in this room."

"You're right." Vinnie's old man walked to the bookshelves. "There's a lot of stuff here. Are these books the same as well?"

I looked at the titles. The killer must have spent a lot of time designing this virtual room. She had even got the detail of King's first repair task right. But there was an addition. "The scroll."

"Where?" Colin leaned closer to the screen.

"On the coffee table that King's dad helped him restore."

"So it is." Colin's avatar walked to the coffee table and picked up the scroll. Without any other action, the scroll rolled down. Colin frowned. "It's in English."

"And it's not even encrypted." Francine's voice was a pitch higher in surprise.

"She's not been hiding from us." The more I thought about it, the clearer it became.

"You're right." Andor scratched his unshaved chin. "If anyone had paid closer attention and had looked into the murders before us, they would've seen the pattern."

"She didn't really hide the livestreaming either. And she hid it rather badly." Francine tilted her head. "The only thing she hid was her identity." Her eyes narrowed and she grabbed her laptop and began to type with single-minded focus.

"What does the scroll say?" Nikki squinted at the screen, but didn't move closer.

"'You're too late.' And, 'Come and get me.'" Colin's voice was a mere whisper. "Why did she write this in English?"

"Huh." Andor coughed once, then put his hand over his throat. "That's a bleeping good question."

"If she's Romani, why isn't it in Hungarian?" Roxy asked.

"Because she knew we were coming for her." I pointed at the family photo on King's desk. The one he had of his family was replaced with a photo of Colin, Manny and Andor standing outside Antal Udvaros' house. "That photo was taken the day before yesterday. It must have been a few seconds before I left the house to join you outside."

"It's from a very high angle." Pink stared at the television. He leaned forward. "Yup. Most likely a security camera on a lamp post or something like that."

"She knows we've been looking for her."

"Then we'd better go and bloody get her." Manny turned to Francine. "Tell me you have her name and her address."

Francine's mouth was slightly agape as she looked at the monitor of her laptop. "I do. I have her name, her address and… wow… quite a bit more."

"Name first." Manny leaned forward.

"Lila Farkas."

"Lila? That's mighty close to Lilly, as in the same name she used for her avatar." Colin blinked. "That's brazen."

"She's been brazen the whole time." Andor rubbed his throat. "She wanted us to find her. Maybe even wanted us to stop her."

"Or she just wanted to be noticed," Roxy said softly.

I didn't take part in their speculations, but it was easy to agree with Roxy. If Lila Farkas had been bullied by the likes of Ms Taikon and the others who were known for their racism, it was likely that she craved recognition for who she was as a person, not her race. But that would apply if she was neurotypical. And I wasn't convinced that she was.

"If she's been watching us, then she also knows that we have the scroll." Colin got up. "And she's waiting for us. Where is she?"

"Hold your horses, Frey." Manny sat back in his chair. "We have to be smart about this. How much do we know about this Lila?"

Francine shook her head in disbelief. "Lila Farkas is the designer of Drestia and she also owns Arany, the gaming company."

"Bloody hell." Manny turned to me. "You were right, Doc."

I nodded, but my attention was drawn back to Francine. "You have something else. Something that's disturbing you."

"Disturbing might be the understatement of the year." She turned her laptop so we could see the monitor. "I found her YouTube channel."

"Bleep!" Andor coughed once then got up and leaned in to see the monitor. "She has recordings of the last… six, no, seven deaths." He straightened. "How did you find this? Was it the same as that numbered account?"

"No. But I tried using that recording you found of István Koltai dying. I searched for more videos with the info you sent from that video, but I didn't find anything." She pushed her hair over her shoulder. "Just now I thought about how open she's been with her crimes. So when I searched variations of her name in YouTube, I found this channel under LilKas. It's like—"

"—she wanted us to find it," Andor said.

"Can you put that on the telly?" Manny nodded at Francine's laptop.

"In a sec." She worked on her laptop for a few seconds. Then the image of King's office on the television screen was replaced with a list of videos. "Shall I play them?"

I really didn't want to watch people die, but this was important. "Yes."

"I'll play the most recent first." She tapped on the touchpad of her laptop and a video filled the screen. We were looking at Minister Tibor Bokros' recreational room. He was sitting on the sectional sofa, looking straight at the camera which led me to believe he was looking at the television.

The game controller in his hands and the focus on his face made it clear that he was playing a game. Drestia. The next six minutes were uneventful. The minister shifted a lot while playing the game and exhibited nonverbal cues similar to Vinnie, Pink and the others when their focus was solely on a game.

Then he pushed a controller button and winced. He pressed his fist against his chest, his eyes widening in fear. He looked around and his eyes focused on something to his left. I remembered seeing a house phone against the wall there.

The minister got up, but stood still for three seconds, his facial muscles contracted in pain. Then he grabbed his chest again and collapsed. His head hit the coffee table, which twisted his body as he landed on the floor. He didn't move. He was dead.

I forcefully pushed Mozart's piano concerto in my mind to keep the darkness from taking me. Around me, the others were exclaiming their shock and disgust at what they'd seen. I was just trying to keep my mind from shutting down so I could watch the other videos.

It took me three minutes before I was ready. Francine played the others without pausing between victims. The videos had been carefully cut to only show the last ten minutes in each victim's life. They also appeared unedited or altered in any way.

None of the videos revealed any actionable information that we could use to find Lila. The focus of each video had been only on the victim and his last moments. Watching these people realise they were dying was deeply disturbing.

"Why would anyone want to do this?" Roxy's quiet question broke the horrified silence after the last video finished. "Why watch someone die?"

"To feel vindicated?" Olivia raised one shoulder. "Or it's like you said. She recorded this not so she could watch, but so that she could be caught. Maybe she just wants someone to take notice of her."

"Well, we're bloody taking notice now." Manny pressed his fists against his eyes for a second, then looked at me. "What do you make of this, Doctor Face-reader?"

I stared at the television screen. It was displaying the seven videos in her channel. There were no other videos. Manny asked for my opinion again, this time with irritation in his tone. I didn't answer. My mind had registered something important on the screen and I was waiting for it to reach my cerebral cortex.

I blinked a few times in shock. "The tags she added to each video."

Francine narrowed her eyes. "Yeah, it doesn't make sense. CME1, CME2, CME3. What does that even mean?"

"Did you Google it?" Andor asked.

"Yes, but it came up empty." She shook her head. "The only thing about those tags that makes sense is that they are numbered in chronological order."

"When were they uploaded?" Colin asked.

"All at the same time. Huh. This is recent. They were uploaded after Antal Udvaros' death."

"She knew we would be looking for it." Andor sounded certain of this. "Just like she's been brazen with everything else."

"See me." I pointed at the television screen. "Those tags are asking us to see her."

"Oh, my God!" Francine straightened. "How did I not see this? Of course. 'C' for see and 'ME' for me."

"Am I the only one that thinks this is incredibly sad?" Roxy pushed a curl behind her ear. "She's making sure you guys can find these videos so she'll be noticed. That's heart breaking."

"I know of a case where the serial killer carved 'help me' on all his victims' chests." Andor stared at the television. "There was also the man with paedophile tendencies who committed armed robbery and shot the shop owner in the thigh to make sure he would go to jail. He didn't want to act on his urges and thought kids would be safer if he was in prison."

"Wow." Roxy put her hand over her heart and nodded towards the television. "Maybe this woman is also asking for help. That's sad."

"She's a bloody killer, Roxanne." Manny turned to Francine. "What else do we have on her?"

"Not much yet." Francine was tapping on her tablet. "There are quite a few articles about her. But they're all in Hungarian."

"I'll translate," Andor said.

"In the car." Manny nodded as if he'd come to an agreement about something. "We'll first go to King. He mentioned one of his people who'd become successful in the tech industry. He'll give us more intel on her."

"Why do you need more intel?" Roxy asked.

"Because we don't want to walk into a booby-trapped ambush." Vinnie pointed his controller at the television. "If she created all of that, I won't underestimate her. She's most likely been planning her arrest for years."

"And then we'll go to Arany." Manny nodded again. "If she's not there, at least we'll get to see where she works and speak to the people working for her."

"May I make a suggestion?" Olivia's lips twitched as she looked at Manny's slippers. "You all might want to get dressed."

Chapter EIGHTEEN

"LILA?" KING SAT down heavily on one of the wingback chairs in his office, his face losing colour. "Our Lila? Lila Farkas?"

"We have irrefutable proof, King." The regret on Andor's face was genuine. "I'm truly sorry to bring you this news."

"How? Why?" King shook his head. "This has to be wrong."

Colin sat down on the chair next to King and leaned forward. He rested his elbows on his knees, his posture harmless, his expression kind. "Tell us about Lila."

Manny held out his open hand towards the other chairs and I sat down as well. He remained standing and glared at Andor until the detective took the last wingback chair. I supposed Manny had also noticed that Andor was not looking well.

We'd come here in two SUVs. Andor had arranged with King for a visit while we'd readied ourselves for the day. I felt disconcerted by the change in routine, but had mentally finished writing Mozart's Piano Concerto No. 5 in D major on the way here. It helped, but still I had the most irrational need to start the day again. This time with my routine.

Vinnie and Francine were waiting outside for us, Francine working on three laptops in the back of the second SUV. Vinnie had reluctantly agreed not to join us in the mansion, acknowledging that four of us were already plenty to interview King.

I'd been keen to observe King's reaction. That was going to give us an indication of King's complicity in Lila's crimes. From what I was witnessing at the moment, I could say with confidence that King had no idea Lila had been killing people.

"How many?" King looked at Colin. "First tell me how many people."

Colin glanced at Manny, but didn't heed the latter's warning gaze. "We've found links to fifteen people. Strong links."

"Oh, Lila." King put his hands over his face and shuddered.

"Doc?" Manny's question and inquiring look was becoming more common and familiar.

"He didn't know." I leaned a bit forward to inspect King as he looked at me. "But you're not completely surprised."

He shut his eyes tightly for a few seconds—typical blocking behaviour. Then he straightened his shoulders and rubbed his palms along his thighs a few times, building courage through this self-comforting behaviour. This was not easy for the leader of these people. "I never suspected she would do something like this. But I was surprised—pleasantly surprised—when she became successful and seemed to be content."

"Tell us about her," Colin requested again.

"Lila didn't have an easy start. Her mom was forced to marry really young." He blinked a few times, seeming to organise his thoughts. "You see, those days the leadership had different ways. There are some conventions in our culture that I value above all. But there are a few that I never agreed with."

"And you changed it when you took over the leadership." Andor cleared his throat and held his breath as if trying to avoid coughing.

King's fists pushed into his thighs. "Forcing young girls to marry is simply not right. I won't start a debate about the morality or ethics if girls choose to get married young, but forcing is out of the question for me. Well, Lila's mom was forced. And Lila was the result of that union."

"Why was she forced?" I thought this might be important.

"Because of their family history." King paused. "You see, Lila's great-grandfather died in 1966. He had some business that his wife should've inherited, but there were other business partners involved and she lost everything. In those days, the courts weren't kind to Romani people and gave the white people everything. So a couple of years after the great-grandfather's death, the great-grandmother had even less. The little she'd had, she'd lost in the legal battle. Lila's grandmother must've been about sixteen or seventeen then."

He looked up and left, recalling a memory. "I remember her. She was a quiet girl, a few years younger than me. Her mother was bitter and angry about losing everything. She also saw Lila's grandmother as a huge burden. She wanted to get rid of Lila's grandmother. She married her off to a man in his early twenties and the poor young girl became even quieter.

"Lila's mother was born soon after. History repeated itself and as soon as Lila's mother was old enough, the grandmother married her off too. About five years later, Lila's father died, leaving the mother alone and vulnerable. But she surprised us all. She broke the family cycle. She was one of the first in the community to push her child into early education." He narrowed his eyes. "It was around that time that I became 'King'. Those were funny and hard days. But that's a story for another time.

"Lila wasn't too badly bullied at school. Unlike my Erika." He glanced at the open door leading to the reception area where his niece had received them. "Actually, those two were friends at some time. Then something changed in Lila. Something happened in her first year at university. It broke her. She refused to talk to anyone about that. I couldn't get her to tell me what had been so terrible."

"What do you mean it broke her?" I needed more detail.

"She changed." He shook his head. "No, change might not be the right word. She became worse."

"Worse than what?"

"Than the psychologically unstable girl she was before." He took a moment to control his emotions, wiping his hand over his mouth a few times. "She was always strange. And not in a good way. She'd take pleasure in damaging the other kids' toys and would often set the kids up against each other. A few times I caught her watching the boys beat each other up because of something she'd done. It was her watchfulness and the smile on her face that made me realise there was something not quite right with her.

"And that event that happened at university made it worse. For a few weeks she had that same smile. And then a few students were involved in an awful scandal. This was about nine years ago. Yes, yes. Nine years. These students' social media accounts were hacked as well as their phones. All their private messages, all their posts and texts were published online and also sent to everyone in their contacts list.

"The fallout was horrifying. Two boys were expelled from the university because of photos and boasting about how they had sex with girls after drugging them. That in itself was bad enough. But soon after they were expelled, the one boy killed himself. The next day a boy who wasn't expelled did the same. His emails and online history revealed that he had homosexual interests. It was devastating to everyone.

"The father of the first boy who killed himself is a very rich lawyer and he paid a private investigator to look into what happened. The police didn't have the ability to look into this type of cybercrime then. Long story short, they discovered links to Lila, but nothing the prosecutor could use to charge her with. It was enough for the university though to expel her."

He sighed. "She moved into her own apartment and for a year didn't come home at all. When she finally did, it was with the news that she'd started a business and she was doing well."

"The gaming company," Colin said.

"Yes. Arany. Do you know that the word 'Arany' means gold? She was going for gold when she registered her company name. But that was before she developed that bestselling game. The first few years she built her reputation and success with different games." He laughed softly. "Once she tried to explain these things to me, but I just don't get it. I'm not really interested in these game things, you know?"

"Hmm." Manny's sardonic expression made King laugh again.

"About four years ago, something else bad happened. Again I don't know what. But for a year Lila again avoided us.

When she came back, it was with that successful game and her smile. That smile that told me something was very wrong with her."

"Is there anyone who might know what happened to her?" This information would give me valuable insight into Lila's motivation. "Anyone she trusted?"

King thought about this. "The only one I ever saw her spend time with was Erika." He got up and walked to the reception area.

"Do you think she's a psychopath?" Andor was looking at me.

"I don't have enough information to make that diagnosis." I registered his expression and held up one hand. "Or any other diagnosis for that matter. People read a few articles in psychology magazines and think they can easily diagnose or spot a psychopath or sociopath. It is not that easy. Sometimes their behaviour makes it easy to recognise these traits, but often these people learn how to integrate very well into society. Their family and friends might just think that they're very passive-aggressive or narcissistic. On the other hand, gifted individuals and even people on the autism spectrum can often be misdiagnosed as psychopathic or sociopathic."

Colin's hand on my forearm stopped my diatribe. It didn't happen often, but there were times that I would start on a topic and find it extremely difficult to stop, even when I registered the disinterest of my audience. I swallowed a few times while staring at the strong hand on my forearm.

"Erika says she doesn't know what happened to Lila." King walked into the office, followed by his niece. Today she was wearing bright blue linen trousers and a colourful top.

Her hair was in a ponytail which made her look young and feminine.

"She never spoke about it." Erika stood next to King's chair and put her hand on the back of the chair when he sat down. Her fingers tightened around the upholstery until her knuckles were white.

This got my attention. I studied her face. She was trying to appear relaxed, but the tightening of the *orbicularis oculi* muscles under her eyes and the *orbicularis oris* muscles around her mouth was revealing. I tilted my head. "You know something else. Something important. Something dangerous. Ah, dangerous indeed."

Her hand flew up to cover her suprasternal notch—the visible dip between the neck and the sternum. "I don't know where she is."

"I didn't ask you where she was."

Erika looked close to tears. King twisted in his seat, took her hand and pulled her to stand next to him. His hand on hers was gentle. As was his voice. "Erika, Lila's been killing people. We need to stop her."

"I didn't know she was killing…" A tearful hiccough stopped her denial. She wiped her cheeks with the back of her free hand. "I swear. I didn't know."

"I believe you." It wasn't only her nonverbal cues that convinced me. That level of distress was almost impossible to fake.

Her shoulders slumped. "Thank you."

"Tell me what you do know." My tone might have been harsh, but I didn't care. "What dangerous information you have."

She sat down on the armrest of King's chair and crossed her arms in a full self-hug. "Lila is planning something. I don't know what, but she wanted me to join her."

"Tell us exactly what she told you." Colin's tone was gentle.

Erika responded to that and relaxed marginally. "Lila and I bonded when I was bullied at school. She phoned me almost every day to remind me that I was strong and smart and could do and be anything I wanted to. Those were the nice things she said. The rest of it was rants against everyone else. Against all men, all white people, all leadership, all institutions, all authorities. Basically, she hated everyone who wasn't Romani and female."

"Because of her own experiences," Colin said.

"I think she was bullied much more than me. She once mentioned a dragon teacher who used to pinch her until she had bruises all over her back."

"I didn't know about that." King's frown was deep. "Why didn't she tell us?"

Erika blinked a few times. "There's a lot she didn't tell anyone. She was terribly bullied at school. Especially by that teacher."

"Ms Taikon," Manny said.

"Yes!" Erika looked at Manny. "That was the teacher's name. But when I asked her about it, she refused to say anything else. When that thing happened at uni, she refused to tell me what those students did to her."

"You have a suspicion." I could see it clearly on her face.

"All the students whose stuff were published online were male. They were all boys from the same group of friends."

"Holy hell." Manny's words were whispered, but sounded loud in the quiet room. "You think she was raped?"

Erika's *mentalis* muscles contracted in her chin, making it quiver. "I have no proof, but there were rumours."

"Why didn't you tell me?" King looked devastated by these revelations.

"What could you have done?" Erika wiped her cheeks again. "I know Lila. The more you try to get closer to her, the more she'll push you away. If you or anyone had tried to get her to talk, she would've withdrawn completely and she needed us. She needed you."

"I've failed her." King dropped his head forward, emotional pain plainly visible on his face. "I should've done something."

"When?" My question was sincere. "If she'd always shown a proclivity for creating hostile situations and taking revenge on people who wronged her, when would you have been able to do something?"

"She's right." Manny pushed his hands in his trouser pockets. "These people seldom respond to interventions."

"You can help her now." Colin addressed both King and his niece. "Help us find her so we can stop her from hurting anyone else."

"She's going to hurt a lot of people," Erika whispered.

"How?" Manny asked.

"I don't know. A few months ago, she asked me if I wanted to get back at everyone who'd ever bullied me. I was so shocked by her unexpected question that I didn't answer immediately. She took that as a 'yes' and told me that she was planning something big. Something that everyone will remember forever. She was tired of always having to defend being Romani and being female. She was going to show everyone that they shouldn't screw with her."

"Do you know what she's planning?" King asked.

"No." Erika shook her head. "When I told her that I didn't feel like I constantly needed to defend being female and Romani, she acted as if I'd slapped her. I felt awful. I told her that I was still her friend, but she shouted at me that I'd betrayed her. She's refused to speak to me since."

We waited a moment while Erika wiped her cheeks and took a few shaky breaths to control her emotions. She looked at me. "But I know that she's planning it for today."

"How do you know that?"

"She told me that it would be on the day that everything changed."

"Oh, my." King glanced at his watch. "Today is the twenty-seventh. It's the same day her roommate at university phoned to say something bad had happened to Lila. I remember because today is my wife's birthday. I went to her university, but couldn't find Lila for two days. When we eventually found her three days later, she refused to tell us what happened. She said everything was okay and we should leave so she could focus on her studies."

"Today." Manny looked at Erika. "Is there anything else you can think of that could help us stop her?"

She thought about it. "No. I don't know where she is and I really don't know what she's planning."

"She might be at her office." King moved to stand up. "I'll get you the address."

"We have it." Manny turned, his feet pointing to the door.

"And we're going there right now."

"Please take care of her." Erika's voice sounded raw from her emotional anguish. "She was a good friend to me once."

Manny nodded, but I saw the deception. He wanted to stop Lila from killing or hurting anyone else. He didn't plan to take care of her.

We spent another three minutes in King's mansion. Andor spoke to King in Hungarian for another minute. His body language told me he was reassuring the older man. He then joined Manny and Francine in the second SUV. Vinnie got into the SUV with us. No one said anything until we were on the main road leading into Budapest city centre.

"What the fuck happened in there?" Vinnie leaned in between the two front seats. I moved closer to the door.

"Lila's had a rough life." Colin gave Vinnie a brief version of what King had told us.

"Yeah. I can see how she wants to take revenge." Vinnie looked at the road in front of us. It was eleven minutes after ten, the morning traffic no longer influenced by workers commuting to their offices.

An annoying ringtone came from my handbag. Colin had explained that it was the theme song to a female superhero animation movie. I sighed, took the phone from my bag and swiped the screen. "You're on speaker."

"Hi, girlfriend." Francine's friendly tone was false. "How are you? I'm well, thank you, and you? I'm well."

"Why are you phoning?" I didn't have the emotional energy for her jesting.

She laughed. "Mister Joy-and-Peace told me you might be interested in what I found."

"I don't know anyone by that name."

"Thanks, Doc." Manny sounded vexed.

Everyone laughed.

"Okay, then. Manny wanted me to tell you what I discovered about Arany."

"Only the relevant parts." Manny's warning made Vinnie snort.

"Quick bio of the company: Started nine years ago by Lila Farkas. She released her first online game two months later. It was an extremely simplified version of Drestia. She employed her first staff member six months later. Then she released another two online games over the next three years. She also employed more people. By the time she released Drestia she had nine people on staff and her company's annual turnover was in the seven figures. In euros, of course.

"Drestia changed everything. Within three months, she hired a full-time accountant and another two people who solely handled social media and customer relations. Arany's turnover that year was in the low eight figures and has been growing like crazy since."

"I hear a 'but' coming on." Vinnie smiled at me when I glanced at him.

"Indeed, my muscled friend. The year after Drestia became big, Lila was invited to World-E."

"What's that?" I asked.

"It's only the third biggest gaming tournament in the world." Francine sounded disappointed in me. "E-sports is huge. And World-E is one of the biggest international tournaments. But with its prize pool it cannot compete with the International. Last year, the International 6's prize pool was twenty point four million dollars. World-E has an attendance of tens of thousands, but online viewers for the tournaments number in the tens of millions."

"What happened with Lila at the event?" I wasn't interested in gaming statistics at the moment.

"Oh, I remember." Andor's voice was slightly muted. He was most likely in the back seat, not close enough to the phone's microphone. "It was a huge scandal in the gaming industry. Even though the majority of gamers came to the tournament to meet Lila and also to take part in her Drestia event, the organisers treated her so badly, it made headlines."

"What do you mean badly?" I asked.

"There were three major attractions, Lila and Drestia were the biggest. The other two were men and their games. The guys got five-star treatment—hotels, limousines, gorgeous VIP rooms at the venue and so on. Lila was told that since the event is taking place in Budapest and she lives here, they weren't approving accommodation or transport for her. She was also put in a tiny, windowless office where she was supposed to meet fans and industry VIPs."

"Why would they do that?"

"Lila hacked their emails and discovered that the organisers—who were all male—were pissed off that she's female. One of them wrote a long rant about how women were infesting the gaming industry and weakening the business with their emotions and biology." Andor coughed. "That also caused an outrage, but by that time everyone was on Lila's side. The organisers paid out an undisclosed sum to Lila in an out-of-court settlement, but it exposed the strong discrimination against women in the gaming industry."

"Not much has changed since then," Francine said. "Female gamers are still discriminated against and female game designers even more so. They are seldom nominated for awards or receive any kind of public acknowledgement."

"Again with the sexism," Manny said. "Is Lila going to kill everyone who ever discriminated against anything?"

Vinnie's phone ringing loudly interrupted our conversation. He looked at the screen before swiping it. "Dude, you're on speaker."

"Hi, all." Pink's voice sounded strained. "I've got Nikki with me."

"And we've got the others on speaker as well." Vinnie looked at my phone and brought his closer so everyone could hear.

"I'm sorry, Doc G! I swear I didn't know." The panic in Nikki's voice brought immediate darkness into my peripheral vision.

Vinnie's hand tightened on his phone. "What's happening, Nix?"

"She got hacked," Pink said.

"Oh, honey." Francine's voice was muted, the sound of her working on her laptop barely audible in the background. "I so hoped I was wrong."

"Someone better tell me what the bloody hell is going on."

Pink cleared his throat. "Francine was worried that Lila could've hacked your devices and asked me to double-check."

"The protection I have on our devices is unhackable." Francine sounded angry and scared. "But with Lila having such success accessing so many people's devices and proving to be really good at hacking, I thought it best to ask Pink to check everything we have in Strasbourg."

"And you're sure all our laptops, tablets or phones are clean?" Manny asked.

"Yes." She sounded sure. "I've been checking every day and I checked again while the guys were playing earlier. Lila might be really good, but I'm better. She wouldn't be able to hide code, a virus, anything from me."

"She wouldn't hide," I said. "If she did, it would be badly concealed, enough so for you to easily find it."

"That's exactly what the virus looked like in Nikki's phone," Pink said.

"Your new phone?" Francine asked. "Did you update the antivirus apps like I told you?"

There was a long pause. "No."

"Ah, Nix."

"I'm sorry, Francine. I was just having so much fun with you guys and then coming back with Émile. I didn't think anyone would want to hack me."

"I've removed the virus and updated all the programs and apps running on her phone." Pink's tone was worried. "But Lila cloned Nikki's phone."

"Which means that she has access to everything Nix has online."

"No." Nikki's voice was thick with emotion and I heard a soft sob. "What if…"

"I know, Nix." Vinnie glared at the phone. "Pink?"

"Daniel is already on his way over and Émile is sending two of his bodyguards. Nikki and Eric will be safer than the president."

"Um…" Andor sounded confused. "Why is this a problem?"

"Because of my dad," Nikki said. "He was a very successful criminal with many enemies. Some of them lost a lot when he died and wouldn't think twice to claim it from me. I've been extremely careful with my social media and online life to keep my identity private. If some of those people find out about me, my life and Eric's life… Oh, Doc G."

"You're safe, Nix." Vinnie's statement sounded like an order. "No one will fucking touch you or Eric."

I couldn't speak. I knew Nikki well enough to know that she was seeking reassurance from me. I couldn't give it to her. I could barely keep the looming shutdown from taking me to that dark safe place.

"Jenny is doing everything she can to stop this woman, Nikki." Colin slowed the car down and turned into a quiet street. He stopped and put his hand on my forearm. "We are all doing everything we can to stop this woman."

"But what if she publishes my life? Shit, I have photos of me and my dad on my phone. And of my dad and some of his old friends." Nikki barely stopped another sob. "Doc G?"

I inhaled to speak, but no words would form in my mouth. The frustration was bringing the darkness closer and I slapped my hand on my thigh. Then I couldn't stop. Vinnie took my phone and Colin used both his hands to grip mine. "Deep breaths, love. Deep breaths."

Vinnie continued speaking to Nikki, Pink and the others, but I was focusing on Colin's hands holding mine. More than ever, Nikki needed me. As welcoming and safe as a shutdown was, I couldn't afford to lose a minute. I needed to know that Nikki and Eric were safe and the only way to do that was to find Lila and prevent her from using whatever data she'd found on Nikki's phone against her.

I inhaled deeply and held my breath for ten seconds. Then I exhaled and tried to relax my hands. It didn't work until the third deep breath. I turned my hands in Colin's and looked into his concerned face. "I'm okay."

He studied me for a few seconds and nodded. "Did you hear that, Nikki?"

"Yeah." She sniffed. "I'm also okay now, Doc G. Go out and kick her butt!"

Vinnie snorted, his expression softening. "We'll all go and kick her butt, Nix. You just listen to Pink and Daniel. And tell Eric he cannot use my aftershave."

She laughed and more of the tension left my muscles. Pink ended the call with reassurances that he was doing everything he could to help us find Lila and keep Nikki safe.

"Ready?" Colin waited for me to nod, then started the SUV again. At the next cross street we turned left.

"What the hell?" Manny grunted. "Garas, what's going on here?"

I didn't hear Andor's answer. Colin stopped the SUV and we stared at the four police cars parked outside the office building that hosted Arany's headquarters. Their lights were flashing and two officers were guarding the door to the building.

There was no place to park, so Colin pulled the SUV next to a parked sedan. "I hope this is nothing bad."

Manny parked behind Colin's SUV and together we walked to the front door. The moment the taller officer noticed Andor, he frowned and said something in Hungarian.

Neither his tone nor his nonverbal cues were friendly.

"Hmm." Andor responded to the officer respectfully, then turned to us. "Captain Palya is inside and waiting for us."

"Did he phone you?" Colin asked. "Do you know what's happening here?"

"No." He turned back to the officer and asked something in Hungarian. The response was clipped. Andor nodded once and pointed us to the door. "They arrived only ten minutes ago. Captain Palya said no one was allowed in unless I managed to show up."

"Curiouser and curiouser." Francine's expression was familiar. Her eyes and mouth moved in that specific way only when she was creating a conspiracy theory.

I was pleased when she didn't share it with us. Instead she followed Andor into the building. The elevator was already on the ground floor and we were on the fifth floor within a minute.

The doors opened to chaos. Two police officers were at a modern reception desk in front of a huge colourful logo. To the left of the desk was a large open space office with slides, a pool table, bright blue, yellow and green sofas and even a trampoline. It looked like a children's playground.

Andor spoke to the officers who pointed us to the end of the open office.

Gathered around a strangely shaped conference table were twelve people, including Captain Palya. Two of the women sitting at the table were crying, one young man was constantly pulling at his full beard and another man was breathing heavily through flared nostrils. We made our way there.

Captain Palya met us halfway. "Ah, my shining star." He

frowned when he took a closer look at Andor. "What's wrong with you?"

"Seasonal allergies." Andor shrugged. "Nothing serious."

"Huh." Captain Palya looked at Manny. "So? What are you doing here?"

"What are *you* doing here?"

"Garas has kept me updated on your progress. So when I heard that there was commotion at Arany, I made sure to get here as soon as I could."

"What commotion?" I hated nebulous statements.

The captain looked at me for a second. "The owner of the company called everyone in for an early meeting this morning. Apparently, that in itself is very strange. She's one of those who works until three in the morning, then wakes up in the middle of the morning and starts working again in the early afternoon."

"The meeting?" Manny asked.

"She told them that the company was bankrupt, she was closing shop and they could all go and fuck themselves."

"What?" Francine's eyes were wide.

"Those were her exact words. These people said she even said the last part in English."

"Where is she?" Colin asked.

"Don't know." Captain Palya looked at Andor. "Now tell me why you're here."

"She's our killer, Cap." Andor was losing even more colour in his face, perspiration beading on his forehead. "And she's planning something for today."

"Today, huh?" The captain rubbed his chin. "These people told me that they are devastated at what this Lila woman did.

Especially since they have their big event tonight."

"What event?"

"The World-E tournament." A man in his late twenties walked to us. He was dressed in what Colin would describe as hipster clothing. His hair was long, but gathered at the top of his head in a man-bun. Vinnie had explained that term to me. He stopped next to Manny. "I'm Rad. And I was Lila's assistant until two hours ago. That bitch! I have no idea what she thinks she's doing."

"What do you think she's doing?" Colin asked.

"Screwing us all." He took a calming breath. "Look, we all knew something was off with her the last few months. Not that she's ever been normal, but hey"—he tilted his head towards the conference table—"it's not like any of us are normal."

"Go on." Colin rolled his hand in a gesture to encourage the man to continue.

"Yeah. Well, she's been even more distant than usual. Normally we have a lot of projects to work on, but the last few months has only been the tournament. She wanted to make sure that the Drestia version we created especially for the competition was going to work flawlessly."

"What competition?" I asked.

"There is a huge competition tonight. Only the best of the best gamers are taking part and the winner will take home three million euros."

"Bloody hell."

Rad looked at Manny. "There's a lot of money in the gaming industry. Guys like you don't know about it, but Lila knew. And she knew how to make even more. That's why I don't believe the bullshit that Arany is bankrupt."

"Then where is the money?" I asked.

"Eva, our accountant, looked. It's all gone. Lila transferred everything last night." He leaned in. "Eva is good. She's not only the best accountant for this type of work, she's also computer-smart."

"Aha." Francine smiled. "She's a hacker."

"I didn't say that."

"Didn't have to. Did she find out where the money went?"

He closed his eyes. "Lila transferred over eleven million euros to several accounts in Switzerland."

"Switzerland?" Andor frowned. "That used to be the go-to country for criminals to hide their money."

"And the obscenely rich to hide their money from the tax man," Francine said. "But Lila putting her millions in Switzerland is a stupid move. Switzerland has been changing their secrecy laws since 2008 and more recently, they've agreed to come in line with international standards of taxation which means more transparency. Her money isn't untraceable there."

"Doesn't matter right now." Rad put his hands on his hips. "We're without money, without a boss and we don't know what to do about the tournament." He looked towards the conference table. "We've worked so hard to make this a success. Everything is set up. Everything is perfect. Tonight's competition will be epic."

"Thank you, Rad." Captain Palya nodded to an officer who took the young man back to the conference table. He looked at me. "So?"

"So what?"

He pushed his glasses up the bridge of his nose and glared at me. "What is your ever-so-expert opinion?"

"About what?"

Vinnie snorted and Manny chuckled. "You have to be more specific when you want answers."

"Was he telling the truth, love?" Colin took my hand and interlaced our fingers.

"Yes."

"Do you have any hypothesis about Lila's motivation for transferring the money?"

I looked at him. "It's the behaviour of someone who has planned their escape. But in this case, it appears that Lila only wanted to create that impression."

"It's like she wants us to find her." Andor looked at me. "To stop her."

"Holy hell." Manny turned to Captain Palya. "How secure is the tournament venue?"

"Completely secure." There was no hesitation in his answer. "With all the terrorist, immigration and political crap going on, we've been on full alert. The place has been cleared by the bomb squad twice. We have numerous measures in place to control who and what goes in and out. All the participants know that there will be extra security procedures and it's generally been accepted in good spirits. These guys just want to go and play games and meet their idols. They don't care that we have anti-terrorist squads moving among them."

Andor's phone rang and he glanced at the screen. His eyebrows lifted. "Gotta take this."

He walked towards the elevators, speaking into his phone while Captain Palya described in detail the security the city had arranged for the tournament. Something in Andor's posture caught my attention and I watched his back as he slowed to a stop. He swayed to one side, then the phone dropped from his hand a moment before his legs collapsed under him.

I couldn't speak. My breath caught in my throat and darkness pushed in on my vision. I shook Colin's hand holding mine and with my other hand pointed towards the elevators.

"Shit!" Colin let go of my hand and ran to Andor. He was lying on the floor. Not moving.

"What the fuck?" Vinnie joined Colin while Captain Palya shouted instructions into his two-way radio. Manny snapped at two of the employees when they got up to see what happened. They sat down immediately, fear in their eyes.

This was too much for me. First Nikki and now Andor. I forced the overture of Mozart's *Don Giovanni* into my mind, but it didn't work. The music that usually calmed me had no effect. The darkness that preceded a shutdown was winning. There was nothing I could do.

Chapter NINETEEN

"JENNY?" COLIN'S WARM hand rested on my forearm. I didn't stop writing Mozart's Piano Sonata No. 8 in A minor. I wasn't ready yet. I'd already written the first two movements and was thirteen bars away from completing the Presto. Colin's hand tightened. "Love?"

I shook my head and carefully added the quaver rest on the music sheet.

His phone rang and he squeezed my arm. "I'm going to take this in the living room. I won't be long."

I didn't respond. He got up and I heard his footsteps against the Italian tiles. We were at the villa. My shutdown had not been as severe as others. With some shutdowns, it was a complete blackout where I had no recollection of the time I'd been rocking and keening. This time I'd been mostly aware of my surroundings, but had wrapped my arms around my torso and had refused to let go.

Colin had managed to get me into the SUV, where I'd wrapped my arms around my knees and had started keening softly. In that moment I'd so deeply despised being a prisoner to my own mind. No amount of Mozart or deep breathing would release me from that powerful hold my mind had over my body. I'd learned the only course of action was to wait it out and work as hard as I could to stay calm. It hadn't been easy.

Even as I was writing the staccatissimo harmonic triads, my mind kept straying back to Andor's prone body on the floor in front of the elevators. In the short time he'd been in my life, I'd come to respect him and like him. There was a time I hadn't allowed myself to have personal connections to other people. I'd suffered fewer shutdowns in that time. Caring about people made my mind more vulnerable to overstimulation and shutdowns or, even worse, meltdowns.

My concern over Nikki's safety was putting immense strain on my mind. Since the first day when I'd given her the news that her dad had died, she'd become an integral part of my life. She'd never allowed my need for personal space, my character and my discomfort with emotions to stop her from loving me and pushing her way into my life.

I loved her. And the thought of Lila putting Nikki's life in danger by revealing her whereabouts to the ruthless enemies of Nikki's father Hawk brought the darkness back. I forced my mind to focus on Daniel and Pink keeping Nikki safe, and Émile's bodyguards making sure no one came close to her.

Knowing that Andor was being taken care of by the best doctors in Budapest aided in calming me. I recalled very little of what Colin and Vinnie had told me in the SUV while driving to the villa. But I did remember Colin repeatedly telling me that Captain Palya had vowed he would make sure Andor had the best care possible.

I drew the final crotchet rest in the F-clef and tilted my head while studying the page in front of me. All the note stems were angled exactly the same, the flags as well. One semiquaver rest was not to my liking, but everything else pleased me. I took the other seventeen pages of handwritten music and added this page to the bottom. I exhaled deeply.

"I wish I could do that." Olivia's quiet observation drew my attention to the chair next to me. It looked like she had been sitting at the dining room table with me for a while. She was smiling at the music sheets in my hands. "My parents sent me to piano lessons when I was seven or eight and I hated it. Actually, I hated the teacher. I lasted a whole three months before I begged my mom to let me take chess lessons instead. That was the end of my music career."

"I had piano lessons from the age of four until I turned sixteen." It had been a marvellous escape from the pressures my parents had put on me. "Then the professor teaching me retired. I wasn't interested in having a new teacher."

"And I bet you were already at concert pianist level." She wiggled her fingers as if typing on a keyboard. "Do you still play?"

"I haven't played since the day the professor left."

Her eyebrows shot up. "Why not?"

I thought about it. "I don't know."

"Huh." She glanced at the sheets now lying in front of me. "Does writing it out help you?"

"Yes." I registered her expression. She was waiting for more. I looked for a way to describe my process to a neurotypical person. "When too much information or emotion bombards my mind, it rebels. It's like the lines in binary code when encoding data. Instead of the bit-strings of zeroes and ones flowing in neat rows, I have all the numbers including decimals rushing in uncontrolled patterns through my brain."

"That would paralyse me." She rested her chin on her hand, her elbow on the table.

"I suppose that is almost what a shutdown is. My mind just refuses to take in any more information and blocks everything out." I touched the music sheets. "Writing Mozart's compositions replaces the numbers with zeroes and ones and pulls them back into flowing in organised lines."

"Huh. That makes complete sense." Her smile lifted her cheeks. "I think my brain's zeroes and ones are much, much slower than yours. And possibly large print."

I didn't understand her last statement, but her laughter relaxed me. "You're unique for a neurotypical."

"Uh. Thanks." She straightened. "And you're perfect. I'm so glad I met you. I mean, it was a huge shock at first to see Colin. And it's still weird to call him that. I suppose he'll always be Jackson to me. But I can see how good you are for him."

My eyes widened. "He's good for me. And good to me."

"Yeah. I see that too. But he's different with you. I mean, it's obvious that he would've changed since the last time I saw him, but there's something special when he's with you." Her expression softened. "You make him happy."

I started to respond, but then decided against it. Philosophically, I didn't agree that any person or place or thing could make one happy, but I understood her sentiment. "He's a good man."

"Oh, that and more." She leaned back in her chair and looked towards the living room. "When we were together, there was always some kind of sadness following him around.

He never said anything, but I think something big, something traumatic happened in his childhood. Something that gave him this strong need to take care of people."

Again I didn't respond. When Colin had told me what he'd been through, he'd also said that he'd never before had the need to tell anyone about this. I'd reminded him how hard it was for me to be deceptive and he'd laughed. He'd been convinced there would never be another reason for him to bring up his childhood. I wondered if he'd been right.

"Here you are." Francine walked to the chair on my other side and sat down. She stared at me. "You're okay?"

"I am now." I turned the music sheets over.

"At bloody last." Manny came in and sat down next to Francine.

"Andor?" My breathing shallowed as I waited for Manny to respond.

"He'll be fine." Manny rubbed his hands over his eyes. He looked tired. "I spoke to Palya a few seconds ago. He's on his way here from the hospital. Andor had a severe reaction to his allergy medication. Apparently he used meds that he knew would worsen his allergies. The doctors gave him stuff to counter it and he'll be up and running and saying 'bleeping' in a day or two."

I took two deep breaths and exhaled slowly in relief. Then I frowned. "His allergy medication?"

"Yes."

"Oh, shit." Francine's eyes widened. "You think Lila did this?"

"I don't know." I really didn't. "But it would be in line with her previous methods."

"Find a way to get to someone's medical situation and kill them with it." Manny got up. "Bloody hell! Palya said Andor swore high and low that he bought his usual safe meds, not the stuff that will make him worse."

"At least Andor is in hospital and being taken care of." Olivia looked at Manny and relaxed when he nodded.

"Palya posted two officers outside Garas' room just to make sure no one else gets in there." Manny smirked. "He said it was hard to find two officers who wanted to protect Garas and not throw him to the wolves."

"Hey, you." Colin walked in and kneeled by my chair. "How're you feeling?"

"How long?"

His smile was gentle, his voice quiet. "An hour and a half. Not too long. We were at Arany for about thirty minutes, waiting for the ambulance and seeing Andor off. Then we came straight here. You haven't missed much."

I nodded, grateful that he understood my need to know how long my shutdowns lasted and what had occurred in that time.

"Who phoned you, Frey?" Manny asked.

Colin straightened, then took Olivia's seat with a smile when she moved to the next chair. "Pál Elo."

"You spoke to him?" Olivia's pitch rose in excitement. A few times she'd mentioned that she was concerned about the owner of the gallery she'd visited the day she arrived in Budapest. "Is he back at the gallery? What did he say?"

Colin turned to face Olivia. "He had a look at the photos you sent him of Netscher's *A Woman Feeding a Parrot.* He said that he recognised it. Not just because it is Netscher's work, but because decades ago Rubique Art offered it to him to display in his gallery."

"I was right." Olivia looked pleased and worried at the same time.

"Yes, you were." He leaned back in his chair to face everyone around the table. "It took some coaxing to get him to talk more. He's scared of negative publicity, haters and everything that comes with the revelation of Nazi crimes that have been hidden for generations."

"There were a few cases of that," Francine said.

"The most talked-about and recent example is of course the discovery of almost one thousand five hundred art works in Munich," Colin said. "The art collector Hildebrand Gurlitt stored these in his apartments. Monet, Matisse, Renoir, Chagall—so many masterpieces. It was a wonderful discovery for the art world and yet…"

"Don't care about that, Frey." Manny slapped his palm on the table. "What did this Pál person say?"

"When Rubique Art offered him that painting, he started making discreet inquiries. He discovered that Gyula Koltai—the grandfather from the old pictures—bought that Netscher painting from a János Nagy in 1940."

"Smack bang in the middle of the Second World War," Vinnie said.

"Wait." I held up one hand while I recalled our previous findings and conversations. I looked at Olivia. "Didn't you say that your research showed that this painting had been sold by a Jewish family?"

"I did. But I seldom believe everything I read." Olivia smiled when Francine held out her hand to give her a high-five. "It would've been easy to enter whatever they wanted into the records."

"János Nagy?" Manny paused and looked towards the front door. "Hold that thought."

Manny got up, his usual posture replaced with alertness, his hand on the weapon holstered at his hip. No sooner had he disappeared into the next room than he returned with Vinnie, Roxy and Captain Palya. Vinnie looked at me and winked before he sat down next to Roxy.

Captain Palya's eyes immediately went to me. His scrutiny held an uncharacteristic concern. He opened his mouth twice to say something, but hesitated. Then he grunted and sat down in the only chair still free. "I don't know what to ask you without sounding insensitive."

"Why would you sound insensitive?" I didn't understand his concern.

He frowned when there were snorts and laughter around the table. "Are you okay?"

"I'm well. How is Andor?"

"That little shit is fine." He wasn't able to mask his relief. Then he became uncomfortable again. "Um… can you… um?"

"She's fine, Palya." Manny sat down and slumped in his chair. "Can we get back to how the fifth man in the photos and friend of four of our victims' grandfathers owned that bloody painting?"

Colin gave Captain Palya a brief explanation of his conversation with Pál Elo. "Here's the kicker. János Nagy was Lila's great-grandfather."

"Holy bloody hell!"

"Okay, that's even better than my theories." Francine sat back in her chair, her eyes wide.

"Was he Romani?" I didn't think it impossible, but it was most improbable for a Romani person to have had a thriving business in those days.

"No." Colin's expression turned hard. "His wife was. She was apparently completely shunned from her Roma community when she married Nagy, but didn't care. She was living a good life and was happy. I'm sure if we look, we'll even find photos of those two at the same parties as the grandfathers."

"What happened to him?" Roxy asked.

"He was rounded up by the Nazis because of his wife. Pál said that a few weeks before that Grandpa Koltai warned Nagy about this. Because they were all such good friends, the four grandpas apparently offered to take over Nagy's leather business and sell it, then keep the proceeds from the sale as well as all of his assets for him until things with the Nazis settled down."

"He was betrayed by his friends." Olivia shook her head in disgust.

"Not exactly." Colin raised his hand to push it through his hair, then dropped it back on his lap. "Nagy signed everything over to his friends and they did exactly what they said they would. They put all the money in some kind of trust and all his art and other possessions in storage. Pál didn't have all the detail, but Nagy and his wife survived the concentration camps and the friends gave everything back to him as soon as they got the paperwork done. Including his two houses, his art, everything."

"So where's the catch?" Francine asked.

"Nagy died when Lila's grandmother was eighteen years old. About twenty years after the war. Pál said that his sources told him that those men never liked János's wife, Lila's great-grandmother. The moment Nagy was gone, they started legal proceedings to claim everything back. Lila's great-grandmother was Roma, didn't have much of an education and simply stood no chance against them. It wasn't even a lengthy legal battle. They got everything and left her with nothing."

"Exactly what King told us," Manny said.

"Yes."

"What happened to her?" Roxy sounded upset.

Colin looked at her. "I don't know how and can only imagine it wasn't easy, but she was somehow accepted back into her old Roma community. Lila's great-grandmother was left with nothing. That was why she married Lila's grandmother off as soon as she could. Lila's grandmother did exactly the same with Lila's mom. The rest we know about Lila."

It was quiet around the table for a few seconds. Manny rubbed his hands over his face. "Well, this is one hell of a thing."

"So, I thought I would ask Pál if there were any other rumours about Rubique Art. He told me that there were many rumours about them selling Nazi-looted art. That's why he never did any business with them. That was also why he immediately took an interest when Liv contacted him." Colin glanced at Olivia. "He sends his apologies for not being able to meet you."

She smiled. "Thanks."

Colin paused. "There's a cache of paintings stashed somewhere."

"What do you mean cache?" Manny frowned.

"Pál said he'd heard that the grandpas never got rid of their entire inventory. They'd kept a lot of the artworks—mostly paintings—in some secret location. We're talking about Griebel, Rubens, Picasso, Van Gogh and many other works by the masters."

"Bloody hell."

"Where is this secret location?" Captain Palya got up.

"Pál didn't know." Colin looked at the captain. "You have to remember that these are rumours. We don't know how much of this is truth, how much legend and how much the art industry's love for dramatic gossip."

I looked at the clock on the opposite wall. "We have six hours until the gaming tournament starts. Do we know yet what changes Lila made to Drestia?"

Francine held up one finger and grabbed her tablet. She swiped the screen a few times, then set it up on its cover to face the table. Pink answered the video call on the second ring. "My quee… oh. Hi, everyone. Huh. Another newcomer. And who might you be?"

"That's Andor's captain." Francine waved at the tablet screen and smiled when Pink winked. "Captain Palya. He's very friendly."

Roxy giggled and Captain Palya glowered at the tablet screen. "Who is that?"

"A trusted colleague," Colin said. "Pink."

"Hiya. What's up?" Pink smiled.

"I was about to tell them about Drestia," Francine said.

"Oh." Pink's shoulders dropped. "Yeah."

Francine faced us. "Pink and I looked at the copy of Drestia the people at Arany gave us. They promised us that was the copy Lila tweaked for the tournament tonight. If it is, we have a huge problem."

"It's one trap on top of another trap," Pink said. "Francine and I tried, but if we touch the programming, we might just set something off that we cannot come back from."

"Set something off like what?" Manny asked.

"That's just it." Francine's bracelets jingled as she flipped her hair over her shoulder. "It could be a national network shutdown, it could be a virus sent to every single computer ever connected to Drestia that could wipe everything off those devices, it could be ransomware that locks every computer."

"It could really be anything." Pink's frustration was as clear as Francine's. "We didn't even get very far before we realised that the risk would be too great."

"Even for you?" Manny looked at Francine, his expression serious.

She pouted. "As much as I hate to admit it, yes. Look, I'm going to try. Pink's going to help me, but I really don't think we'll be able to safely tread through the programming before the tournament begins."

"Do you at least know what changes she made to the game?" I asked.

"Traps," Francine and Pink said at the same time. She smiled when he gestured for her to continue. She looked at me. "Remember the rope trap next to the carpet in the mediaeval room? Well, multiply that by about twenty and you'll get a rough idea."

"Shit." Colin frowned. "No one's going to get to the last level then."

"They might, but I can think of only a handful of gamers who might manage that."

"There's something else." The tone in Pink's voice sent a spike of adrenaline through my system. "It looks like she set a final trap in the tower room—the last room in the game. From what I can see, it will be triggered when someone lifts the scroll."

"Do we know what will happen if that scroll is lifted?" Captain Palya asked.

"Not yet." Francine's jaw tightened. "But we will find out."

"Tell them what you found in the boosters, Francine," Pink said.

"Oh. Yes. Pink helped me look through all the software from the victims' computers and devices. We found the same virus in all of them. The same virus Pink found in Nikki's phone." Francine inhaled deeply. "But it was what I found in the victims' hardware that's more interesting."

"A chip." It looked like Pink couldn't wait any longer to share the finding.

Francine smiled. "Yes. It wasn't in any of the other boosters from Három, only in the ones from the victims that I saw."

"What does that chip do?" Olivia asked.

"It gave Lila complete access to every device connected to the wifi enhanced by the booster—phones, televisions, tablets, e-readers, security systems, computers and by extension anything connected to these devices via Bluetooth. That means any appliances, printers, anything with Bluetooth. And if those devices connected to another network after that, she would've been able to access those networks as well and worm her way in there too."

Manny glared at his smartphone lying on the table in front of him. "The good old days without all this bloody technology."

"Have you received the results from the autopsies?" Roxy was looking at Captain Palya. It didn't surprise me that she was interested in the medical side of this case.

"Yes." The captain cleared his throat. "The medical examiner confirmed that Minister Tibor Bokros died from a heart attack. But it was brought on by some medicine that made his blood pressure go very high, very quickly." He shook his head at Roxy. "Don't ask me the name of these medicines. The doctor told me, but I have no memory for those stupid names."

Roxy laughed and nodded. "What about the other victims?"

"Let me think. Was it Kolta… no, it was Udvaros who died two days ago. He was given some drug that overstressed his heart or something like that. There were traces of it in the tumbler Garas insisted the crime scene guys test. And Szell, who died before you people joined the investigation, well, he had high levels of…" Captain Palya said something in Hungarian that was most likely expletives. "He also died from being given a drug that would make it look like he died of natural causes."

"Only someone with knowledge of their medical histories would know the effect the drugs would have on them." There was no more humour in Roxy's expression. "What an awful person."

"She definitely would've had access," Francine said. "Even just being able to get into someone's email would already give someone a lot of information about that person. Nowadays, people receive their medical results via email."

"Email." Colin straightened. "Andor said something about emails just before the paramedics came."

"What are you talking about, Frey?"

Colin dropped his head back and faced the ceiling for a few seconds. Then he looked at me. "It was before I knew you were in a shutdown. When Andor had just fallen to the floor."

"The guilt on your face is misplaced. I don't understand it."

He huffed a soft laugh and kissed me on the cheek. "When I got to Andor's side, he was still conscious. I thought he was talking nonsense, but he said 'friend's dad,' 'boost,' 'gift,' 'email'. He repeated 'email' a few times before he passed out."

"Huh." Captain Palya took his smartphone from his trouser pocket. "If Garas told you that, it means it's important."

"What are you doing?" Manny glared at the captain's fingers tapping his smartphone screen.

"Reading Garas' emails."

"Oh, my God. That's a total invasion of privacy."

Captain Palya looked up and stared at Francine. "Really? You hack everything and everyone and you have an opinion about me reading the emails of my subordinate, who is also a public servant?"

"He's kinda right, Franny." Vinnie's expression was mischievous.

Francine scratched her temple with her middle finger and raised an eyebrow at Captain Palya. "So? What is in Andor's emails?"

Captain Palya looked at Manny who only shrugged. "Let me see. Hmm. Yes. Wait. There's a… Okay. The CEO of Három sent Garas an email with a list. Let me… Huh. Apparently, the CEO is very unhappy that his brand is associated with a serial killer. He's spent the last twenty-four hours going over all client accounts. He's had his whole team search for irregularities and found that all the boosters that were in our victims' homes were gifted to them."

"Gifted." Manny scowled. "We already know that."

"Looks like they got it as some prize at a function or a cold call or something. None of them bought their boosters." Captain Palya pulled the phone closer then moved it back, his expression showing surprise. "I might just have to employ this CEO. He'd make a good detective. He went a step further and looked at the postage information for all the gifted boosters. Seems like they keep track of everything. And all the boosters were sent from the same address. And it's not any of Három's distribution centres."

"That doesn't make sense." Francine's *corrugator supercilii* muscles pulled her brows in and down. "Only a really stupid criminal would do that. She could've given any address."

"This is consistent with her behaviour throughout." I wondered if anyone would ever have discovered her crimes if it hadn't been for Andor. "She's never tried to hide any of her crimes. With the exception of the actual murders, she made little effort to mask her online presence, her name, her connection to these people."

"Oh, my God!" Francine's loud exclamation made me jerk back. She turned wide eyes from her laptop screen to Captain Palya. "What's the address?"

"It's here in Szentendre."

"Berek Street?"

He frowned. "Yes. What do you have?"

"János Nagy owned a summer house here in Szentendre until it was registered in a trust belonging to Rubique Art."

"Holy hell." Manny got up and looked at Captain Palya. "You better have an extremely good SWAT team."

"I do. And we call ours TEK." Captain Palya also got up, already swiping his phone screen. "You think Lila's at that house?"

"My gut tells me she's there."

This time I didn't disagree with Manny's use of that expression. All evidence led me to believe the same. I glanced at the clock again and wondered if we would have enough time to find her, detain her and get enough information to know what she was planning and possibly prevent it.

Chapter TWENTY

THIS WAS MY first visit to the residential part of Szentendre. I was not disappointed. The streets were extremely narrow, lined with hedges and trees obscuring the houses. It was still beautifully green. Only a few trees started showing signs that the season was changing. János Nagy's property was one of the largest on the street, the hedge higher than those in front of the other houses. It was only the automated wooden gate that gave us some view of the front of the two-story house.

The TEK team had arrived in two SUVs and one armoured vehicle, and were currently surrounding the property. More police officers were going from house to house, warning the residents to stay inside. I had the impression that this was the most activity this street had ever seen. The neighbourhood was quiet, only the sounds of children playing, dogs barking and the birds in the trees filling the air. And the sound of booted feet on the street.

I was sitting in the SUV with Colin and Vinnie, parked in front of the house diagonally across from János'. Colin was staring at the house, his *orbicularis oris* muscles contracting his lips to thin lines. This case, this killer, was affecting Colin more than any case we'd worked before.

"Dude!" Vinnie laughed into his phone. "Please tell the old man that. In those words. Hah. Okay, I'll put you on speaker."

"Hi, Genevieve." Daniel's calm voice with a hint of laughter brought a feeling of warmth to my chest. As the leader of the GIPN team in Strasbourg, he'd played a pivotal role in the resolution of many of our cases. He'd also become a good friend.

"Daniel. Is Nikki safe?" I knew Daniel would be honest.

"Yes. She and Pink are in her room, changing Eric." His voice lowered. "She's worried about you."

"Why?"

He chuckled. "I told her there was nothing to be worried about."

"How's Pink?" Colin asked.

"Happy." He was quiet for a second. "Thank you for asking for his help on this case. It seems to have boosted his recovery a lot. I haven't seen him this upbeat in a very long time."

"Tell them about the Budapest TEK team." Vinnie shifted impatiently in the back seat.

"I already spoke to Manny and reassured him that George and his team are really good. We trained with them last year at a European emergency response conference. You're in good hands." He paused. "Uh… I'm with Nikki and Pink and she's nagging me to talk to you. I'll put you on speaker."

"Doc G!" Nikki's voice sounded as if she wasn't close to the phone. "Have you found Lila?"

"Yes." Hearing Nikki's voice brought the debilitating concern over her and Eric's safety rushing back. I took a shaky breath. "You must stay safe, Nikki." I didn't know if I would ever recover if something were to happen to her.

"Don't worry about me, Doc G. Eric and I are in great

company. Pink is busy moving all my personal photos and documents to a secure server with crazy passwords." She cleared her throat and whispered, "And Daniel has three guns."

Vinnie chuckled. "Good. That will keep my punks safe."

"I miss you, Doc G. Eric misses you. Come home."

I placed my hand over my heart before I realised what I was doing. I leaned towards Vinnie's phone. "We will be home as soon as we're finished here."

"Stay safe and hurry."

"I'll keep them safe, little punk." Vinnie's tone was gentle. "You just make sure the tiny punk doesn't go into my room and try on any of my clothes. I don't share."

Nikki laughed and made kissy noises, then proceeded to speak to Eric and tell him that his Uncle Vinnie was a selfish oaf. Despite the ridiculousness of that conversation, I smiled. It amazed me that Nikki could stay so buoyant while this life-changing danger loomed over her and Eric.

Movement from the street caught my attention. Captain Palya and Manny were talking to a uniformed man who looked to be the TEK leader. I turned my attention back to the phone. "Have you been updated on everything, Pink?"

"Yup, I have." It sounded like he moved closer to the phone. "Francine and I are online and we're ready to act the moment we have more info."

Francine was sitting in the back of the second SUV with three laptops and her tablet. She'd suggested that we should engage with Lila as soon as we found her in an effort to get her to disable the traps she'd set in Drestia's programming. Francine had hacked into the tournament's server and had given Pink access. Together they were ready. But, as Francine had rightly pointed out, they didn't know what they were ready for.

We didn't know who Lila was targeting and what the traps were supposed to do. Pink and Francine didn't consider it wise to look around the coding of the game in case they set off one of the traps.

A knock on the window next to me sent a small spike of adrenaline through my system. Captain Palya was standing next to my door, staring into the vehicle. When I didn't react, he scowled and gestured for me to get out.

Vinnie got out first and placed himself half in front of me when I got out. Colin joined us and took my hand. "What's happening?"

"TEK went in and found Lila. They're asking what to do about her."

"What do you mean?" I didn't detect any alarm, but his ambiguous statement didn't give me any information about Lila's condition or state of mind.

"You'd better come and see this, Doc." Manny nodded towards the open wooden gate.

I inhaled deeply, pushed Mozart's Violin Sonata No. 3 in B-flat into my mind and nodded. Colin and I followed Manny and the captain into the property. Vinnie walked behind us, his hand resting on his holstered weapon.

There wasn't much of a front garden. Only a narrow strip of lawn separated the house from the voluminous hedge. The grass looked like it hadn't been cut in two or three weeks, but the garden wasn't particularly neglected. Two TEK members were standing in the open front door, chatting.

Their nonverbal cues were relaxed. They didn't consider there to be any threat inside the house.

They moved aside when we stepped onto the veranda and nodded respectfully at Captain Palya. The latter didn't say anything, just walked straight through the house without even glancing into the other rooms. I couldn't do that. Colin slowed down with me and also looked into the three doors leading to a dining room, formal sitting room and bedroom respectively.

All three rooms looked clean but old. The curtains were torn in a few places, not from abuse, but rather from the fabric having grown weak over the years. Colin's breathing changed a few times and I knew the paintings on the walls had got his attention. Artwork in old frames covered most of the surface of every wall. Each room looked like an individual art exhibition of the most famous masters.

"Jenny, that Courbet looks authentic. My God. That Rubens too. They look like original works." His voice was low, his mouth slightly agape. "But they can't be. There can't be this many masterpieces in one house. That Picasso is listed as lost. It was taken during the Second World War."

"Frey!" Manny's whispered shout drew our attention to the back of the house. "Get your arse over here. You can look at the pretty pictures later."

Colin's hand tightened over mine, but he nodded. We joined Manny, the captain and the TEK leader in the old-fashioned kitchen. They were looking out the window at the spacious backyard. Captain Palya's *corrugator supercilii* and *zygomaticus major* muscles contracted into a textbook expression of confusion. "What is she doing?"

"Swinging." It was obvious to me.

Under an old oak tree, a young woman dressed in jeans and a red t-shirt was sitting on a swing, moving back and forth. Her hair was sheared close to her scalp and dyed dark blue. She had a row of earrings in her left ear and only a diamond stud in the other. Her olive skin sported a healthy summer tan. Her features were such that she could've passed for many nationalities. She was a beautiful young woman.

Her feet pushed on the ground, sending the swing even higher. She was studiously ignoring a man trying to engage with her. He was wearing a police uniform, but not the same as the TEK team.

"Who's talking to her?" Vinnie asked.

"Rudolph Hajos." Captain Palya didn't take his eyes off the backyard. "He's the best negotiator and interrogator we have."

"She's not responding to him." I didn't understand why that man would continue to speak to her when her nonverbal cues so clearly communicated her disinterest in and disrespect of him. "You're wasting time and antagonising her."

"Well, what do you recommend?" The captain turned around and put his hands on his hips. "We need information from her and fast."

"Doc and I will speak to her." Manny lowered his brow when I started shaking my head. "Think about it, Doc. You will know what to say to her because you'll read her reactions to everything. I'll be there with you."

"No."

"Bloody hell, Doc." Manny shook his index finger at the backyard. "That female has already killed more than a dozen people. We know that she's planning something crazy for tonight and we need to stop her. You have to talk to her."

I blinked at him. "I will talk to her. But not with you."

"You're not bloody going in there alone."

"Colin will come with me." I turned away to face the backyard. "Lila has been intimidated and discriminated against her whole life. By men. By forceful males. That man talking to her exhibits all the nonverbal cues of a dominant male personality. She won't respond to it." I turned back to face the men in the room. "She won't respond to you either. Only Colin."

Vinnie snorted and punched Colin in the shoulder. "Softy."

I narrowed my eyes at Vinnie. "A man can be an alpha male and not overwhelm others. Colin is more sensitive to body language and linguistic nuances than any of you. He would know how to act around Lila to put her at ease. Your forceful nature would have the same result as that negotiator. She would become defensive and wouldn't engage."

"You're on, Frey." Manny turned to me. "Make sure, Doc. Study her now and make sure she's not a danger to you. I'm not bloody sending you out there with Frey if it's not secure."

I didn't need to study her. "She's not a physical threat."

"It might be a good idea for everyone else to fall back." Colin glanced back into the house. "They can secure the art in here. It's worth hundreds of millions, if not more."

Captain Palya said something in Hungarian. I was sure it was yet again an expletive. "I'll get more backup. Get what you need from that woman."

"We need to wire you up, Jen-girl." Vinnie reached into

one of the many side-pockets of his combat trousers. "Franny will have my head if she can't immediately hear anything Lila tells you."

I took a step back. "I'm not wearing an earpiece. Or a wire."

"You should know better, Vin." Colin took the small box from Vinnie. "I'll wear the earpiece and mic."

It took three minutes for Captain Palya to clear the backyard and for Colin to test the communication devices. Once satisfied that he could clearly hear Francine and Pink, and they could hear our conversation in the kitchen, he looked at me. "Ready?"

"As ready as I can be." I would've felt more confident if I'd had a lot more information on Lila. But we didn't have time for that.

Colin and I stepped out of the house into the late afternoon sun. Lila was still swinging, but not as focused as when the negotiator had been with her. We stopped a metre in front of her and Colin put the two kitchen chairs he'd brought down.

"So they send out a woman." The corners of Lila's mouth lifted in a smile as she studied me. But her cheeks didn't lift and the corners of her eyes didn't crinkle. It was a false smile.

"I'm Doctor Genevieve Lenard." I frowned. "How did you know to speak English?"

Her eyes widened slightly. "I didn't. I just wanted to irritate you."

"Like you did with the negotiator."

"He's an idiot." She glanced at Colin. "Like all men."

Colin sat down on one of the chairs. "I'm Colin."

"Are you the bad cop to her good cop?" She glanced down at his Italian loafers, then took careful note of his slacks and his tailored linen shirt. "You are way too pretty and well-dressed to be a cop. You were also outside that Udvaros prick's house. With all the other pricks."

Colin smiled. "Yeah. The old man with the constant frown can be a real prick."

It was interesting to watch Lila respond to Colin instead of me. I wasn't completely surprised. People seldom responded well to my presence. My natural nonverbal cues didn't invite any form of social interaction, whereas Colin never had problems building immediate rapport with people. Without any formal training, he had an innate ability to read, understand and respond to the nuances of verbal and nonverbal communication.

Lila and Colin stared at each other for a while. Colin was a master at deception and could mask his true reaction to people and situations very well. Lila was not that skilled. As she stared at Colin, myriad emotions flittered across her face, one of which was intense sadness.

"What are we doing here, Lila?" Colin's tone was gentle. He leaned forward, rested his elbows on his knees, his hands dangling.

"Waiting."

Colin raised one eyebrow. "For the disaster you set up for the tournament?"

"Huh." She put her feet on the ground to stop her movement. "You know."

"Not everything."

Colin's honesty had the desired effect. Lila's shoulders

relaxed even more, her hands no longer gripping the swing ropes tightly. She liked him. "What do you want to know?"

"How did you find all the paintings in the house?" Colin's question didn't surprise me. Knowing him, it was not only because he was truly interested, but also to establish a baseline with Lila.

"It was in the house." She raised one shoulder, but her attempt at nonchalance was not successful. "Do you know whose house this is?"

"It used to belong to your great-grandfather. János Nagy." Colin paused. "Is that how you found the house? You looked into your great-grandfather's history?"

"You're smart for a pretty man." Her condescension was an obvious effort to regain distance. "Yes. I first wanted to take care of everyone who'd made my life hell. But then I started thinking about the bigger picture. I remember the stories my granny used to tell about the wonderful life she had before her father died. Before those bastards took everything from us."

"Szabo, Szell, Koltai and Udvaros." As Colin named the grandfathers, Lila's nostrils flared, colour creeping up her chest.

"You know what they did, right? They took everything from us. Everything my great-grandfather had worked for. And why? Because his wife was Romani. They didn't like her. Didn't approve of her."

"That should never have happened."

"You think?" Her voice rose. "Did you know they made it look like my grandfather had asked them to protect his life's work from falling in the hands of *those degenerates*?" She spat out the last two words. "We are not degenerates."

"No, you're not. You are an extremely smart and successful young woman."

"If only all those idiots realised it, they wouldn't be dead."

"You're talking about Ms Taikon and the other people you killed?"

"I didn't kill them." Her nonverbal cues told me she believed what she'd just said. "I only hastened what was coming to them in any case. All of them had their health problems. Why not find a way to make it bigger and better so they could stop hurting people?"

"They really hurt you badly, didn't they?" The empathy in Colin's tone was reflected in his expression.

"I was ten years old when that Taikon witch dragged me across the classroom by my hair. She shook bunches of hair from her fingers and told me she would have to disinfect her hands. Then she made me disinfect the classroom. To get rid of my Roma dirt. She told me I shouldn't bother trying to disinfect myself, because I would never get rid of the dirt of my race."

Her pain triggered emotions in me that didn't feel comfortable. I was intimately familiar with discrimination. My parents hadn't handled my non-neurotypical condition well. They'd permitted endless medical tests and experiments to cure me. I couldn't recall my mother once holding me with the love Nikki exhibited when she handled Eric. All because I was different. I wasn't going to break the momentum Colin had gained with Lila by telling her how deeply I understood her suffering.

"What did Andor Garas do to you?" Colin asked.

"Oh." She shrugged. "He was getting too close. He was

going to ruin everything and I needed more time."

"So you tried to kill him?"

"Nah. I just slowed him down." Her laugh was disdainful. "People have no idea how much information they give away online. I only had to gain access to his private email to find out about his allergies. He really complains about it a lot. That was the easy part. It always is. The fun, but harder part was to find ways to make his allergies worse. The security in his apartment is not very good. Only two locks? It was too easy to get in there and swap his meds." She paused. "He isn't like the other men. He's surprisingly nice for a man. And smart. I underestimated him. He worked much faster than I anticipated. I decided to let him live."

"What about Olivia Webster?"

She thought for a moment, then her eyes widened. "The lawyer from New York. Yeah. That was a surprise. I didn't expect someone from America to link Szabo, Szell and Koltai. I followed her closely and got worried when she came here. I was about to do something to slow her down as well, but then she just disappeared. So I decided to let her live as well."

"But the others had to die."

"They were hurting people. I was watching them. I saw how they spoke to their wives, their cleaning ladies, their assistants. These were bad men." She raised one shoulder in a half shrug. "They were also arrogant. Their houses were never that hard to get into, their medication easy to swap. With enough patience, I found everything I needed from watching them."

"Is that why you livestreamed their deaths? Why you recorded it?"

Her eyebrows shot up. "You found my YouTube channel."

"We did." Colin moved a fraction closer to her, his eyes locked on her face. "And I see you, Lila. We all see you."

Her blinking increased as did her breathing. She swallowed. "You might be the first."

"What do you plan to do with the information you got from Nikki's devices?" Colin's tone lost some of its gentleness. A cold feeling entered my body. I held my breath waiting for her answer.

She straightened her shoulders. "That's my insurance policy. If you try to stop me, I'll destroy her. It didn't take me long to see how much she loves you people. And all the things you've done for her." She looked at me. "She worships you, you know?"

I pressed my lips tightly together and nodded. I didn't want to open my mouth in fear that I would blurt out my observations. The evidence of love Lila had discovered in Nikki's devices had brought her great sadness. And an even stronger resolve. That was visible in the tense muscles in her jaw. This was the flawed reason so many people employed: If they couldn't have something, no one could have it.

"The minister?" Colin's tone and micro-expression once again revealed kindness and patience. I was glad he'd moved the conversation away from Nikki. I didn't know if I could bear listening to Lila threaten Eric's life.

"Tibor Bokros?" Her *risorius* muscles moved her mouth into a sneer. "That fucking bastard denied my business application three times. Three times. So I hacked his email and found out it was because I'm Romani. He got what came to him."

"Aha." Colin nodded. "You applied to register your

business when he was on the approval committee."

"Idiot."

"But what about Gabor Szabo, Ferenc Szell, István Koltai and Antal Udvaros? They were the grandsons of the men who took everything from your family. But it was their grandfathers, not them. What did they do to you?"

"They lived the life I should've had." She shifted on the swing. Had I not paid such close attention, I might not have seen the micro-expressions of guilt. Interesting. "Three of them didn't even know what monsters their grandfathers were."

"István knew." I spoke before I could stop myself. As Lila had spoken, I'd remembered Olivia's conversation with István Koltai on the first day she'd arrived in Budapest.

Lila glanced at me, but addressed Colin. "That slimy bastard. He knew. He knew his grandfather had stolen from my family. He knew about the paintings. He knew about everything."

"He knew about the house." Colin must've also noticed the quick glance Lila had thrown at the house. "That's how you found out."

"He told me about the house. He said that I could have everything inside the house. He didn't want it."

"But doesn't the house belong to the trust and therefore to all the grandsons?"

"No." She shook her head. "I don't know how or why, but only the Koltais had this property. István told me they never changed anything. When his father found out what his grandfather had done, he'd locked the doors and had never come back. István came here a few times, he said to clean and make sure the paintings were still okay. He wanted me to take everything because he didn't want this to be connected to his family and to his business. Hypocrite! Of all of them he deserved to die the most."

"But you do realise that you took a father from his children, right?"

"I don't care." Her smile was the same false one she'd affected when we'd approached her.

"That's not true." Colin glanced at me, but immediately put his full focus back on Lila. "I can see on your face that you care. A lot. You hide it behind your smile."

This time her smile was sad, but genuine. "You mean the smile everyone says makes me look psychotic?"

Colin nodded, then leaned even closer to Lila. "What are you planning for tonight, Lila?"

"I want everyone to feel what it feels like to be looked at as if you're a freak."

"How are you going to do that?"

Her top lip curled. "By showing the world who these people really are."

I had many questions for her, but held my breath. I could see Colin's mind working as he thought about Lila's words. He straightened. "The people at the tournament. You're going to make their emails and social media public. Like you did with the boys who raped you."

Lila's hands tightened on the swing ropes. "You know about that?"

Colin nodded.

"You believe me?"

"Why wouldn't I?"

"My professor didn't. The police didn't. The officer wouldn't even take my statement. He told me that dirty Romani girls don't get raped. They get what they asked for." Her eyes glistened from unshed tears, the corners of her mouth pulled down. "That police officer died before I could get to him. But I would've made him suffer more than the others."

"How do you feel right now?" Colin's question was unexpected.

Lila frowned. "Why?"

"I want you to make an effort and think about how you're feeling at this moment. You've killed everyone who ever made your life hell. You've even killed the grandchildren of the men who wronged your family." Colin paused for a second. "Do you feel more accepted now? Do you feel happy? Did killing them make you feel recognised as the smart, beautiful young woman you are?"

Lila's eyes filled with tears. This young woman was not a psychopath. She was a severely traumatised individual without the emotional tools and social support to deal with her internal agony. Her compulsion to kill had come from a desire to feel normal, the irrational reasoning being that removing those who'd made her feel unaccepted and unacceptable would make her feel included, would make her feel like she belonged.

"What do you know, pretty boy? You with your expensive clothes. You've never experienced a single day of discrimination against you." She pulled her shoulders back and pressed her lips together. "You don't understand."

"I do." Colin touched his shirt button where Vinnie had

attached the tiny microphone. He inhaled deeply and dropped his hand. "I took revenge and lost a lot because of that."

It felt like something heavy fell onto my chest when I witnessed the painful memory on Colin's face.

"I don't believe you." Lila was lying. She was leaning forward, eager to hear more.

Colin inhaled, but I stepped closer and sat down next to him. "There has to be another way. You don't have to tell her."

"If it helps to stop her hurting more people, it's worth it, love."

"What did you do?" Now Lila's curiosity was undisguised.

"I was nine." Colin swallowed, touched the button again and let go. I understood his reluctance. Francine, Vinnie, Pink and probably Manny, Daniel and Nikki were listening. "My mom had just bought me the coolest handheld computer game and I loved it. All my friends loved it too. I was one of the coolest boys and everyone in my class envied me for having such a great game.

"One Sunday, we had a huge family lunch and my cousin wanted to play with my game, but I wouldn't let him. I was being a little shit. My cousin was also a little shit. He grabbed my game, ran out the house and threw it in the pool. I was so angry. He had just taken away a status symbol from me. So I retaliated. I threw him into the pool"—Colin's voice wavered—"and walked away."

"So?"

Colin looked away and blinked a few times, stress forming fine lines around his mouth. "He'd told me he couldn't swim. I didn't believe him."

I reached out and put my hand on Colin's arm. He grabbed my hand and held it tightly between both his.

"He drowned?" Lila's question was quiet.

Colin nodded. He swallowed a few times. "It destroyed my family. My uncle and aunt didn't want to accept the prosecutor's decision that I wasn't going to be charged or prosecuted. They cut off all contact with my parents. My mother was devastated. My aunt was my mother's twin sister. They were extremely close." Colin took a few deep breaths. "My parents decided to send me away. They wanted to send me to a military school, but my grandmother intervened. She wasn't really up for it, but she took me in. And saved my life."

"Why wasn't she up for it?"

"She was disabled." Colin's smile was soft. "But would have your hide if you ever thought she was weak. You see, my grandmother's surname was Landau. She was born in Poland in 1935."

"And was there during the Nazi horror." Lila shuddered.

"Yes. Her whole family was taken to a concentration camp. All of them died, except for her. She was beaten so badly once that it caused permanent damage to her spine. When she was in her thirties, she became a complete paraplegic, but before that she managed with crutches."

"Did she leave Poland?"

"Yes. When the war ended, another family lied and said she was their daughter. They'd had family in America and left Poland the moment the war ended. My granny told me of many people who selflessly helped others, never asking for any recognition, doing it because it was the right thing to do, because they wanted to help. She spent the rest of her childhood in a loving family and was lucky enough to be in a community where there was no discrimination."

"That doesn't mean you understand what it means to be discriminated against." Her argument didn't hold as much power as before.

"No, I don't. Not in the same sense as you and my gran experienced discrimination. She told me many stories of the race hate they were exposed to even before the war. Then of course the concentration camp. She taught me that it was never acceptable to think yourself superior to anyone for one second. And she helped me see that revenge would never heal the original wound." He swallowed again. "She also helped me forgive myself for causing my cousin's death. And she helped me find my purpose in life."

"Fighting crime?"

Colin laughed softly. "In a way, I suppose. Although my first action was more criminal than anything else. My gran told me about a painting that used to hang above the piano in their living room. She remembered asking her dad about it a lot and every time he would tell another story. It was the *Place De La Trinité* Paris by Renoir. Her dad loved talking about the times he visited Paris and the people he'd met there. And she loved telling me about it. Then one day, I was at the dentist and was looking through an interior designer magazine when I saw the painting. It was hanging in some celebrity's house in the hallway."

"You stole it."

"I did." Colin's smile was unrepentant. "It took me weeks to build up the courage and plan it. But I planned it really carefully. When I eventually broke into the actor's house, I took the painting, but left something else in its place. It was a copy of a list of Nazi-looted art that I had found at the university. I had highlighted the listing of that Renoir painting. They'd bought an artwork that had been stolen. They never reported my theft to the police."

A tear rolled unchecked down her cheek. "What did your granny say?"

"After she cried a lot and hugged the painting to her chest, she told me she was proud of me. And if I chose to do something like this, I had better make sure I never got caught." He closed his eyes for a second, grief drawing the inner corners of his eyebrows in and up. "She died the day after my eighteenth birthday. That day I vowed that I would never cause anyone pain again. Not if I could help it. And I would always try to protect the innocent."

Colin got up and went down onto his haunches in front of Lila. He took her hands from the swing ropes and looked up at her. "Help me keep that vow, Lila. Tell me how we can stop your plan."

"You can't stop it." Her voice was hoarse from emotion. "I just wanted everyone to see me. Me. But they wouldn't. Not even when I started hurting them."

This young woman had never been given the guidance and emotional means to communicate her need for acceptance, belonging and love. It was the case with so many young people all over the world. And so often it ended in tragedy when they made symbolic attempts to gain that love from others by force.

She swallowed and wiped her cheek on her shoulder. "I can't even stop it. Not now. The programming is such that I would need at least three hours to get through the layers of security and traps I planted to get to the final trap."

"Who will be affected?"

"Everyone who's connected to the tournament at the moment."

"Online viewers as well?"

She nodded. "It will be millions of people."

"What about cancelling the tournament? Cancelling this Drestia game?"

"You think I didn't plan for that?" Her laugh held no humour, only malice. "Of course I did. At last count, I've been able to infect over thirty-seven million computers with my virus. It's been dormant in their computers, but if no one plays the game at the tournament tonight, that virus will activate and publish all the private and intimate details of thirty-seven million people. All over the planet. So which will it be? The tournament with only a few million people or all thirty-seven million?"

"What's the final trap?"

"The scroll." She smiled at Colin. "I was impressed when you got the scroll. It was really good playing. But this time there are more traps and the moment the winner lifts the scroll, a virus will be released which will access and publish everyone's social media and emails."

"How can we prevent that from happening?"

"By playing the tournament game, winning it and not lifting the scroll, but destroying it."

Chapter TWENTY-ONE

"I CAN'T." THE sight and sound was so overwhelming that darkness shot into my peripheral vision at an alarming rate. I closed my eyes. "No. No. No."

"Bloody hell." Manny stood in front of me to cut off my view of the inside of the arena. "Frey, do something."

We were in the László Papp Sports Arena, the largest in Budapest. It could hold up to twelve and a half thousand people. It felt like ten times that to my overwrought mind. We had walked past the crowds outside lining up to enter the arena area. Other long lines were leading to the arena itself. There was a festive atmosphere as everyone went through the numerous security checks. At one check point, the security officers had collected an array of costume weapons, locking them up for safekeeping. Most people didn't complain.

Special tents had been set up between the street entrance and the main entrance to the arena. A glimpse inside the tents had made me cringe. Lights were flashing and people crowded around gaming stations where players competed against each other. Nobody seemed to care about the many police officers whose eyes were roaming the crowds, looking for the slightest hint of a disturbance.

I managed to stop shaking my head and opened my eyes. A man dressed in an eerily familiar costume rushed past us, waving at a friend. He was dressed in the exact same uniform as some of the mediaeval guards from the Drestia castle. There were many people wearing bizarre costumes. Vinnie had pointed out each game they'd used as inspiration for their attire as we'd walked past them.

"Jenny, love." Colin pushed Manny away and put his hands on my shoulders. It was strange to look into the face of the man I loved when he didn't look like that man. Colin was dressed as his avatar from the game. Captain Palya's wife had taken great pleasure in sourcing a Robin Hood costume. Colin had made a few adjustments, then had used make-up to obscure his features. The authentic-looking beard hid his age and his posture made him appear ten years younger. He lowered his head until our noses almost touched. "Vin can walk in front of you, scaring the people away. I'll be next to you and Millard will be on your other side. No one will touch you."

"It's the only way to the security room, Jen-girl." Vinnie had undergone an even larger transformation than Colin. It wasn't as much the loose-fitting pants and cardigan as it was what Colin had done to his face. With the help of the captain's wife, Colin had transformed Vinnie into an old man. His face was lined with wrinkles, his nose larger and the bags under his eyes looked real. Vinnie rounded off the metamorphosis by walking with a limp, his torso hunched over. All this had been done to obscure their identities. Vinnie winked at me and moved to the front of our small group. "Don't worry. No one will get close."

"We've got your back, girlfriend." Francine and Captain Palya were behind me.

"Come on, Doc. We have to get moving." Manny moved to my side like Colin had said and waited. He glanced at Colin yet again. He'd done that numerous times after the conversation with Lila. We'd left Lila on the swing to be guarded by the TEK team. The moment we'd entered the kitchen, Colin had looked at Manny and Vinnie and said only one word: "Later." Both had nodded, but there had been a newfound respect in their expressions.

I inhaled deeply, pushed Mozart's Minuet in E-flat major into my mind and nodded. Colin kissed my nose and grabbed my hand. I wished for sound-cancelling headphones as we made our way through the arena. I'd not been prepared for the onslaught of sound. I'd only focused on the plan we'd hastily put together. It was a solid plan.

Everyone had agreed that Colin and Vinnie should be the ones taking part in the tournament. Even though Pink was greatly skilled at the game, we needed his IT skills more. As soon as we reached the security facilities of the arena, Francine was going to set up her computers and link Pink into the whole system. The tournament organisers had agreed to give us everything and anything we needed as soon as Captain Palya had explained the severity of Lila's actions.

Lila hadn't given us any other useful information. Francine had asked Colin a few questions to relay to Lila, but her answer had been the same: None of the traps could be removed. And if they attempted to touch the virus, it would be set off prematurely. Nothing could be removed from the program.

I shuddered to think of the immediate and long-term consequences of all these people's private messages being published. Francine had told us about a dating site whose data had been published after the site had been hacked. It had been a dating site for people who'd wanted to cheat on their spouses. When all the names, credit card and other details had been made public, it had resulted in many divorces, criminal charges and even a few suicides.

We were surrounded by young people. The average age of a male gamer was thirty-five and female gamers were on average forty-three years old, but it seemed to me that the majority of the audience here were in their early twenties. Too early to have a fully developed cerebral cortex. And too early to have all their personal thoughts, their private emails, their photos and anything else on their devices made public. I feared for the psychological impact it would have.

But my biggest fear was Nikki's data being made public. Her father had protected her from his unscrupulous and often brutal business dealings by sending her to the US to finish her secondary education. She was such a loving and bubbly young woman who'd turned out to be a responsible and fun young mother. If her father's old enemies found out where she was and, even worse, that she had Eric, her life would be in incredible danger. It would change her and I didn't want that. It would also have the possible outcome of her having to move away. That thought caused my heart rate to increase exponentially.

I focused on the back of Vinnie's gray wig and followed him through the crowds. At first the organisers had been resistant to adding any more players to the main event. But when they'd found out the players were OMM and RHood, they'd been most pleased. Vinnie and Colin apparently both had fans. Their presence was not only going to please the fans, but also heighten the excitement and tension in the main event. The organisers were hoping for record online attendance.

Colin had looked embarrassed at his avatar's name, but Vinnie had looked straight at Manny when he'd explained OMM stood for Old Man Millard. Manny hadn't been amused.

We reached the other side of the arena and I took a shuddering breath. I was already in a constant battle to remain calm and keep the looming shutdown at bay. Walking through that arena had brought the blackness much closer than I felt comfortable with.

Captain Palya walked around us and spoke to the police officer guarding the heavy-looking steel door. The officer nodded and stepped aside. We followed the captain into the well-lit hallway and the door closed behind us. Immediately my muscles relaxed as the chaos was muted to bearable levels.

The security room was at the end of the hallway. It was smaller than I'd hoped. Even though the room could easily hold all of us, combined with the equipment, I hesitated to enter. Colin's hand on my forearm helped me focus on my breathing and the Trio of Mozart's Minuet. A few seconds later, I followed Manny and the captain into the room.

On the wall to the left of the room were more monitors than I had in my viewing room. It made me feel simultaneously at home and homesick. I would be watching the game being played on some monitors, looking for Három's logo—the same as I'd done yesterday. Nikki would be online as well, helping me. Even though Olivia had been helpful the day before, Nikki had been playing the game and, as Colin had rightly pointed out, was very observant when it came to art. She'd developed that skill through her studies as well as spending a lot of time with Colin. And she'd begged to help. She wanted to do something to help keep herself and Eric, as well as millions of others, safe.

"Doc, will this do?" Manny pointed to a simple desk at the back of the room.

"Yes." I relaxed a bit. I would be facing the three monitors set up against the wall and not seeing the room or how crowded it was.

I walked to the desk and sat down. It was spotless. As was the keyboard and the mouse. I glanced at the other desks and saw that every piece of furniture and all the equipment were without dust and clutter. My muscles relaxed even more.

"Okey-dokey." Francine put her bag with three laptops and her tablet on an empty desk against the wall to my right. She looked at the man who'd watched us enter. "I'll set up here. That okay?"

It was the first time I'd given the head of security my full attention. He was nondescript. Average height, average build, average looks, brown hair, glasses. There was nothing that would demand attention about him. Yet now that I was studying him, I noticed the alertness in his eyes. He'd already assessed all of us and had come to his own conclusions. He nodded at Francine. "You have full access to whatever equipment you need."

Captain Palya walked over to the man and talked to him in Hungarian. I wasn't interested in what they were saying and turned back to the monitors. The one in the centre displayed the welcome screen of Drestia. The monitor to the left was an overview of the whole arena and the one to the right was focused on the empty seats on the stage. That was where Colin and Vinnie would be in another twenty minutes.

"I got Pink," Francine called from her desk. I got up and joined Colin and Vinnie standing behind her seat. Pink was on Francine's tablet screen, his face in total concentration.

He glanced at the camera and smiled. "Hey, everyone. I think I have a plan, Genevieve."

"What plan?" Manny walked over from where he'd been watching the head of security speaking to Captain Palya.

"Well, Genevieve gave me an idea when she asked Lila whether the only limitation was not tweaking or removing anything from the coding of the programming." He turned away from the camera and typed something on his laptop. "I'm thinking that we could add something."

"Genius!" Francine worked on her laptop for a few seconds. "Okay, I'm seeing what you're seeing… huh… are you… I think this might work."

"Full sentences and normal English." Manny issued the order through clenched teeth.

Francine swivelled in her chair to face us. "We're going to blow the whole place up."

"What?" Captain Palya's voice was louder than I'd heard it before—even when he'd shouted at Andor. "You're not blowing anything up. Not in my town."

"No, honey." Francine's tone was husky. She flipped her hair over her shoulder and lowered her gaze at the captain. "We're going to blow up the game."

"Explain." Manny's lips were in a thin line.

"I don't know how yet," Pink said. "Francine and I will try to build a bomb that you guys can use to destroy everything."

"How long will this take you?" Colin asked.

"Don't know." Francine turned back to her laptop. "Hopefully before anyone enters the final room and lifts the scroll."

"You'd better win this bloody game, Frey." Manny pushed his hands into his trouser pockets. "We can't have this virus go to thousands of computers and publish all their private stuff."

"Millions." The head of security's quiet word got us all to turn around and face him. "We already have six point seven million viewers online watching at the moment. The organisers just announced online that RHood and OMM will take part in the final game. We reckon that will push the numbers up to about ten million."

"Bloody hell." Manny took a step closer to Colin. "Can you do this?"

"With help." Colin looked at Francine's tablet. "Pink, is Daniel there?"

"I'm here." His answer sounded a moment before his face came into view.

"Can you help Millard look for traps?"

"No problem. We'll keep you and OMM safe."

Vinnie snorted. "Punk?"

Nikki's hand entered the tablet screen. She wiggled her fingers. "I'm here. And ready to kick butt."

"Where's Eric?" It was an hour after his bedtime and I didn't want Nikki to be distracted with the game if he needed her.

"With his dad." She pushed Daniel away, her face filling the screen. "Martin is in your living room with Eric at the moment. He was very understanding when I said I needed a babysitter, but that he can't leave."

I exhaled in relief.

"Ten minutes!" The call came from the hallway and the head of security reacted immediately. He moved back to his desk with the bank of monitors. "Get your people in place, Captain. The show is about to start."

"Win this thing, Frey." Manny stared at Colin for a few seconds, then nodded once.

"See you when it's done, love." Colin kissed me softly on my lips and followed Vinnie into the hallway.

I glanced once more at Nikki, then returned to the desk with the three monitors and sat down. Manny took a chair and sat down next to me. He noticed my expression and grumbled when he moved a few centimetres away. "You and your bloody fifty-centimetre rule."

"It's not a rule."

"Ladies and gentlemen!" The dramatic voice of the master of ceremonies drew my attention to the screen. "It is with great pleasure tonight that I welcome you to the fifth international World-E games."

The audience responded such that I could only describe it as a roar. I shuddered.

"As you all know, this year we chose the game that has been taking the world by storm. Drestia." Again he had to wait for the crowd to quieten down before he could continue. "Few players ever get to the third-last level. Even fewer players have ever reached that elusive tower room."

Shouts went up and he smiled. "No, my friends. You are wrong. There have indeed been players who reached the last level. But a bit about that later. Let me first introduce our players tonight."

It took a full five minutes of him dramatically introducing each person, citing their numerous scores in different games as well as their score on Drestia. Then he paused. "Tonight we have a special bonus for you! At the very last minute, we got these guys to agree to take part in tonight's epic tournament. These are the guys who have reached the tower room. These are the guys you have all begged us to get here tonight. And here they are. Please welcome RHood and OMM!"

People jumped up from their seats, screaming and cheering as Colin and Vinnie walked to the stage. Vinnie tried to walk like an old man, but it looked comical. Colin hadn't attempted to create real-to-life identities, but rather recreate their avatars as closely as possible. And the audience was responding to that.

It took almost three minutes before the audience calmed down enough for the master of ceremonies to list the rules. "A quick recap. Five teams, two members per team, each team playing their own game. The goal is to reach the last room first and get that elusive scroll. So without any further ado… let the games begin!"

I looked at the monitor that showed Vinnie's and Colin's faces. They both appeared calm, but focused.

"To your left, Frey," Manny said the moment Colin's avatar entered the first room. A groan went up in the arena as a few of the other players set off the trap in their rooms, causing the ceiling to come down on them. I wasn't interested in their games and turned my attention back to the monitor in the centre. Colin and Vinnie needed my full attention if we were to give Francine and Pink the time they needed to find a way to prevent an online tragedy that would destroy many young lives. Including Nikki's.

The first level was more difficult than it had been when we'd played it in Émile's villa. There were more traps and in two rooms I had to look really hard to find the Három logo. Colin's Robin Hood and Vinnie's old man finished the first level with seconds to spare ahead of the only two Hungarians taking part in the tournament. The next few levels increased with difficulty.

"Carpet under the little coffee table." Daniel's measured tone came through the speakers.

"Bloody hell. There's no reprieve." Manny had lost all pretence—his shoulders were straight, he was leaning slightly forward as his eyes took in every detail on the monitors.

"On it, guys." Colin sounded calm. I studied his profile on the monitor to the right and blinked at the relaxed smile around his mouth. He was enjoying this challenge. Vinnie too, but his enjoyment came from the many battles his avatar entered into while protecting Colin's avatar and giving him time to find the bonus points, weapons and, ultimately, the key to the next room.

I searched the Baroque-era room for the Három logo. It was an era of great decorative arts. The walls, the ceiling, even the door frames were painted with swirls, wreaths, flowers and chubby angels. Looking for a triangle with one open corner was not easy. But my brain had registered something above the decorative mantelpiece.

I moved closer to the monitor, inspecting every centimetre until I saw it. "The mantelpiece. One third from the left are two angels playing musical instruments."

"The second one's got the triangle." Colin's avatar nocked an arrow and immediately shot an oversized soldier dressed in a colourful uniform. The arrow entered the eye socket of the warrior, but Colin was already on the move.

Vinnie's old man threw daggers and axes at the men trying to stop Colin from reaching the mantelpiece while using his sword to fight off the warriors trying to kill him. "Motherfuckers! Dude, get that key."

"Got it!" Colin's avatar put his open palm over the triangle on the mantelpiece and all the soldiers dropped to the ground.

The wall behind the mantelpiece fell away to reveal a room with furniture and art from the nineteenth century. I counted three paintings from Cézanne. Colin and Vinnie fought the soldiers as Colin's avatar made his way around the room.

"Floor!" Manny spoke only that one word and Colin reacted immediately.

His avatar jumped into the air, landed on the beautiful upholstery of a French walnut armchair and stilled. "Thanks, Millard."

The floor was a mosaic of encaustic and geometric tiles that was typical of the Gothic Revival in the nineteenth century. Framing the floor about half a metre from the walls was a line of dark blue tiles that formed a square. The thin rope pulled tightly across the floor was almost invisible, a mere two centimetres above that dark blue line. Colin's avatar had been heading straight for it.

"The Pissarro landscape." Nikki's voice was clear, but

excitement and stress was evident in her words. I'd become used to the feeling in my chest when it came to her. It was pride. I'd known she would find the logos. "The triangle is bottom left on the frame."

"On your six, Colin." Daniel's warning caused Colin and Vinnie to react. Colin fell to the floor and swung around in a move he'd done a few times, immediately pulling a bow from his quiver and shooting at the soldiers streaming into the room. Vinnie pulled another sword off his back and ran towards Colin, both swords raised in the air. This time their avatars had to fight a lot harder than before to get enough time for Colin's avatar to run to the painting and slam his hand on the triangle.

My mind was no longer separating reality from the game. My breathing shallowed and my muscles tensed as I feared for the lives of the avatars as if they were real. I gripped the narrow arms of my chair, trying to push the darkness away so I could help Colin and Vinnie survive this room and get to King's office.

Colin's avatar stood ready for attack when the walls fell away to reveal a room from the Neoclassicism era. Again it looked the same as in the game they'd played yesterday, but there were a few more details.

"Only two teams left, guys." Nikki's voice interrupted my inspection of the room. "The others have all died."

Adrenaline rushed through my system at her words. I didn't waste time rationalising with myself that it had been their avatars who'd died. There wasn't time. I looked for the triangle in the same place as it had been before, but it wasn't on the marble statue in the corner.

Soldiers rushed into the room, attacking Colin and Vinnie. They were at least fifty percent larger and more powerful than before. Within the first minute, Vinnie's hand was severed and Colin was bleeding from a long, but shallow cut to his torso.

I still couldn't find the triangle. Or the key.

And the temptation to hide in the safety of a shutdown was becoming stronger by the second. I couldn't stand the stress of watching these avatars. Knowing that Nikki and Eric's safety depended on Vinnie and Colin winning held me together. Then I saw it. "The key is on the floor, next to the large table's leg. The triangle is on the lower part of each leg."

"Watch out for the trap next to it, Frey."

Colin shot an arrow at a soldier who was swinging a curved sword at him and jumped on the table in the centre of the room. He jumped again just in time to save his legs being severed by the sword of another soldier and ran to the end of the table. Another arrow and another dead soldier later, he landed just left of the trap and fell onto the key.

The walls fell away to reveal the anteroom.

"The other team is already here." Nikki's voice sounded strained. "And it looks like they're fighting towards the painting on the left."

My eyes immediately went to the door Colin had closed. I inspected the handle, but couldn't find the triangle or key where it had been before. Then I looked at the painting Nikki had mentioned and didn't see the logo—not anywhere on the painting or the frame.

"Got it!" Francine's shout startled me. I hadn't known she was also looking for the triangle.

"Where?" Manny didn't take his eyes off the monitor. "Frey, left corner of the carpet."

"Colin, Vin, we have a bomb." Francine's excited statement sent more adrenaline through my system. I glanced back to see Pink's triumphant expression on the tablet. It wasn't a real bomb. Francine was still typing on her laptop. She hadn't found the triangle. She'd found a solution to having the audience's data published, a way to protect Nikki and Eric. "It will blow everything to high heavens, but you need to grab it before you enter King's room. I put it on the second bench against the wall. It is the Robin Hood statue. It will blow eight seconds after you lift it off the table, so you'd better get to the scroll as soon as possible."

"Bloody hell."

"You guys need to hurry." Nikki's words were tense. "The other team…"

It felt like I was in the grip of a boa constrictor. It was hard to breathe, even move. My muscles felt locked in place as I searched the room for the triangle. Vinnie was fighting off three soldiers, a fourth rushing towards him.

Colin was running out of arrows, but still had a supply of daggers and throwing knives. "Jenny?"

Something made me look up. The triangle wasn't on the floor or any of the furniture. "The chandelier!"

Vinnie beheaded a soldier and continued the momentum with his sword to behead a second soldier. Then he jumped into the air, his sword raised above him to kill another enemy. Colin ran towards Vinnie. He jumped to meet Vinnie mid-air and used Vinnie to push him even higher. He landed awkwardly on the chandelier, but it was enough.

The walls fell away.

"The bomb!" Francine's panicked warning sent Colin jumping off the chandelier and running towards the wooden benches lining the wall. The first bench had already disintegrated with that part of the wall. The disintegration reached the bench in the middle. Colin snatched the Robin Hood statue just in time and ran into King's room as the wall completely disappeared.

"Stop." Daniel's order had an immediate effect.

Colin stopped, the statue in his hand.

A centimetre in front of his left foot was a trip wire. I didn't know how Daniel had seen it this quickly.

"Six seconds, Colin." Francine's words were low, her voice tense.

The coffee table King and his dad had restored was about two and half metres in front of Colin, the scroll on top of it.

"Fuck, dude. It's everywhere." Vinnie was standing behind Colin, not moving. There were trip wires centimetres apart all the way to the coffee table. To the scroll.

"Three seconds."

"Catapult me." No sooner had Colin spoken the words than Vinnie grabbed him from behind and threw him.

Colin twisted mid-air and aimed for the coffee table. I wasn't breathing. It seemed like time had slowed down as gravity claimed Colin and brought him down to the table. A millisecond before he touched the surface of the coffee table, the monitor lit up in a spectacular explosion.

I jerked back in my chair, my eyes wide. On the monitor to my left, the audience were on their feet roaring. Whether it was in excitement or anger, I didn't know. I couldn't get my mind to accept that the bomb hadn't been real. That Colin and Vinnie hadn't died in that explosion.

"Did it work?" Manny turned away from the monitors to look at Francine.

"I don't know yet." She was typing on one laptop, then switching to the second. "Pink?"

"Looking."

"It… Oh…" Francine typed some more. Then her whole body tensed, her fingers hanging above the keyboard.

"Shit!" Pink's nose was almost touching his computer monitor. "It worked. Fuck it! It worked!"

"Jenny?" Colin's voice drew me to the monitor to my right. He was looking into the camera. "You were amazing. Are you okay, love?"

I wasn't. Even though seeing Colin onscreen alleviated some of the irrational belief that he'd just died, it didn't take that shock away. And knowing that Nikki and Eric were safe exacerbated the overstimulation that was pounding my mind. I could no longer fight the shutdown.

Chapter TWENTY-TWO

I SANK DOWN on my sofa with a sigh of bliss. It was good to be home. The trip to Hungary had been the first time I'd been away from my own environment in years. I hadn't realised how set I had become in my routine, in the safety I felt being surrounded by my own things.

"Want to go to your Auntie G?" Phillip's amused tone made me look to my right. My previous boss was sitting next to me on the sofa, Eric wriggling to get out of his arms. Phillip's smile was warm. "I love that Nikki is calling you Auntie G."

"It was either that or Auntie Doc G." I glanced at Nikki where she was in deep discussion with Manny. "I refuse to be called that."

"Want him?" Phillip was still holding onto Eric, but the baby was getting increasingly more frustrated at being held captive. He pushed out his bottom lip and stretched out his hands towards me.

"Yes." Of course I wanted to hold Eric. Only when we'd arrived home last night had I comprehended the extent to which I had missed him. And Nikki. And how desperately I needed to see with my own two eyes that they were safe. Not even my dislike for physical touch or Eric's constant drooling were strong enough deterrents. Not now. Maybe tomorrow my mind would once again rebel against Eric's need to be with me.

The moment Phillip let go, Eric crawled over to me and pulled himself onto my lap. He stretched up, but I pulled my head back. "No kisses. No kisses."

Eric seemed to understand and plopped down on my lap facing me. I put my hands on his back, holding him in a light embrace and preventing him from falling off. He noticed the colourful embroidery of the traditional blouse I'd bought in Szentendre and touched his index finger to it. I was fascinated by the gentleness in his touch.

"You've come such a long way, Genevieve."

"Hungary is not that far." I glanced at Phillip and frowned. "That's not what you're referring to."

"Not at all." He straightened his tie that I was sure Eric had grabbed and pulled out of place. Even though it was the end of a workday, Phillip still looked impeccable in his tailored suit and silk tie. His expression was filled with affection when he glanced at Eric and looked back at me. "When I first met you almost twelve years ago, I would never, not in a million years, have imagined you like this."

I agreed with him. "The change has not been easy."

"I can't even begin to imagine what a challenge all this must have been for you."

"It still is." I followed his gaze and took in the chaos that reigned in my apartment. Vinnie and Pink were in the kitchen. Pink refused to use a wheelchair and moved around with an aluminium walker, but he insisted on using his 'own two damn legs'. Currently, he was sitting on a high chair, chopping tomatoes for a salad. Vinnie was taking something from the oven. Another dish to add to the growing selection on the dining room table.

Nikki and Manny were now arguing about something inane, Francine watching them. I recognised her expression. It was the one she tried to hide when she'd caused a misunderstanding and had aggravated it by goading people into arguments.

Colin was in the shower. He'd gone for a run, but I hadn't joined him. It hadn't been part of my routine and after the last week, I desperately needed to get back into my safe routine. Colin had promised to fit into my schedule tomorrow and join me for a run.

Phillip was right. I had indeed moved far away from the person I'd been before all these people had entered my life. And every single day had been a struggle. I didn't always win, but most days I derived much more pleasure from my new life than the discomfort I suffered from navigating my way through new emotions and relationships.

I carefully pulled Eric's hand from my earring and turned him to face the others. I looked at Phillip. "I miss seeing you every day."

"I miss you too." The affection on his face brought warmth to my chest. "We should make a point of visiting more often."

"Who's visiting whom?" Colin leaned over and kissed me on my head. Then he leaned over even more and blew kisses on Eric's cheek until the baby giggled. "Hey, little man."

"I was saying to Genevieve that I miss her and you guys working in my offices." Phillip dismissed that topic with a wave of his hand. He leaned forward and watched as Colin sat down on the armrest of the sofa. "I've been burning with curiosity. What happened to all the paintings you found in Szentendre? Are they real? Were they looted? I'm not seeing anything in the media."

"They're all authentic, Phillip." Colin's face took on that dreamy expression he'd had since he'd returned to János Nagy's house to assist Captain Palya in taking care of the art-works in the house. "I got to see a Rembrandt that everyone thought was lost forever, a Vermeer, a Gauguin and a Raphael. And all of them are real."

"What's going to happen to them?" Phillip asked.

"Well, I gave Captain Palya names of the best people and institutions that will authenticate these works."

"People who don't use aliases." Manny and Nikki had stopped arguing and were listening with interest.

Colin ignored him. "They will authenticate the paintings. In the meantime, Captain Palya is setting up a task force that will search for the original owners and return as many as they can. Or put them in museums. It will be a lengthy process."

"Does that include Netscher's *A Woman Feeding a Parrot*?" Phillip asked.

"It does." Colin nodded. "Olivia got Nathan Donovan's family to cooperate with Captain Palya and his task force."

"And I can imagine they want to keep it out of the news to keep all the chancers away." Francine raised an eyebrow when Manny looked at her. "What? It's not a conspiracy theory. It makes sense."

"It really does," Colin said. "Captain Palya was extremely pissed off when he discovered exactly how legally complicated the whole process is going to be. He swore that he was going to make Andor take lead on this and suffer for uncovering this case."

"And Lila?" Phillip asked. "What's happening to her?"

"Palya doesn't even know if her case will go to court," Manny said before Colin could answer. "Apparently, she confessed to everything and is co-operating with the police on only one condition."

"That they treat her with dignity." Francine shook her head. "This must be the weirdest case ever. I'm so confused. On the one hand I think Lila is evil and on the other hand I think she's a sad little girl."

"She killed a lot of people." Manny put his hands in his trouser pockets. "She's evil."

"Motivations are never that clear-cut." I wished they were. It would make understanding people so much easier. "There are too many nuances to Lila's motivation to say it was only the discrimination against her race that drove her."

"It seems like Hungary is feeling very divided about her actions." Phillip had been following the news coverage closely. "Some people sympathise with her and others are screaming for life in prison or even the death penalty. This case is a nightmare for the politicians as well. No matter what they say, they're alienating supporters."

"All because this girl was bullied." Francine raised one hand and winked at me. "I know it's much more complex than that, but as far as I'm concerned it's what started her slide down the crazy-hill."

"What's happening with that virus?" Phillip asked.

"The one she threatened to unleash on millions of computers?" Francine rubbed her hands. "Pink and I decimated it. We killed it, crushed it, eradicated it, vaporised it."

"The bloody melodrama." Manny turned to face Phillip and nodded towards Francine. "The two of them created a virus that infected the computers with Lila's virus and destroyed the bad virus."

"Ooh. Look at you talking tech." Francine put her arm through Manny's and fluttered her eyelashes. When he leaned away, she laughed and looked at Phillip. "It's exactly as he said, just much more complicated. But the computers of the world's gamers are safe from Lila and her desire to expose everyone's secrets."

"And my phone is safe." Nikki sighed. "I'm so embarrassed about this."

"No worries, Nix. Pink made sure no one will get access to you again." Francine lowered her chin and mock-glared at Nikki. "As long as you always update your software."

Nikki put her hand over her heart. "I promise. Promise, promise, promise."

"Good." Francine looked at me. "Do we know how Andor is doing?"

"Much better." Roxy walked into the kitchen and immediately left when Vinnie flicked a dishcloth in her direction. She blew him kisses, then walked to the table. "I spoke to his doctor an hour ago. Andor should be released within the next three days."

"He says his mommy is driving him crazy." Vinnie chuckled as he put a ceramic dish on the table. "He phoned me last night. His dad is seriously pissed off that Andor didn't loop hi… sorry, Jen-girl—that Andor didn't inform him that there was a serial killer in his jurisdiction. And even more pissed off when he found out about the art and the tournament from his aide."

"Garage is big and ugly enough to handle his dad," Manny said. "He'll most likely get a promotion out of this."

"I hope so." Vinnie stood back from the table. "He's a good cop. He deserves all the credit given to him."

"Can we eat, please?" Roxy cuddled against Vinnie's side and blinked up at him. "I'm starving."

Vinnie chuckled. "Food's ready. Come eat, everyone."

We had to add an extra two chairs to accommodate Pink and Daniel. I had to take a few deep breaths to accept the change. Seeing the unfiltered pleasure on Pink's face and the relief on Daniel's every time he looked at his team mate and friend was worth it.

"A toast!" Nikki raised her glass of wine and waited until everyone raised their glasses. "To the best people anyone could ever ask for to have in their life and to keep them safe."

"Hear, hear." Francine winked at her.

Nikki looked at me. "To the absolute best person I could ever rely on."

"Hear, hear." Everyone followed Francine's initiative.

Nikki looked at Colin. "And to the kindest, most caring person I'd ever want to emulate."

It was quiet around the table. Colin tensed, his carefree expression losing its truth.

Manny got up and pointed his glass at Colin. He inhaled to speak, but didn't say anything. He did that three more times. Emotion tightened the muscles in my throat as I watched the stoic man struggle for words. His jaw moved back and forth, his mouth working as he tried to gain control over his emotions. Then he pulled his shoulders back, pointed his glass again at Colin. "You're a good man."

Francine, Roxy and Nikki were wiping tears from their cheeks. The affection on Vinnie's face was for Colin even though he pulled Roxy against him and kissed the top of her head.

Colin rubbed his hand over his eyes and focused on where my hand rested on his arm. His smile trembled when he took my hand in his and kissed my knuckles. That gave him time to compose himself. He raised his glass to Manny for a long moment, then to everyone else. "To family."

A rude sound came from Eric's bottom where he was now sitting on Phillip's lap and everyone burst out laughing. Manny sat down hard on his chair. "The mouths of babes."

"That didn't come from his mouth, handsome." Francine laughed and took a sip of her wine.

The heaviness of the moment had been lifted, but not the depth of affection around the table. Bantering, insults, swearing and arguing ensued, but all was done without malice. I was fortunate. Lila had never known this. And now she never would. No matter what injustices had led her to commit her crimes, she was going to spend the rest of her life paying for them.

Vinnie had prepared a completely traditional Hungarian meal. Cook had given him the recipes only after Vinnie had threatened him with the most of violent deaths. I didn't understand it, but Cook had seemed happy and proud to receive those threats. Vinnie had even made miniature lángos for Nikki to enjoy. His chest had puffed when Nikki had rolled her eyes in pure enjoyment of the deep-fried dough.

My phone pinged and I was surprised that it was a normal notification. Curious who it was, I swiped the screen and realised why Colin had not yet assigned ridiculous tones for this contact—she was new.

"Who's that?" Colin leaned closer to look at my phone's screen.

"Olivia." I tilted the phone so he could see. "A selfie with her children."

"She looks happy." He was right. The woman in the photo, her face pressed together with her kids', looked truly happy. Her smile was genuine, as were the children's. "When did she get home?"

I minimised the photo to read her text. "Her flight landed five hours ago. She's exhausted, but very happy to be home."

When we'd seen her off at the villa, she'd told me that she'd asked Colin for advice, then she'd warned me that she was going to hug me. Her hug had been unreserved and her words of thanks genuine. I liked her. She'd hugged everyone, Colin last. He'd told me that this case had brought him closure on many levels, seeing Olivia happy and living a fulfilled life being one of the highlights.

"I have an announcement to make," Nikki said when we'd settled in the sitting area, waiting for Vinnie to bring the coffee. Excitement brought colour to her face and she shifted from side to side, Eric swaying on her hip. "There was a reason I came home earlier."

"I knew it!" Vinnie put the tray with steaming mugs on the coffee table and straightened. "Helping Pink, my ass. Why did you come home early, punk?"

Her smile widened. "To help Pink."

"She's telling the truth." I knew all Nikki's deception cues. None of them were evident.

"So?" Manny lowered his brow. "Do we have to wait all day for your announcement?"

"Nope." She looked towards the other side of the apartment, the part where she, Vinnie and now Pink lived. She held out her arm towards the arch that connected the two apartments. "Show them, Pink."

Pink entered through the arch without his walking aid. His posture was straight as he slowly walked towards the sitting area. Francine gasped and Daniel put his hand over his mouth as they watched him make his way to us. Roxy squealed and jumped up. "Ooh! Look at that!"

I was looking. But the unexpected tears in my eyes were obscuring my view. I blinked them away to study Pink's face. There were no nonverbal cues of pain visible on his face, only concentration. Twice his left leg wobbled, but he quickly righted himself. He stopped next to the dining room chair Daniel was sitting on and punched him hard on his arm. "You owe me a thousand euros, sucker!"

Daniel got up and grabbed Pink in a strong embrace, slapping him on his back. Then he stood back and looked Pink up and down. "Arsehole. You made me think your progress was much slower than this."

"I need that money." Pink laughed. "Want to buy the new game controller coming out this week."

"Really?" Roxy walked around Pink, poking at his legs. "You're really walking like this?"

"With shitloads of work, yeah."

"And swearing," Nikki added. "A lot of swearing."

"Congratulations, Pink." Phillip got up and shook Pink's hand. "You are an inspiration."

"Talk about inspiration." Vinnie put a large cake on the coffee table. "I made Dobos cake to go with the coffee."

"Ooh!" Roxy and Francine burst out laughing when they spoke at the same time.

"What's Dobos cake?" Phillip asked.

Vinnie cut into the cake and put a slice on a small plate. "Six layers of special sponge cake with chocolate-flavoured buttercream between the layers."

"And caramel on top?" Roxy rubbed her hands when Vinnie nodded. "A large piece, please."

"Can you take him for a moment?" Nikki put Eric on my lap without waiting for an answer. "I want to enjoy this cake without that little monster trying to take it out of my mouth the whole time."

"And Jenny should just wait?" Colin asked with a laugh.

"Uh." Nikki looked from the cake on the coffee table to me. "Please, Doc G?"

Eric wiggled on my lap and turned around to look at me. I nodded at Nikki, but quickly turned my attention to Eric. I looked at his eyes, which were focusing on my lips. "No kisses. No kisses."

~ ~ ~ ~ ~

Be first to find out when Genevieve's next adventure will be published. Sign up for the newsletter at http://estelleryan.com/contact.html

~ ~ ~ ~ ~

Look at the paintings from this book, find out about the true provenance of The Woman Feeding a Parrot, *learn more about Nazi-looted art, the gaming industry, Hungarian cuisine and the Roma culture at:* http://estelleryan.com/the-netscher-connection.html

Other books in the Genevieve Lenard Series:

Book 1: The Gauguin Connection

Book 2: The Dante Connection

Book 3: The Braque Connection

Book 4: The Flinck Connection

Book 5: The Courbet Connection

Book 6: The Pucelle Connection

Book 7: The Léger Connection

Book 8: The Morisot Connection

Book 9: The Vecellio Connection

Book 10: The Uccello Connection

and more…

For more books in this series, go to
http://estelleryan.com/books.html

~ ~ ~ ~ ~

Please visit me on my Facebook Page to become part of the process as I'm writing Genevieve's next adventure.

and

Explore my website to find out more about me and Genevieve.

CPSIA information can be obtained
at www.ICGtesting.com
Printed in the USA
LVHW030317270319
611982LV00001B/54